MISSISSIPPI NOIR

EDITED BY TOM FRANKLIN

Published by Akashic Books
©2016 Akashic Books

Series concept by Tim McLoughlin and Johnny Temple
Mississippi map by Sohrab Habibion

Hardcover ISBN: 978-1-61775-472-2
Paperback ISBN: 978-1-61775-228-5
Library of Congress Control Number: 2015954059

First printing

Akashic Books
Twitter: @AkashicBooks
Facebook: AkashicBooks
E-mail: info@akashicbooks.com
Website: www.akashicbooks.com

MISSISSIPPI NOIR

ALSO IN THE AKASHIC NOIR SERIES

ORANGE COUNTY NOIR, edited by GARY PHILLIPS
PARIS NOIR (FRANCE), edited by AURÉLIEN MASSON
PHILADELPHIA NOIR, edited by CARLIN ROMANO
PHOENIX NOIR, edited by PATRICK MILLIKIN
PITTSBURGH NOIR, edited by KATHLEEN GEORGE
PORTLAND NOIR, edited by KEVIN SAMPSELL
PRISON NOIR, edited by JOYCE CAROL OATES
PROVIDENCE NOIR, edited by ANN HOOD
QUEENS NOIR, edited by ROBERT KNIGHTLY
RICHMOND NOIR, edited by ANDREW BLOSSOM, BRIAN CASTLEBERRY & TOM DE HAVEN
ROME NOIR (ITALY), edited by CHIARA STANGALINO & MAXIM JAKUBOWSKI
SAN DIEGO NOIR, edited by MARYELIZABETH HART
SAN FRANCISCO NOIR, edited by PETER MARAVELIS
SAN FRANCISCO NOIR 2: THE CLASSICS, edited by PETER MARAVELIS
SEATTLE NOIR, edited by CURT COLBERT
SINGAPORE NOIR, edited by CHERYL LU-LIEN TAN
STATEN ISLAND NOIR, edited by PATRICIA SMITH
STOCKHOLM NOIR (SWEDEN), edited by NATHAN LARSON & CARL-MICHAEL EDENBORG
ST. LOUIS NOIR, edited by SCOTT PHILLIPS
ST. PETERSBURG NOIR (RUSSIA), edited by NATALIA SMIRNOVA & JULIA GOUMEN
TEHRAN NOIR (IRAN), edited by SALAR ABDOH
TEL AVIV NOIR (ISRAEL), edited by ETGAR KERET & ASSAF GAVRON
TORONTO NOIR (CANADA), edited by JANINE ARMIN & NATHANIEL G. MOORE
TRINIDAD NOIR (TRINIDAD & TOBAGO), edited by LISA ALLEN-AGOSTINI & JEANNE MASON
TWIN CITIES NOIR, edited by JULIE SCHAPER & STEVEN HORWITZ
USA NOIR, edited by JOHNNY TEMPLE
VENICE NOIR (ITALY), edited by MAXIM JAKUBOWSKI
WALL STREET NOIR, edited by PETER SPIEGELMAN
ZAGREB NOIR (CROATIA), edited by IVAN SRŠEN

FORTHCOMING

ACCRA NOIR (GHANA), edited by MERI NANA-AMA DANQUAH
ADDIS ABABA NOIR (ETHIOPIA), edited by MAAZA MENGISTE
ATLANTA NOIR, edited by TAYARI JONES
BAGHDAD NOIR (IRAQ), edited by SAMUEL SHIMON
BOGOTÁ NOIR (COLOMBIA), edited by ANDREA MONTEJO
BUENOS AIRES NOIR (ARGENTINA), edited by ERNESTO MALLO
JERUSALEM NOIR, edited by DROR MISHANI
LAGOS NOIR (NIGERIA), edited by CHRIS ABANI
MARRAKECH NOIR (MOROCCO), edited by YASSIN ADNAN
MONTANA NOIR, edited by JAMES GRADY & KEIR GRAFF
MONTREAL NOIR (CANADA), edited by JOHN McFETRIDGE & JACQUES FILIPPI
NEW HAVEN NOIR, edited by AMY BLOOM
OAKLAND NOIR, edited by JERRY THOMPSON & EDDIE MULLER
PRAGUE NOIR (CZECH REPUBLIC), edited by PAVEL MANDYS
RIO NOIR (BRAZIL), edited by TONY BELLOTTO
SAN JUAN NOIR (PUERTO RICO), edited by MAYRA SANTOS-FEBRES
SÃO PAULO NOIR (BRAZIL), edited by TONY BELLOTTO
TRINIDAD NOIR: THE CLASSICS (TRINIDAD & TOBAGO), edited by EARL LOVELACE & ROBERT ANTONI

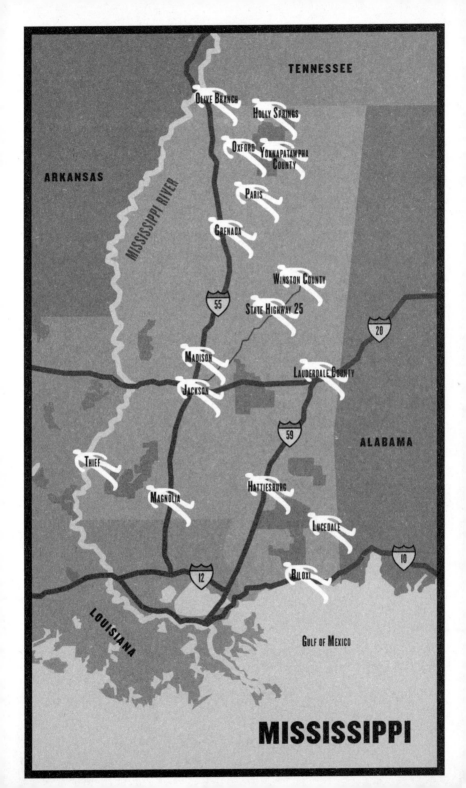

TABLE OF CONTENTS

INTRODUCTION
Welcome to the Bottom

Welcome to Mississippi, where a recent poll shows we have the most corrupt government in the United States. Where we are first in infant mortality, childhood obesity, childhood diabetes, teenage pregnancy, adult obesity, adult diabetes. We also have the highest poverty rate in the country.

And, curiously, the highest concentration of kick-ass writers in the country too.

Okay, maybe that's not a Gallup poll–certified statistic, but we do have more than our fair share of Pulitzers and even a Nobel. William Faulkner lived and wrote here. Richard Wright is from Mississippi. Tennessee Williams, Eudora Welty, Larry Brown, Ellen Douglas, Shelby Foote, Richard Ford, Ellen Gilchrist, Barry Hannah, Kiese Laymon, Willie Morris, Walker Percy, Kathryn Stockett, Donna Tartt, Jesmyn Ward, Brad Watson, Steve Yarbrough, etc. Also, the Crooked Letter boasts perhaps the heaviest-hitting trio in the crime/thriller biz: Greg Iles, Thomas Harris, and John Grisham. I could go on, and in fact I do, in this very anthology.

Faulkner said that good writing is created by "the human heart in conflict with itself." Maybe that's why so much art comes out of Mississippi—a state in conflict with itself in so many ways. The legacy of slavery has left wounds that are slow to scab over, not even close to healing. The South's position of loser in the Civil War has left Southerners to "brood," as Shelby Foote says.

"The winner of a conflict goes on. But the loser . . ." Finish this quote. We all know it's healthier to be the mover-oner, the winner, skipping off with a shrug. The state of brooding is a painful one, but it's one that produces great books.

Maybe when you think of noir, you think of cities shot in grainy black-and-white; alleys and fire escapes and blinking neon signs with a letter or two gone dark. That's part of it, sure. But noir often reveals a down-on-his/her-luck person going from bad to worse. And where can one find more wonderful "worse" than here in Mississippi? This isn't, and hasn't ever been, a land purely of moonlight and magnolias. Because in that moonlight, under those magnolias, terrible things happen. And in the cities, too, in the Jackson alleys and strip malls, down along the casinos on the coast, in Tupelo, home of Elvis, or the Delta, home of the blues, or along I-55, where there's a Nissan plant almost a mile long, where trios of crosses dot the highways.

Here are sixteen stories from seasoned noir writers like Ace Atkins and Megan Abbott as well as Mississippi's new generation of noirists, authors like William Boyle and Michael Kardos. You'll also find unknown, first-time-published writers like Dominiqua Dickey and Jimmy Cajoleas, who won't remain unknown for long. I'm thrilled to bring these writers to you. In Alabama, where I grew up, we had a saying: *Thank God for Mississippi, otherwise we'd be at the bottom in everything.*

Welcome to the bottom.

Have fun.

Tom Franklin
Oxford, Mississippi
May 2016

PART I

CONQUEST & REVENGE

COMBUSTIBLE

BY ACE ATKINS

Paris

"I shouldn't be doing this," I said.

"Hell you shouldn't," Shelby said. "You fucking owe me."

"Why?"

"Don't you want to meet Lyndsay Redwine?"

"Since I saw her in a bikini at the city pool."

"Then shut the fuck up and drive."

Shelby was fourteen. And she talked like that.

She'd crawled into my tall Chevy Silverado without even asking. Maybe because she liked my truck, riding high on a Rough Country lift kit and new set of 295 Firestones. I gave her rides to school sometimes from the bottom ass of the county down in Paris. People tried to make something of it, which was bullshit.

I was seventeen and a senior. Shelby was a freshman, chubby, and mean as hell.

"Wasn't your momma picking you up?" I said.

"I don't care."

"This comin' down on me."

"I ain't goin' home."

"Suit yourself," I said, waiting for the deputy directing traffic to wave me onto 334.

He stared at me through mirrored sunglasses like he knew I was trucking jailbait. But he waved me on as Shelby got some Bubblicious out of her backpack and offered me a piece. She had on faded jeans and a Walmart T-shirt that tugged at her belly, saying, *Amazing Grace. How Sweet the Sound.*

"Well, I'm screwed," I said, driving south, back to Paris. I used the cut-through by the Yellow Leaf Church where my kin were buried.

"Hunter, don't be such a pussy," she said. "You want, just let me out. I'll walk."

"It's ten miles to Paris."

"I don't care," she said. "I don't care about nothing. I've gone way past that road."

She smacked her gum and started texting. I let down my window and drove on. It was late November, already deer season and cold, but it felt good to air out the truck. "That ought to do it," she said as she finished the text.

She held out her phone, proud as hell. I glanced down as we hit the stop sign at County Road 418. *I FUCKING HATE U.*

"Yep," I said. "That ought to do it. Your momma will love it."

"She's fucked in the head."

"Yep."

"She didn't used to be that way. He's the one who led her into all her fucked-up-ed-ness."

"He" meaning Randy. Randy being Shelby's stepfather. 'Course I always liked Randy. Him and my daddy had gone to Lafayette back in the day, and I'd heard that Randy got in a year at Ole Miss before tearing up his knee. He was big and potbellied, always tan and grinning with large white teeth. He built barns from wood he'd milled himself. One time he bought me a Coke at the barbershop.

"I ain't goin' home," Shelby said.

"Then don't go home."

"Let me out up at the cemetery," she said. "I don't give a shit, long as it's not home."

I dropped her at the old Paris cemetery, crooked and rolling and alone on the hills.

As I drove away, it started to rain. I watched her in my rearview as she sat down near a headstone. She looked worn-ass out.

WHERE U AT? WORRIED. MOMMA.

Shelby sat on a big slab of marble and texted back. *I'M NOT FUCKING COMING HOME. EAT SHIT.*

She got up, walked to a cedar tree, and uncovered a rock. Under the rock, and under a couple inches of dirt, she found a half-drunk pint of Aristocrat vodka. Shelby spit out her watermelon gum and took a swig, walking back to the headstone. Probably been better if she'd known any of the dead folks around her. But her people were from Olive Branch, her daddy was buried there, and she wished to hell she could move back.

She drank.

Randy. Fucking A-1 asshole.

Their old house had been colder than shit all week and he wouldn't get his fat ass up and fix that propane leak. Just crawled under the house and cut off the heat. Said if he hadn't noticed that fart smell the other morning, his first cigarette could've killed them all. Randy said it like he was some kind of fucking hero. Her daddy had been a hero. A hero doesn't smell farts. A hero gets blown to bits out in the desert.

The phone buzzed in her lap.

I'M CALLING THE LAW.

Shelby downed some more vodka, warming her up in the cold rain and, by God, giving her strength. The ground all bumpy and uneven with skinny old headstones and thick new ones. A few old lambs for kids and tree stumps for the loggers. Must've been something to be a logger back in the day. Lots of dead folks here seemed to be real proud of it.

CALL EM, BITCH.

The rain come on hard, splatting off the headstones and dripping off the pine trees surrounding the cemetery. *Fuck her. Fuck him. Fuck it all.*

She heard a motor and looked up to see Hunter's dumb ass driving back to where he'd let her out. She tucked the vodka in her pink camo backpack and walked down to where his Chevy idled.

"What?" she said.

"You just gonna sit out here all night in the rain?" Hunter said. "Jesus."

"Maybe."

"Get in."

"I ain't goin' home."

"You said that. I'll take you to my cousin's. Grab that damn towel. Shit, girl. Don't get my seats all wet."

She put on a pair of red sunglasses flecked with rain, and climbed in. She felt good and in control. "Okay," she said. "Your cousin is cool."

Kids only thought Rebecca was cool 'cause she was eighteen and had her own trailer. But she also had a two-year-old baby, bills, and a tenth-grade education. She'd ditched school about the time she got knocked up. When me, her, and the baby went shopping at the Walmart, folks stared like she was straight trash. Maybe it was all the bracelets she wore and the nose ring. People in Mississippi really got upset by that nose ring.

"What the hell, Hunter?" she said, walking barefoot from her trailer when she heard my truck. "What do you want?"

"To get out of the rain," I said.

"This look like a motel to you?"

I shot Rebecca a look. She lit up a cigarette, stared down at Shelby all wet and chubby, and blew out some smoke. "Shit," she said. "Come on in. Be quiet about it. Braden's asleep."

Rebecca tossed Shelby a clean towel as the rain drummed on the trailer. Shelby walked back to the bathroom while Rebecca pressed a hand on the kitchen counter. She was tall and thin and wearing a black T-shirt with the sleeves cut out. A tattoo on her right arm said, BRADEN. She'd gotten it done one night on Beale Street when she decided to quit drinking and smoking weed.

She looked to me and shook her head. "Y'all are screwed."

"Why?"

"Johnny Law just called here about five minutes ago," Rebecca said, smoke streaming from the edge of her mouth. "Sheriff's looking for your girlfriend."

Deputy Ricky Babb spent nearly a half hour with Leanne Dalton while she talked about how her daughter was a stupid, selfish shit and maybe crazy too. She said she wasn't above committing Shelby, if things come to it. Leanne said her little girl didn't make no sense most of the time and maybe she belonged in Whitfield. Babb wanted to tell her that if you could take a pill or do an electric shock for being a pain in the ass, he wouldn't have a damn job.

But Babb just sat there on her tin-roofed porch, nodding along with problems kids got today, and waited to get some religion thrown in there. Just as he thought the woman had shut up, she mentioned a quote from *The Purpose Driven Life*. "God sometimes removes a person from your life for your protection. Don't run after them."

Babb never thought of God protecting a momma from her own child. But Leanne was pretty sure of it, saying that she didn't have the money or time to put up with all Shelby's bullshit and lies.

"How's she lyin'?" Babb asked.

"'Cause that's who she is," Leanne said.

Babb sucked on his tooth, listening to the crackle of a radio call. A bunch of cows had broken out of fence on County Road 381. *Son of a bitch.* Nothing like herding cattle with a busted-ass Crown Vic. Least it wasn't nighttime. Herding was a bitch at night. "What's that, ma'am?"

"She accuses my husband of all kinds of things."

"What kind of things?"

"What's it matter?" she said. "Shelby's a liar."

"Yes ma'am," Babb said. "These kids need to realize the road they're paving to their future."

Babb thought about all those cows heading down the county road, trying to break for the highway where they'd run out in front of semis and splatter the pavement with meat and blood.

He walked back to his patrol car, which he'd left running, and knocked her into drive.

"What do you think of that man your momma been seein'?" Shelby asked. "Jimmy or J.J. or whatever the fuck his name is."

"Mac."

"Yeah, Mac."

"I guess I don't think much of him," I said. "He's not my daddy or nothing. And he knows he's not my daddy. My daddy lives in Jackson. He'll always be my daddy."

"My daddy is dead, but that doesn't make it stop being a fact," Shelby said. "Half of him is half of me."

I nodded.

"Problem with Randy is he acts like he's charge of me, my momma, and my brother," she said. "Only reason he's living with us is he's paying the rent."

"Yeah?"

"You bet," Shelby said. "Payin' it to my momma six inches at a time."

"Shit, Shelby."

"It's true," she said. "I hear him at night. His fat ass riding her like an old bicycle. I thought something was wrong with her one night, and I gone into the bedroom and seen her and him watching a dang porno movie and them doing it like dogs. His old fat, hairy ass on her, nasty breath in her ear. She seemed like she trying to get away. But him locking her down, holding her ass till he finished what he started."

"Randy ain't that bad," I said. "They got a picture of him back in the day by the principal's office. I heard he could bench-press three hundred pounds."

Shelby looked like she was going to throw up. I slowed the truck.

"You okay?" I asked.

"Shit yeah."

"You don't look okay."

"Just fucking drive, Hunter."

"Doesn't your momma work?" I said, hitting the gas, the dually pipes growling behind us. "I mean, she don't need him."

"She was working as a receptionist at an eye clinic for four years," Shelby said. "She was real good at fitting glasses."

"Where do you want to go?"

"I don't care," she said. "Somewhere. Anywhere. Put me out. Hell, it's all the same."

"Why are you crying?"

"I ain't fuckin' crying."

"Ma'am, the school resource officer said Shelby Littlejohn rode off with Hunter this afternoon," Deputy Babb said. "Have you heard from your son?"

"No sir," Hunter's mom said. "He do something wrong?"

The woman wore a big blue flowered dress that didn't hide

her big blue flowered ass, which was blocking the entire door. She looked down from the mouth of the trailer, soap opera blaring on the television, waiting for him to leave. The rain was in his eyes and soaking his uniform good.

"Where does he usually go after school?"

"He comes home," she said. "Except during baseball season. You know he's starting this year. Third base. I think he's got a future."

"Yes ma'am," Babb said. "You think you might try and reach him on his cell phone?"

"He doesn't have a cell phone," she said. "Kids don't need phones."

"Lots of kids have them."

"Good way for them to get in trouble," she said. "With all that twittered and selfie stuff. Girls taking pictures in their panties and passing it around. That can just do nothing but make a teenage boy lose his mind."

"Does Hunter work?"

"He sometimes works at the radiator shop over on old 7," she said. "But that's when he's trying to get some new parts for his truck. You know how much he loves that truck."

"Mmmhmm."

"Even got a name for it," she said. "Calls it the Silver Bullitt. 'Cause of the way it looks like a Coors Light can."

"Shelby's momma is real worried," Babb said, walking back from the steps. "The little girl sent some pretty awful words to her momma."

"What did she say?"

"I can't repeat them."

"Do I look like I sing in the choir?"

"Harsh words, ma'am."

"Don't mix up Hunter in that little girl's crazy family business," she said. "He doesn't have nothing to do with it. Didn't I tell you he's got a future?"

"Your boy didn't have permission."

"Talk to her mother, then," she said. "'Cause I can't raise their daughter while trying to raise my own son."

Babb was soaked through and through. The trailer door slammed. He walked back to the patrol car. *Been easier working with them cows.*

"You ever think about killing someone?" Shelby asked.

"Hell no," I said. "What's wrong with you?"

Shelby's shoulder pressed against the passenger window of my truck. She was still in her cheap sunglasses, chewing gum, blowing big loud bubbles.

"You know," she said, "that your life would be better if someone wasn't on the planet?"

"You want to kill your momma for being a pain in the ass?"

"That's not what I'm saying."

"What are you saying then?"

"I'm just talking, Hunter," she said. "Can't we just talk awhile?"

"I'm taking you home."

"'Cause the law showed up at your mom's house?"

"She told them I didn't have a phone," I said. "She lied for me. She lied for you. And Johnny Law interrupted her afternoon television. That's all she cares to do until I get home for supper. She said the law said I didn't have permission to give you a ride."

"You drove me because I said I'd talk to Lyndsay Redwine."

"I got you here, didn't I? Shit."

"Fine," she said. "Drop me off then. Right over fuckin' there."

"There?" I said. "That's nowhere. That's just an old couch on the road."

"I need to rest."

"I'm driving you home."

"Shit," she said. "I don't even know where the hell that is."

Shelby grabbed the door handle and acted like she was about jump out. And I figured she was just about crazy enough to do it. I slowed onto the gravel shoulder.

My truck pipes growled as she opened the door wide. I revved the engine. She didn't move. She just sat there watching the wipers slap the hell out of the rain. She stared straight ahead, thinking on something.

"What you got in that toolbox?"

"Flowers," I said. "What do you think?"

"You got a wrench?"

"Yeah, I got a wrench."

"Give it to me."

I left the motor running, walked out into the rain, and grabbed a wrench from my Husky toolbox. I looked at her hard as I handed it over in case she had it in her mind to go and hit someone with it.

"What?" she said. "Can't a girl just go and fix her dang house?" She blew a huge pink bubble and it exploded like a shot.

"I guess."

"And Hunter?" she said. "Pick me up for school tomorrow. Little earlier than usual. I got somethin' to do."

"You want me to get arrested?"

"Will you do it?"

I nodded.

She got out and went over to the wet, ragged sofa as I turned the Chevy around and rolled down my window. Shelby was a trip in her sunglasses, taking a seat on that old sofa in the rain. She acted like she owned all of Paris and that the hamlet was her living room.

"You really introduce me to Lyndsay Redwine?" I said.

Shelby smiled back and crossed her legs. She had a phone in one hand and a big-ass wrench in the other. "Just pick me up," she said. "Okay?"

Randy had come in late the night before, racing up from Calhoun County where'd he'd been out with his stupid buddies spotlighting deer. He was red-faced and sweating, wearing an old Carhartt jacket over his T-shirt, when he'd asked Shelby to step outside. He had something he wanted to show her.

She knew her damn bitch momma had called him. She'd told him what she'd said.

"Why you want to upset her like that?" Randy said. "Your momma was crying and blubbering so much, I could barely make out her words."

Shelby just stood there in his headlights, arms crossed over her small chest, in their front yard. Randy opened up the tailgate to his truck and dragged out a dead deer.

"Sometimes a young girl believes things, imagines things that never been there," he said. "Way it works when you're a kid. But you spread them things onto your momma, and your momma calls me up, that's when you need to consider your actions. Brother Davis was sayin' last Sunday . . ." Using his winch, Randy hoisted the doe by the back legs over a tree branch.

"Brother Davis is a cross-eyed hypocrite."

"You need to think on what you're sayin' and doin', Shelby," Randy replied, shuffling back to his truck and cracking open another Busch from his cooler, Adam's apple working while he swallowed most of it.

He wiped his mouth with the back of his bloody hand, and set down the beer on the tailgate. His stomach swelled over the top of his pants. The back of his neck was reddish-brown and hadn't been shaved in a while.

"Are we straight?"

She was quiet. She just stared back at his big, dumb ass, showing she wasn't scared of jack shit. She knew and her momma now knew too. Whether her momma believed it or not wasn't Shelby's damn problem.

Randy pulled a buck knife from a leather sheath and walked to the doe swinging in the wind. There was lightning far off from their neighbors' and a cold wind bringing in rain from down on the coast. Headlights shone on the dead animal.

Shelby wanted to say more but only got out, "Can I go inside?"

"Hold up," Randy said. "Hold up. Listen. Haven't I been good to you?"

"That's what you call it?" she asked, lifting up the sleeve of her T-shirt, fat finger bruises on her arms. "Goddamn you, you fat bastard. It ain't right what you did. I didn't want it."

Randy froze in the front yard, open-mouthed, doe swinging from the pecan, and slit that deer from anus to throat, the insides of the animal dropping down hard and bloody onto the dead grass.

He studied the entrails that had fallen, picked up a cigarette, closing one eye as if to get better focus, and just nodded at her. "We straight?"

Shelby ran into the house and slammed the door behind her.

"Shelby's momma ain't gonna file charges or nothing," said Johnny Law, a.k.a. Deputy Babb.

We sat in the cruiser together that night as it rained like hell outside us. I didn't say nothing.

"But she and her stepdaddy wanted me to talk to you," Babb said. "They wanted you to understand the exact nature of what you done today. That girl is fourteen years old."

"Yes sir."

"And she's real impressionable," Babb said. "You being a senior with a big, nice truck like that. I ain't too old that I don't recall what a young girl would do for an older boy. But your cousin sure as hell understands the consequences of her actions."

"This don't have nothing to do with Rebecca."

"You don't want to be changing diapers while trying to play ball," Babb said. "That little girl is messed up in the head. Shelby would do anything for some attention. That's why I'm talking to you like a man. Let you know all the things that come with spending time with a girl like that."

"Shelby's just my friend," I said. "She needed help."

Babb smiled. He had yellow, crooked teeth.

"She didn't want to go home."

"How come you went over to your cousin's trailer?"

"'Cause we didn't have nowhere else to go," I said. "It was raining."

"Y'all were together nearly four hours before she got home."

"We were riding around. Shelby likes to take the back roads."

It was the wrong thing to say. Babb just smiled bigger. He put a hand on my shoulder, leaned in, and said, "Keep it in your pants, Hunter. Don't go throwing away your life on a little ol' fat girl."

I didn't answer. I just crawled out of the cruiser and walked back to my house and the supper my momma had laid out. Field peas, greens, and hamburger steak that had grown cold.

Momma was back on the couch, laughing at something she'd seen on television.

The morning was bright and cold when Shelby removed the skirting around the front porch and crawled under the tin-roof house. She was quiet about it. All she needed was Randy to wake up from a twelve-pack coma and start asking a lot of questions.

The house was old and slat-boarded, nothing but dirt and trash up underneath the floors. Running above her was a mess of old copper pipes and new PVC water lines. So many cracks and breaks in the bottom floor of the house, she could see the light inside bleeding through clear as day. It took her awhile but she soon found where the gas line ran up into the living room and then along the back of the house to the stove. Shelby reached for Hunter's wrench in her back pocket and turned the screw in the pipe, letting the propane run free.

She listed for a hiss, but didn't hear a thing.

The rotten egg smell didn't come to her until she put the wrench back in her pocket.

It took her twice as long to crawl backward into daylight, the back of her jeans and jacket covered in reddish dirt. She dusted herself off best she could and just started walking down the curved road toward what used to be Paris. The old general store was just a heap of boards and broken glass. The post office was an empty cinder-block building where they'd sometimes have a flea market on Saturday, selling old and useless things. Across the street was a volunteer fire station and a few trailers on a muddy, eroded hill.

Shelby kept walking, camo backpack over her shoulder, listening and looking for Hunter's truck. She figured the house would be good and filled with gas in about an hour, filling those deep, dark places and far corners of that damn drafty old house. Her momma had gone to town. Her brother was already on the bus to school.

She'd left Randy's cigarettes and lighter right where he liked them. Right by his bed.

LORD OF MADISON COUNTY

BY JIMMY CAJOLEAS

Madison

"Are y'all ready to worship?" says Pastor Jerry. He's got his eyes shut, one arm raised high to Jesus in some weird half–Nazi salute. Frosted hair slicked back, bald spot barely showing. Graphic T-shirt that says, *Lord's Gym,* and has Christ bench-pressing a cross on it. Cargo shorts that he still thinks are cool.

I'm a little ways back in the youth room, chewing on a pen cap. The worship band kicks in; it's all reverbed guitar and concert lights and the bullshit praise lyrics projected onto a screen behind them. You know, the songs that are the kind of crap you say to your girlfriend but it's supposed to be about God? *You alone are beautiful. You alone are my rock. You alone are my one and only.* Oh Jesus, baby!

Out in the crowd of youth-groupers are my customers. The girl with her hands up in the air, giggling, singing louder than anyone? That's Theresa. Everyone thinks she's weird, that maybe she's one of God's holy fools, but they all agree that she's on fire with Jesus.

Nah, she just popped a molly.

Don't get me wrong, Theresa loves Jesus. She says drugs just help the experience. She's from Seattle, her parents are hippies, it's a weird thing. But just look at that girl worship!

And the bro with the mullet up front? The one who's all glassy-eyed for the Lord? That's Dennis. I smoked him up about fifteen minutes ago.

I could go on. There's Fran and Baskin and Hillary and Scottie. The youth group is about one hundred strong, and I sell to 30 percent of them.

The praise song ends. The guitars ring out. Pastor Jerry speaks: "The Lord reigns over our city. Can you feel Him all around us? Can you feel Him in this very room? It's good to feel the presence of the Lord. The peace that passeth all understanding. Do y'all feel the peace of the Lord?"

Well, they're feeling something, that's for damn sure.

"Amen," I say.

Pastor Jerry looks out to me and smiles. "Douglas, will you lead us in a word of prayer?"

It's funny. Pastor Jerry has no clue about me. In fact, he believes I'm his greatest success story. I'm fully converted, and Pastor Jerry was the one who did it. I bet that asshole gets a holy boner in his cargo shorts every time he thinks of me.

Not to mention all the converts I brought. Once word got out I was dealing at youth group (they leave all the areas inside the church unlocked, so once you're in, the place is an abandoned labyrinth of dark, closed-off rooms, perfect for private business), all sorts of riffraff started showing up. All of a sudden Pastor Jerry thinks I'm the Apostle Paul to a bunch of stoner kids.

"Sure, Pastor Jerry," I say. "Let us pray."

I used to go to school at Parkside Prep, along with every other rich kid in Madison. I was an okay student, I went to class, whatever. My dad was long gone and my mom started dating this guy, Dillon, who was a total pothead. I caught him at it one day while Mom was at her tennis lesson. I threatened to tell her that Dillon's been selling me weed for months unless he gave me the number for his dealer.

So I went and met the guy, this white dude named Kroner.

He had a shaved head and a nasty scar down his cheek, but he was a smooth guy, kind of soft, like everybody else in Madison. And I pitched him. *You want an in at Parkside? It's all rich kids with trust funds. They'll buy anything to look cool.*

He said sure. It was that easy. He said, *Sure, but if you fuck this up, if you fuck with my money, I will fucking kill you. I will kill you and your entire family. I will cut your mother's lips off and staple them to my dick.*

And it was hard not to laugh. Just think about stapling something to your dick. That's the stupidest shit I ever heard of in my life. Kroner was a fucking moron, and he was going to make me rich.

Everything went smooth at Parkside for a while. I was making all kinds of money. I was a hero. I got every kid the high they wanted. Even Kroner was impressed. All was golden until this fat fucker named Bill Widdleton did a line too many and had a seizure in Mrs. Bilson's art class.

I'd never seen a kid have a seizure before. It was like watching a computer reset. He made this weird stuttering noise first, his chin bobbing up and down like the picture when a DVD skips. In seconds he was flopping on the floor, foaming at the mouth, legs kicking. It was a thing to see.

I shouldn't have stayed to watch though. I should have run my ass to my locker and dumped everything I had in a toilet. Because the ambulance came, and then the cops arrived with the drug dogs.

Even though my dad flew in for a week to pay off half the county, I got kicked out of school. I got a month in juvie. I got mandatory rehab and parole for a year. Mom took my car so I had to walk thirty minutes just to get home. Every shop and gas station I passed made me hate this bullshit town more and more.

It's all about the looks in Madison. Like how every store is made out of bricks. I mean everything, even the Walmart. It's a city ordinance, I don't know. You can't tell if you're at a bank or a gas station half the time. It's like they fling up these cheap strip malls, throw a layer of bricks on them, and act like they're going to last. When they won't last at all. They're just as disposable as everything else in this white-flight town.

My first day at the new school, Kroner drove up in his Mustang with the tinted windows. He had his thug Ty in the passenger seat. Kroner told me if I didn't make it up to him, if I didn't sell enough to cover everything I'd lost him, he would cut my dick off and feed it to his dog.

"You got a dog?" I said.

"A big dog," he said. "A Doberman."

"I figured you more for a dachshund kind of guy."

"A what?"

"You know, a wiener dog."

Kroner didn't think that was funny. His thug Ty—this big blonde-headed county boy, complete with cowboy boots and brass knuckles—stepped out of the car and beat the shit out of me. He took my wallet and my shoes. He kicked me so hard I shit my pants.

There I was, crying my eyes out in a Walgreens parking lot, when I had my idea.

I called up Pineywood Baptist Church, the biggest church in Madison. It's the one my mom and all her friends go to. They have the big church barbecues where everybody gets hammered and figures out who they're going to cheat on their husbands with next. It's a horrible church full of horrible people and everyone knows it.

I asked to talk to the youth pastor. I didn't know his name, I didn't know a thing about him. His secretary said he wasn't in, but I told her it was an emergency so she gave me his cell phone number.

Bless his stupid heart, Pastor Jerry was there ten minutes

after I called him. Picked me up at the Walgreens in his plum-colored Honda Element. Took me straight to his house and listened to my whole bullshit story: the bullying drug dealers, my desire to come clean, to have a fresh start. He had me say the sinner's prayer, right then and there. Then he fed me dinner.

After we ate, Pastor Jerry went to take a dump and left me in the living room with his daughter Kayla. She's a freshman at Parkside. She's gorgeous. I had no clue how I'd never noticed her before. She was watching fat people yell at each other on the TV. A big smiling family portrait hung over the mantelpiece: a four-year-old Kayla, Pastor Jerry, and a brown-haired beauty with gigantic tits who I guessed was Kayla's mom.

"So where's your mom?" I asked.

"She's dead," said Kayla.

"I'm sorry."

"I bet," said Kayla, then she changed the channel. "Are you serious about all this Jesus shit?"

"Nope," I said.

"I hate my dad."

"He's a fucking tool, and he's about to make me a hell of a lot of money."

Kayla smiled at me. I put my arm around her.

I come home from youth group with my backpack full of cash. Just three months in and I already got ten grand hidden in a Nike box up in my room. I overcharge like crazy but the kids are too rich to know the difference, or even to care. It feels good, knowing I got enough to pay Kroner back tonight. Then I can start making the real money.

Mom sits at the dinner table in a purple dress that shows off her legs. Guess she and Dillon must have had a date night.

"Douglas," says Mom, "we have something to talk about."

Immediately I'm on my guard. Did they find out I'm still dealing? Did Kroner rat on me to Dillon?

Jesus, I must be stoned. That's fucking stupid. What good would it do Kroner to have Dillon on my back?

"Dillon and I are getting married!" says Mom.

"That's awesome," I reply. "Great." Dillon's a jobless parasite, a wannabe rock star with a ponytail. But he seems to like my mom okay, and that'll make her happy. Fuck it, whatever.

"Honey, look at the ring he bought me!" Mom holds out her hand to show me the biggest hunk of diamond I've ever seen in my life. Christ. Either that's fake or Dillon robbed a bank, because that dude is broke.

Oh fuck.

I run upstairs to my room and lock the door. I go up to my closet and unscrew the air vent and pull out my Nike box.

It's fucking empty. My future stepdad robbed me.

I call him on his cell phone.

"Howdy, Douglas, did you hear the news?" says Dillon.

"Can it, cocksucker. You fucking stole my money."

"Oh, that little shoe box full of change? You really should take better care of your things." He chuckles. "Actually, that's my first lesson to you, as your stepdad. Take better care of your shit." Dillon laughs and laughs.

"I need that money, man. I'm not kidding. I know you didn't spend it all on the ring. Just give me what you got left over."

"No can do, kiddo. I'm on my way to Tunica now to celebrate."

"Do you realize you're going to get me killed?" I say.

"Who's going to kill you? Kroner? Come on, that guy's a pussy. I used to give him guitar lessons when he was twelve. He's just some Madison kid, a phony like all the rest of you."

"Yeah, you're real hard core, Dillon. You grew up in North fucking Jackson. Real ghetto, man."

"Hey, I'm not the guy who just got robbed by his mom's boyfriend. And thanks, Douglas. I never could have gotten your mom such a nice ring without your help."

I hang up. If I ever get out of this, if I ever go Scarface, I swear to God the first person I kill will be Dillon.

I'm supposed to meet Kroner at ten o'clock on this dirt road two turns off 463. High school kids call it The Spot, but it's always abandoned on school nights. There's no way I'm meeting him out there alone, with no neighbors or people around. No, I got to force him to meet me in public and try to explain things.

It's eight fifteen. Kroner knows where I live, so if I holler at him now he'll be at my place in twenty minutes. I got to be patient, make sure he's all the way out at The Spot before I make contact.

I light up a joint and crank my stereo and wait. At ten thirty my phone starts ringing. I let him call me for five minutes before I answer.

"Hey, Kroner, dude. What time is it?" I say.

"Ten thirty, you pussy," he shoots back. "That makes you thirty minutes late."

"Shit, yeah, man, I'm sorry. Just fell asleep."

"Do you need me to come and get your ass?" he says.

"Listen. There's a problem." Maybe it's the weed, maybe it's just because I don't know what else to do, but I go for it: "My stepdad stole all your money."

"Are you fucking with me?" says Kroner.

"I had it hid in a shoe box up in my room and he stole it."

"Dillon stole it? The guitar-teacher guy?"

"Yeah, him. He's my stepdad."

"You had my money in a shoe box? With your daddy's old *Playboys*? This is some junior high shit, man."

"I'll get you your money back. As soon as I can."

"No, motherfucker. You get me my money tonight." He hangs up.

That didn't go well. I got to get on the move, somewhere Kroner won't know to find me. I fill my backpack with the rest of my cash and all my bud. Maybe I can bargain with some of it.

Mom's got the TV loud and she's asleep in her pink bathrobe on the couch. I bend down and kiss her forehead. For a second I think about waking her up, telling her everything, asking for her help. But then I remember what it was like after Dad left, the overdose on sleeping pills, how proud she is of me now that I'm Jesus Boy. Besides, all the money she's got is whatever Dad sends her, since he had the good lawyer and won the divorce.

Mom stirs, but doesn't wake up. I ease the door shut behind me. I figure I'll go to Kayla's. Kroner doesn't know her, and even if he did, I doubt he would storm a preacher's house.

On the way I call my dad, just to see if he'll answer for once. He doesn't, but I leave a voice mail asking him to call me, it's urgent. Fat chance of that ever happening, but I give it a shot.

It's eleven fifteen. There's no doubt Kayla's asleep. Both she and her dad have this thing where they conk out at ten, no matter what. She calls it the family curse, says everyone on her dad's side has it. Their house is two stories, in Annandale, but there's a big tree on the back side of her house, facing her window, and it's easy for me to climb.

I knock on the window until she wakes up.

"Hello, sexy," she says, pulling me into her room.

God, Kayla. Only fifteen but with a body like a girl in a rap video. She's wearing one of my T-shirts, that's it, and no bra. We sit down on her bed.

"I'm in trouble," I say.

She's got a happy glazed smile on her face, like she hasn't

quite woken up yet. There's a glow in her window and I can't tell if it's a streetlight or the moon. Outside is the developed half-woods of every Madison neighborhood. The only things out on the streets are kids and rent-a-cops chasing them down.

"What's got my boy so worked up?" says Kayla.

I tell her the whole thing, about Kroner and Dillon and the money, about how royally fucked I am.

"Does Dillon have anything?" she asks. "I mean, he fucked you over. He deserves it. And he's out of town, right? It'll be easy."

"Nah. He's a mooch, been living off my mom for two years now. Had to rob me to buy the ring, remember?"

"But he's got those guitars, right? The ones he teaches with?"

Goddamn, she's right. A 1969 Les Paul Custom Black Beauty. Keeps it in a glass case. I've seen him wipe it down for hours at Mom's house, when he's showing off for her. He won't let anyone else touch it. I could pawn that for a pretty good bit. There's a handful of other ones, seventies Telecasters, a big red Gretsch hollow-body. He's also got an old Fender Strat that he claims he used "for gigs" that's worth a decent amount.

"Kayla, you're a motherfucking genius. You're saving my life."

"Let's smoke a blunt first," she says.

"You know why I love you?"

"Because I'm the tightest pussy you ever had?"

I want to say, *You're the only pussy I ever had.*

I want to say, *You're harder than I ever dreamed of being.*

I want to say, *No one loves me and no one ever did and if you were to die I would have nothing.*

But what I say is, "If the Rapture came and sucked all the good people up, you and me would rule the earth."

"We already do," she counters, and passes me the blunt.

Dillon lives in a shitty brick thing in Gluckstadt. It's got neighbors and a red door and a yard full of weeds. Dillon's car broke down a few times so I've given him rides to and from work, but I've never been inside. The streetlight is burned out and all the neighbors' windows are dark.

I try my debit card on the front door look. Kayla stands there with her arms crossed and a smirk on her face.

"You ever done this before?" she says.

"Yeah," I lie. My card snaps in half.

Kayla walks over to the street and picks up a fist-sized chunk of broke-off concrete.

"What are you gonna do with that?"

"Baby, sometimes you're so fucking stupid," she says.

I follow her around to the backyard where she chucks it through the kitchen window. I flinch, waiting for alarms to sound, for cops to come dropping out of trees and arrest the fuck out of us. But nothing happens. No neighbor lights even flick on. Just the insect whir of summer nights in Mississippi.

"He could have had an alarm system," I say.

Kayla smirks at me. Then she clears the rest of the glass out with a stick and crawls through. I follow.

The nicest thing in Dillon's den is the TV. It's big and flat-screen and mounted on the wall like a goddamn family portrait. He probably watches Asian foot porn on it all day. He's got a record player from the eighties, one of those big battleship-looking ones. The couch is fake leather. There's a Pink Floyd poster on the wall. It's like a shitty older brother's college dorm.

His bedroom is even worse. The bed is big and unmade, with red sheets. He's got boxers and used socks and flannel shirts all over the floor. An opened box of lubed Trojans sits on the bedside table and I gag a little.

"Hey, look at these," says Kayla. She holds up some lacy red panties. "Holy shit, are these your mom's?"

"Don't touch those. That's fucking gross," I say.

"I bet they are." Kayla drops her jean shorts and then her panties, and she's just white V-neck and pussy bare to the world. She's got my mom's panties dangling from her finger.

"Please don't," I say.

Kayla slides them up her legs. "You like me in these?"

"Stop it."

"They're kind of tight. Your mom has the tiniest ass." She climbs up in Dillon's bed. "You want to fuck me in your stepdad's bed?" She reaches her finger down into her panties. "Come on, peel your mommy's panties off and fuck me right now."

Kayla lifts one foot up, a slender, tanned thing. I can see her whole gorgeous leg. Her nipples stand up in the white undershirt.

I'm so hard it hurts. Sometimes Kayla really scares me.

I crawl onto the bed and Kayla pulls my shirt off, then the rest of my clothes. We fuck slow and good. She wants to be on top, and I let her have it. Kayla rides me until she cums. Then I get mine. When it's over she clings to me like I'm the only thing on earth, arms and legs wrapped tight around me, like if she let go she'd fall forever. It feels good to be somebody's only. Too bad I can't let the quiet last.

"Baby," I say, sitting up, "it's time to steal us some guitars."

I dress quickly, conscious of the time we just lost. Kayla only bothers with a T-shirt and my mom's panties. I make a face at her.

"What?" she says. "I like them. They're sexier than anything I got."

In the far back of the house is a little room crammed with music equipment. I guess this is the "jam room" Dillon's always talking about. The guitars are hanging from a rack on the wall. A Marshall half-stack from the seventies stands in a corner with a pedal board that takes up half the floor space. There's also a black light and a minibar.

"What a fucking loser," says Kayla.

"There's the guitars," I say.

"I'm more interested in the booze."

There's a minibar stocked full of whiskey bottles. Kayla grabs the smallest, most pricey-looking bottle. It's got a cork in it. She pops it and takes a sniff. "Smells expensive." Kayla takes a slug and passes it to me and I pass it back.

She wanders off, so I set to work on getting the guitars down. I sling the Les Paul around my right shoulder, like a rifle. The Strat doesn't have a strap so I just hold it by the neck.

A crash comes from the den. Kayla's in my mom's underpants, ripping shit off the walls.

"The fuck are you doing?"

"Well, it'll be pretty suspicious if we bust in and go right for the goods, like we already knew where everything was. Besides," she says, chucking a framed picture of Dillon's mom against the wall, "it's fun. Try it."

I lay the guitars down and walk over to the TV. I grab it with both hands and yank it loose from the wall mounts. I lift the TV over my head and smash it into the coffee table. I smash it like Moses smashed the Ten Commandments. I stomp it and stomp it and stomp it till it's nothing but a mass of glass and wire.

I stop when I feel a hand on my shoulder. Kayla's smiling.

"That's it, baby," she says. "Just like that."

We get the guitars and go back out the window. I never stole anything before. It's fucking easy. You just bash a window, walk in, and take whatever you want. It's that simple. Why does anyone ever get a real job?

We drive off toward town, not a single flashing blue light in sight. Me and Kayla avoid the highway, moving only on back roads toward Madison. There's always a million cops out on 463 and they'll pull you over for nothing. At night, if you got long hair or a sticker on your car or you're not driving a Beamer, you're fucked.

When we get back to town, me and Kayla decide to drive back to her house and wait the night out. To do that, we have to cross the highway, the only time we won't be on back roads. I don't like it, but if we keep driving around, eventually a cop's going to pull us over, and I can't think of a better idea.

Everything's going just fine until we catch a red light next to a new strip of lawyer offices and my passenger window explodes. Glass flies all in my face, in Kayla's hair. Before I can do anything the door rips open and Ty the Thug yanks Kayla out of the car by her hair.

The headlights from a car parked along the side of the road cut on. The door of the Mustang opens and Kroner steps out.

"You trying to bail on me?" he says. "Going out for a stroll with your lady friend?"

"I got half your money here," I say. "Now let her loose, a'ight?"

I pull Dillon's prize Les Paul out of the car. The pickups sparkle in the headlights. Kroner takes it and gives it a once-over.

"What the hell am I supposed to do with a guitar?" he says. "I quit lessons after like two months. I need cash."

"You give me until tomorrow and it will be cash, moron."

Kroner takes the guitar by the neck and smashes it onto the pavement until it's just splinters and strings. "Always wanted to do that," he says.

"Yeah, you're a real fucking rock star," I say.

Kroner pulls an ugly-looking buck knife out of a sheath on his belt and points it at my chest. "You think I'm a pussy, don't you? All motherfuckers around here think because I'm not from Jackson I'm a fucking pussy. Well, I ain't a pussy. And I'm about to show you."

He punches Kayla in the face. I can't believe it. She falls back onto the street.

The big guy kicks me in the knee. I go down on the pavement. He puts a boot on my neck and keeps it there.

Kroner bends over Kayla. "Look me in the eyes," he says to me. "I will rape her. I will fuck her every which way I want to. I will make that tight little pussy bleed. Do you hear me? I'm on a whole new level, Dougie. Nobody's ever gonna fuck with me again." He spits on Kayla. "Get me the money and I'll give you your girl back. Meet me at The Spot in three hours."

Ty takes his foot off my throat and I can breathe again. He grabs Kayla and shoves her into the trunk of Kroner's Mustang. They drive off into the night.

I try to get up all calm and dust myself off. I walk away from the main road, away from where any passing cars can see me, behind a strip of disposable stores, and puke. One of the stores is under construction, they're building a new bathroom or something, and there's all kinds of shit—boards, glass, metal beams, nails—all over the place.

A noise like a window getting busted erupts out of the woods. I think it's Kroner back to kill me or the cops or somebody wrecked a car. But a doe comes bounding out, bewildered and bleeding down its legs. Then comes a buck and a limping fawn, a whole lost family crashing on the construction material, sounding like a pack of looters.

The buck stares me down, its horns like weird fangs jutting out of its skull, like he will charge me at any moment if I so much as lift a finger toward his family.

I know I only got one person I can call.

Pastor Jerry answers on the sixth ring. His voice is rusted, croaking, not the cheerful high-pitched happy routine he gives the youth group. He sounds busted, worn out, and tired.

"Pastor Jerry, this is Douglas. I got a problem. It's Kayla. We need to talk."

He tells me to come over and I'm there in ten minutes. Pastor Jerry's got a look to him like he's halfway between pissed and confused. I sit him down on his front porch and tell him everything, like he's a priest, like he's my dad, like he's God Himself.

"We have to go to the cops, Douglas," he says. "There's no way I'm letting anything happen to Kayla."

"Can't. They'll hurt her. These guys are on some crazy shit." It's the first time I've ever cussed in front of him. If he notices, he doesn't show it.

"How much you need?"

"About ten grand," I say.

"Come inside," he says, flicking his cigarette off into the bushes.

Pastor Jerry takes me to his bedroom, to a wooden trunk he has in the back of his closet. There's a letter in it, some bottled water, canned food.

"It's Kayla's Rapture kit," he says. "You know, in case she doesn't come to Jesus in time. If I get taken and she gets left. It's enough for her to live safely on for a while."

The trunk has a false shelf. When he takes it out, there's got to be twenty grand down there. Pastor Jerry counts out ten grand. We put it in a Walmart bag.

"I got to go," I say.

"I'm coming with you. I'm a pastor, and I want to make sure no one gets hurt. Especially not my baby girl."

"No fucking way you're coming with me," I say.

"If I don't go, you don't get the money."

"Christ, fine, whatever. Let's go."

"Let me pray first," says Pastor Jerry.

"We don't have time for that kind of crap."

Pastor Jerry looks hurt, like a dad whose kid just got caught cheating on a test. It makes me feel kind of shitty.

"Look, you can pray in the car. Let's just go."

We drive without any music, just the wind sliced by my busted window. Pastor Jerry prays to Jesus. He prays with his hands lifted up, same as he does in youth group, in that soft, sincere voice, begging God for the safety of his sweet Kayla, his good daughter who stumbled off the path.

"I know she doesn't believe yet, Lord, but please let my faith be enough. Please let the faith of a parent get her through."

It's pure TBN Joel Osteen horseshit, but you can tell Pastor Jerry actually means it. He asks for forgiveness for all kinds of stuff—for his failure as a dad, as a husband, all his own faults and shortcomings. Never once does he blame me.

That hurts, you know? This guy was never anything but good to me and I have him begging Christ for his little girl's life. Same daughter I fucked earlier tonight and who might get murdered because of me, same one who he doesn't even hardly know, not really. Pastor Jerry never stole anything from me like Dillon, and he sure stuck around longer than my own dad when I was in trouble. I've done nothing but take from him. I've made a fool out of him.

All the while Pastor Jerry prays.

We pull up to The Spot in my bashed car. Kroner's leaning against his Mustang with his arms crossed like a gangster in a movie. A bit-off chunk of moon hangs in the sky half-hidden by clouds. Ty holds Kayla by her arms. He's got sunglasses on even though it's dark. When I get out, I slam the door like I'm a tough guy and the rest of the glass shatters out in shards. Pastor Jerry steps out gingerly over the glass.

"Who the fuck is that guy?" asks Kroner.

"That's Kayla's dad," I say. "I had to get the money somewhere."

"We can do this real safe-like," says Pastor Jerry. He holds out the money in a Walmart bag. "Everybody needs to keep real cool now. I don't want any harm to come to anybody. Christ died for each and every one of you. Even if you don't believe it."

"The fuck is he talking about?" says Kroner.

"He's a youth pastor," I say.

"Oh," says Kroner. "I fucking hated youth group."

"Why?" asks Pastor Jerry.

"The singing. I hate singing."

"Just give him the money," I say.

"Yeah, give me the money," says Kroner.

Pastor Jerry tosses him the bag. Kroner smiles.

The whole time Kayla's got her arms crossed over her tits. Blood's dried all down her face. I can tell she's chewing on the inside of her cheek; she does it whenever she's mad. I've seen her chew herself till she bled out of her mouth before. Ty has his hands on her shoulders, those stupid sunglasses on. Her head barely comes up to his chest.

"I told you not to fuck with me," says Kroner. "I told you I was hard." He grabs Kayla away from Ty and pulls her to him, twisting her arm behind her back, then yanks her head back by her hair. "See what I can do? See what I can do to your girl?" He licks Kayla's neck. "I can do anything I want. I'm the hardest motherfucker in this whole city. Fuck Jackson. I'm the Lord of goddamned Madison County."

Kayla elbows Kroner in the stomach. With her free hand she pulls his knife out of his belt sheath, whirls, and slides the blade across his face. It's quick, but awkward, like she was aiming for Kroner's throat but didn't know how to do it, like she had never really tried to hurt anyone before. She only gets Kroner's ear. It half-hangs off his cheek, mutilated, dangling from a flap of skin.

"You bitch! Jesus, my face!" Kroner reaches out to Ty, but the thug backs away like he doesn't want any blood on him.

"You beat me," says Kayla. "You were going to rape me."

"Baby?" says Pastor Jerry.

"You're fucking dead," says Kroner. He points to Ty. "Kill her."

"If you take one step closer I will cut your dick off." She points the knife at Kroner. "I will cut it off and fuck him with it."

Ty takes his sunglasses off. His eyes are blue and scared. He looks down at Kayla, then back to Kroner.

"You need to leave," says Pastor Jerry. "I'm going to call an ambulance."

Ty nods. He backs up a few steps with his hands in the air, like he's being held up, then takes off running toward the woods.

"My fucking ear," moans Kroner. Blood leaks between his fingers and down his face. "You cut it off."

"Not all the way," says Kayla.

Pastor Jerry pulls a handkerchief out of his pocket. It's the same one he's always wiping his face with when he preaches. He kneels down next to Kroner and presses the handkerchief to the guy's ear, as if to heal him. Kroner cries and cries.

"I can't fucking believe this," says Kayla. "Get up, Dad."

Pastor Jerry shakes his head.

"I said get up."

"No," says Pastor Jerry. "Remember, *There is more joy in Heaven over one sinner who repents than ninety-nine who need no repentance.*"

"You can have that party without me," says Kayla. "If you call an ambulance, the cops will come, and no fucking way I'm going to be around for that." She turns to me. "Keys?"

I look at her and there's no love looking back. There's something else in her eyes, a disappointment. Like I let her down. Like I couldn't handle the situation and I had to go running to her daddy. Kayla finally sees me for what I really am: another goddamn phony Madison kid. Not like her. Kayla's something different.

I toss her the keys. Kayla tucks Kroner's knife in her belt. She picks up the bag of money, gets in my car, and drives off down the dirt road toward the highway. I watch my car disappear into the darkness without me.

Kroner whimpers on the ground. Pastor Jerry's still holding him, rocking him back and forth, praying for him. They seem so close, like they're related, like a father and son. The moonlight hits the shattered glass around them and the pieces glimmer. I feel like I belong there in the dirt with them, wounded and bleeding and maybe about to be healed. Pastor Jerry begins to sing a hymn, one I recognize from youth group. I would join in but I never bothered to learn the words.

LOSING HER RELIGION

BY RaShell R. Smith-Spears

Jackson

it waznt a spirit took my stuff
waz a man whose ego walked round like Rodan's shadow
waz a man faster n my innocence
waz a lover
i made too much room for

> —from Ntozake Shange,
> "Somebody almost walked off wid alla my stuff"

Jada Wallace wrapped her long bronze legs around her lover's waist as he slammed her into the bedroom wall. Her tongue pushed desperately past his lips, seeking the flavor of his mouth. His hands were just as desperate; they ran up her back under her shirt, seeking the hooks of her bra. The release of her breasts was freeing and satisfying. He threw her down on the bed and straddled her waist. He jerked her shirt over her head after his lips found hers again and pressed painfully against them. With equal purpose and intensity, he unsnapped her jeans and yanked them down her legs along with the pink lace panties she had worn for him. She sat up and licked a trail down his stomach, following the path laid out by the soft, dark hair that started at his navel and disappeared into his shorts, while she opened his jeans. Apparently, she was moving too slowly because he pushed her back on the bed and yanked his own jeans off. Having discarded his shirt almost immediately after coming into the house, he now stood before her naked and beautiful. His creamy white skin looked so delicious she wanted to run her tongue all over it; she wanted to bite him everywhere. And she did. As he covered her body and entered her, she put her mouth over the skin of his shoulder and bit down. And as he rocked her hard and fast, flipping her on top of him, then throwing her back underneath him, she found different areas of his body to place her teeth: his neck, his broad chest, the inside of his arm, between his thumb and finger. Anywhere on his body she could get access to, she marked her territory. She laid her claim to him just as his body inside of hers laid claim to her. She was his, all of her.

"Whose is it!" he demanded.

"Yours," she gasped.

"Who?" he growled. His face was red. A vein in his neck stood out.

"Yours, Derek. Only yours."

With a thunderous growl, he took the ultimate claim of her. "God, I love you, Jada!"

With that, she came.

They lay beside one another, both spent and sweaty, holding hands. Jada could not believe how satisfied she was. Was it anyone's right to feel that good?

A slight buzzing sounded from the nightstand by her bed. Derek reached over and looked at his cell phone. Placing it back down, he sat up and swung his legs over the side of the bed.

"Where're you going?" Jada asked.

"Home." He had already found and pulled on his jeans.

"Now? I thought *she* was going to be out all night with her friends." Jada never called his wife by her name. It was hard to keep from calling her by other names.

"Guess the night ended early for her." He was buttoning his shirt, the dark blue button-down Jada had given him.

"So it has to end early for us?"

"Unfortunately," he bent over and kissed her forehead, "yes."

Derek sat on the bed, his back to her, and put on his mahogany slip-ons.

"I thought we had the whole night; I had things planned." She ran her fingers down his back and pulled his shirt out of his pants waist. She slipped her hand underneath, against his warm skin.

He stood up and stuffed his shirttail back into his pants. He gave her an exasperated look. "Jada, I gotta go. You know how this goes."

"Why? Why does it have to go this way? Why does *she* get every damn minute of your time?"

"She's my wife. You know that. I made promises to her. I told you I wasn't looking to end my marriage when we first hooked up. I thought you understood that."

Jada rose up on her knees, letting the sheet fall away to reveal her naked body. "You made promises to me. Every time you bust a nut, you tellin' me you love me. That's a promise."

"C'mon. That's just nuttin' talk." He looked at Jada's body with longing.

"You know you want this. You can have it . . . if you stay a little longer."

Derek leaned over to Jada, his knee on the bed and the other foot still on the floor. He grabbed one of Jada's breasts and put it in his mouth. She threw her head back in pleasure—the physical pleasure of his tongue and the emotional pleasure of winning the battle. Jada didn't beg men to stay—ever. It unnerved her that she begged now. But at least she had him; he was staying. His tongue traveled from her breast to her neck. Jada grabbed the back of his head, and guided him to her mouth. His tongue tasted like mint. She pulled him down on top of her, but he pushed back up.

"I'll see you at work on Monday." He flicked her wet nipple and walked out of her bedroom after grabbing his cell phone.

Jada pulled the cover over her cold, naked body and wondered how she'd gotten into this position in the first place and how she could get out of it.

Gray clouds held the sun hostage at 6:45 in the morning. The sun tried to break free of the rain clouds' prison, glowing faintly on the horizon every so often as Jada sped up I-55 to Madison. She had left later than she intended which meant that she would probably be late all day. She tried not to take this as a bad omen, but the dreary cloud jailers seemed impossible to ignore. But sign or no sign, she would make her pilgrimage; she had made it every Sunday for the past month and would continue to do so until she had reached the nirvana she sought. The journey itself was a sanctifying ritual, working her into a passionate fervor. As she drove, she didn't see the stores—Char, Chili's, Target—that she had grown up with most of her life and which lined the sides of the interstate like silent sentinels. Instead she focused on her relationship with Derek, recounting what they had done and said the week before, smiling at the funny exchange they had on their way back from the pep rally for school-wide testing. She remembered the sex the night before, and a gentle shiver fell over her body. Already she felt sacred.

By the time she pulled over into the driveway of the house next to the two-story brick Tudor, she was almost ready for prayer. She prepared by pushing aside the pocket New Testament and the small pistol she always carried in her purse, and in calming solitude, she pulled out, then applied her Red Revival lipstick. Gently rubbing the velvety color between her lips, she surveyed the house's landscaping, checking whether any changes had been made since the last Sunday. Fresh straw had been laid on the flowerbed that held budding tulips. It seemed a few branches had been cut back from one of the two large trees in the neatly manicured lawn. Jada closed her eyes and imagined she had been working in the yard yesterday morning; she had laid the straw. Dressed in her bright green capris and a peach T-shirt, she had kneeled in front of the flowerbed and removed most of the old, graying straw, placing it in a pile behind her. She worked hard, stopping every now and then to pull up some newly sprouted weeds. It was important to remove ugly, unwanted weeds so that the beautiful could grow. The sun had come out and she had begun to sweat. She wiped her brow with the back of her wrist. One of her neighbors, an older white gentleman, called to her. She smiled and waved at him. Returning to her work, she didn't even notice Derek walking out with a glass of lemonade and her straw hat. He startled her by placing the hat on her head. She smiled up at him and stood. They shared a long kiss before she took the glass from him and drank the lemonade. He took the glass back, slapped her butt, and walked back in their house.

Jada exhaled, willing the fantasy to become reality. She would speak it to the universe so that which she named, she could claim. She and Derek were meant for beautiful things. She had not known it when they first met two years earlier on her first day at the high school where they both taught, but a year later, after they hooked up a few times, it became overwhelmingly clear.

"I want us to be together. God, I claim his love. I claim our love, in the name of Jesus," she declared in the car sitting in the driveway next door to his house. "Please."

Just as she opened her eyes, Derek's front door opened and his wife came outside. *She is so ordinary,* Jada thought. *What does he see in her?*

Jada wasn't sure when she started viewing her as a rival, but as she scrutinized her now, she couldn't help but notice how uninteresting her wild curly brown hair and her pale, oval face were. The only thing that made her interesting was the olive undertone that hinted at her biracial heritage. She was thin and straight, like a boy. Derek said she played tennis in high school. Of course, that was fifteen years ago.

Jada peered a little closer, noting that she was gaining weight; at five four, her widening hips made her look short and sloppy. She certainly was no match for Jada's shapely five seven. Summing her up, Jada assessed that she was not very formidable competition.

She got into her car and blew the horn. That was Jada's cue to leave. Derek's wife was calling him to come out so they could go to church. He probably wouldn't have noticed Jada in the driveway, but she thought it better to leave.

Driving back down I-55, she observed the city coming awake. More cars were on the road even if the parking lots of the stores on the side were still empty. She loved the look of the city, having grown up in it most of her life. She learned to drive on the wide, open curves near Tougaloo College, one of the city's two historically black colleges. In Fondren, the artsy part of town, she and her high school boyfriend went on her first date to eat at Brent's Drugs. At Jackson State University, the other HBCU, she fell in love with biology and decided she would share that love with other generations as a teacher. Now she taught at the same high school she had graduated from and she loved her job and her children. She had watched the city of Jackson progress and regress, decay and rebound, and she loved every inch of it.

Of course, her senior year, she thought she would be on the first plane soaring out of the state. A full scholarship to Jackson State and a summer teaching program between her junior and senior year ensured that she would not only remain for college, but that she would stay after graduation. God had jokes. Just when she thought she had everything figured out, He surprised her.

Like Derek. Jada had never intended to fall in love with him. It had been all about the sex. Like it had been with the others. Since her freshman-year relationship ended badly with a boy who couldn't commit if he were sewn to his girlfriend, she only entered relationships that promised to be beneficial to her financially or sexually. That meant three things to her: one, she was not interested in becoming emotionally involved, opting to see the men on a rotating basis. It also meant that she was perfectly okay with sleeping with a married man if she were attracted. Finally, it meant that she would only date white men. She entertained thoughts of sleeping with black men, but often, if they had any money, it was tied up in some plan for entrepreneurship or worse, some baby mama. White men could satisfy both her craving for the physical and the financial. Hooking up with Derek happened in a perfect storm: he was white, from a well-off family, her first married man, and he caught her when no other men were on her dating horizon.

Jada zoomed down the interstate toward the Byram exit. The small city outside of Jackson had grown up almost overnight, much to the dismay of Jackson's city leaders who wanted to consume Byram in its body. The town had been so rural when she was a little girl attending church. Her grandmother had moved her and her sister Regina to South Jackson when she was ten, but they had maintained membership in the town's little country church. As she drove down quiet roads, lined on one side by a speckling of small, older houses, trailers, and the occasional new stone houses, and on the other side by fenced-in yards corralling horses and cows, a few cars joined her on their way to one of the many country churches. Jada marveled at how quickly things can change. One minute she was surrounded by the signs of city life with the stores, wide pavement, and multiple cars, and then, a few miles down the road, she was in the midst of rural life. One minute she was unattached and unconcerned about any man in her life, and then, a few weeks down the calendar, one man was all she could think about. She didn't like it at all, but like the city leaders of Jackson, she was powerless to stop its progress.

Jada went on to church, but she'd already had her worship service, complete with prayer and praise, outside of Derek's house. If anyone had asked her about why she did this every Sunday, she would have told them she was keeping tabs on her investment, but really she didn't know why she did it. Sometimes it worried her, but she didn't dwell on it long.

After church she drove to her grandmother's house. Nana had been too ill to attend church for the past few months. Jada took her a CD of the day's sermon.

Her grandmother had never been a big woman. Jada inherited her height and size from her grandfather, a man she had never really gotten to know since he died when she was five and her sister seven. By all accounts, he was a big, jovial man who worked hard for his family until the day he died. In fact, he was at work at the Pepsi bottling plant when he had his fatal heart attack.

But Nana was a thin woman who stood at five feet even. She had a big presence, always unafraid to stand her ground and make people acquiesce to her will. Now, however, Nana looked small, in her pink flowered nightgown, lying in the hospital bed they moved in when she came from the hospital. Her steel-gray hair, usually pulled back into a single thick braid, was loose and unkempt. A thin sheet covered her legs, but nothing else. Her eyes were closed when Jada came to the bed and sat in the chair that had been vacated by the home health care nurse when Jada entered the house. The chair was still warm.

"Hey, Nana," Jada almost whispered. It was hard seeing the woman who raised her like this. She fought against the lump rising like dry yeast in her throat.

Nana opened her eyes, the color of watered-down coffee. She rolled her head over and looked at Jada with those eyes. "Hey, baby." Her voice was scratchy and airy at the same time.

It is hardly a voice, Jada thought. "How you feeling today, lady?"

She smiled weakly. "Fair to middlin'."

Jada smiled back. "Well, the nurse said you've had a pretty good day."

"Humph. Did *she* have the day? How is she going to pronounce my day good?"

Jada laughed, glad to see Nana had not lost her spunk, even in her illness. It gave her a little hope; maybe she wouldn't have to face losing her grandmother so soon. She knew it was selfish. Nana was over eighty years old and she was tired. She had been through sharecropping, Jim Crow, struggles to vote, struggles to work. Her home had been attacked by white racists and later by black gangbangers. She had raised two daughters and later two granddaughters. She bore witness to the devastation of losing a child and then, a few years later, a spouse. She had seen her brother and her sister as well as two parents move on to glory. Now, her body was old and shutting down, diabetes and hypertension demanding more of her than was their due. But they were claiming her nonetheless. Jada knew she deserved rest, but Nana was the core of her earth; without her she would spin hopelessly off her axis. The back of Jada's throat stung. Her cheeks grew hot, and she knew if she didn't stop it now, she would soon be a sobbing mess lying in Nana's bed. She switched her thoughts to wondering what Derek was doing.

"How is she?" a whispered voice asked, rousing her from her pleasant thoughts. It was Regina.

"She's fine," Nana answered in a voice strong enough to convey a hint of annoyance.

"I'm glad to hear it, Nana." Regina leaned over the bed and kissed their grandmother on the forehead. Then she hugged Jada. "How long have you been here?"

"Just a little while. I came from church." Out of the corner of her eye, Jada saw her grandmother smile. She knew it would please her to hear that she went to church. Her sister rolled her eyes.

"Have you had anything to eat, Nana?" Regina asked, clearly trying to steer the conversation to some other topic.

"I ain't hungry."

"You have to eat, Nana," Jada gently chastised, losing some of the hope she had before. If Nana didn't eat, she would not have strength to stay around. It wasn't a good sign that she didn't want to eat. "At least drink one of your shakes."

"Okay, baby, I'll get one a little later. You girls sit down and tell me what's going on with you."

Jada sat back in her chair while Regina pulled up another chair beside her.

"I saw that new Tyler Perry movie," Regina offered.

"I likes that Tyler Perry. Madea cracks me up," Nana half-chuckled.

"Who did you go with?" Jada asked.

"Tayshun."

"You two have been going out for like a month now. Is this serious?" Jada teased.

Her sister pushed her playfully in the arm. "Who knows, you might be a maid of honor soon instead of just an old maid."

"Don't worry about me; I get mine," Jada boasted.

"I do worry about you, baby," Nana interjected quietly. "I wish you would find a good man you can settle down with, have me some great-grands. I don't want to leave you here by yourself."

"She has me, Nana," Regina said.

"You can't do for her what a man can do, Gina."

"Nana!"

"I'm sick and old, Gina, not stupid. I remember what your grandpa did for me."

"Nana, I'm not old enough for this conversation," Jada laughed.

"You too old to be by yourself."

"She's picky, Nana. She don't like 'em too dark. Really, she likes 'em, you know . . ." Regina turned one of her palms faceup and rubbed her finger across it.

"White?" their grandmother shrieked. "Oh, Lawd Jesus, where did I go wrong?"

"It's fine, Nana. I've dated black guys before."

"Don't let her fool you, Nana. She hasn't dated a black man in years."

"Jada, baby, tell me it ain't true." She raised up slightly, seeming to gain strength from what she had to say. "You know them white folks near 'bout ran me out of my house that time just 'cause I moved into their neighborhood. And they kept passing yo' grandfather up for promotion at the plant even though he had the knowledge and experience. They don't mean you no good, Jada." She fell back, having spent all of her energy.

"That was then, Nana. I know there were some bad racists in the past, but this is the new millennium. White people aren't all racists. And if they all hated all of us, would any of the men even consider dating me?"

"Yeah. They want some of that sweet brown sugar."

"Regina, you are not helping," Jada countered. "Take the guy I'm dating now. Yes, he told me his family would rather he be with someone white like them, but he doesn't care. He prefers black women."

"What's this fella's name?" Nana asked, still looking disappointed.

"Derek Ross. He's a teacher at my school."

"Humph."

"I really like him, Nana. I like him more than anybody I've liked in a long time." It felt good to talk about Derek to her grandmother. To finally be out in the open with her feelings for him, even if she couldn't tell her everything. But even her sister didn't know he was married or how much she actually cared about him.

"Humph. Regina, go get me a shake. I'm getting thirsty."

They watched Regina leave the room before Jada spoke again.

"Nana, you would really like him, if—"

"Hush, child. I see the crazy way yo' face is lightin' up just talkin' about this white boy. Get that anniversary necklace out my jewelry box."

A little peeved that Nana had interrupted her and said she looked crazy on top of it, she went to the jewelry box and retrieved the necklace her grandmother used to wear only on special occasions—sterling silver with a medium-sized mother-of-pearl teardrop dangling at the end. Nana had polished it once a week ever since her husband had given it to her on their twentieth wedding anniversary. He saved a year to buy it. The chain was now dull, more evidence of her grandmother's failing health.

"Take it."

"Nana?"

"Take it. I know I probably should give it to your sister since she's the oldest, but I think you need it. It's not a diamond necklace, not even pearl, but it cost your grandfather a full year of workin' at the plant and fixin' cars to get it for me. White folks threatened to fire him at the plant when they found out he was working at the car shop on the weekends, so he started just fixin' cars at our house. He didn't give up where he was going for them."

"Don't worry, Nana. I never let these men get in my head."

"Humph. Put it on." Nana watched as Jada clasped it behind her neck. "Don't you give up too much for this white boy. Your grandfather worked that year, made that sacrifice because he loved me. Now, you wear it and remember, don't settle for anything less than a love that will sacrifice for you. Don't lose yourself."

"Of course, Nana. You know Gina is going to be mad you gave me this necklace instead of her."

"I'll deal with Gina. Pull this cover up on me. I need to get some sleep."

The visit with Nana lingered in her mind Monday morning when Jada entered the school building wearing the necklace. She was not as concerned about Nana's health—she felt better about that—as she was about her grandmother's advice to her. She knew she was in deeper with Derek than she had been with any man in a long time, but she certainly wasn't in any danger of losing herself, whatever that meant. She knew Derek would never leave his wife. She didn't expect him to, like silly mistresses did. Their arrangement was solid, secure. She enjoyed being with him, he enjoyed being with her. Except for the occasional annoying demands on his time, his marriage was a good insurance policy, Jada thought. It meant no surprises.

She refrained from her routine second-period visit to Derek's classroom in an effort to prove something. She would wait and let him come to her. But by lunch he had not come by, so she went to his room. That's when she discovered he had a substitute teacher; he hadn't even come to work. She tried texting him, sending an innocuous message about school in case *she* read his messages, but he didn't respond.

On Tuesday, he did come to her classroom between classes. Emerging from the wave of kids filing out of her room, he was like a merking—tall, powerful, and beautiful. His full, blond-streaked, light-brown hair flowed against the wind of people moving past him. It highlighted his strong cheekbones and square jawline underneath tanned skin.

Jada exhaled at his beauty. "Hey, stranger. Where were you yesterday?" She smiled as she silently willed her last student out of her classroom.

Derek glanced around, noticing the slow-moving girl. He looked back at Jada with a pensive expression. "I was, uh, at the doctor's office."

"Are you okay?" Jada asked, sounding too alarmed even to herself.

"Yeah, everything's fine. Um, I, uh, just came by to say hi. I'll see you at lunch, okay?"

"Yeah, sure."

Derek nodded and walked out, leaving even before Jada's student.

He was acting strangely. He seemed distracted and cagey. Jada didn't like it, especially after not seeing him on Monday. Maybe he was really sick. He hadn't said anything about feeling bad. Of course, he hadn't told her he was going to see a doctor either. Maybe it was just a routine visit. He looked healthy enough, Jada thought, calling up the excitement of seeing him walk through her door.

By lunchtime, she was vacillating between worry and calm, finally deciding he was fine. She was on her way to meet him in the lounge when he appeared in her door.

"Are you walking me to the lounge? Did you want to carry my books?"

Derek did not return her smile. He closed the door. "We need to talk."

"Something is wrong with you!" she gasped, and sat back down in her chair behind her desk.

"No, I'm fine. I went to the doctor yesterday with my wife. She's pregnant."

"What?"

He smiled. "Sixteen weeks."

Jada felt like someone had dropped a lead baseball into the bottom of her stomach. She wondered if she were heavy enough to fall through the floor and if that was the meaning of "floored."

"Aren't you going to say something?" Derek prompted after a few moments of silence.

"Congratulations."

"Thanks. I've been reluctant to go to her doctor visits with her because, you know, I wasn't really ready for kids. I deal with these monsters all day; I didn't want to go home to my own. I like my peace and quiet, you know." He came over and sat in the student desk beside her desk. "But I went yesterday and Jada, it was amazing. I heard the heartbeat and then I saw him on the sonogram."

"It's a boy?" she managed to get out.

"It's too soon to really tell, but I know we're having a boy. I feel it." His face was bright and excited. He looked like a little boy himself.

Jada loved him even more in this moment, which made that lead ball expand. It consumed the whole lower half of her body.

"Can you imagine me as a father?"

She had imagined it a hundred times—to her kids. "You're good with the students. They like you."

He nodded solemnly and reached for Jada's hand. "I think, with the kid coming and all, that I need to do better by my family. We have to stop what we're doing."

Jada lost all feeling in her body. She slid forward out of her chair, unable to hold herself upright. Had Derek not been holding her hand, she would have been on the floor, hitting the back of her desk with her face on the way down.

"What?"

"You know I love being with you. What we do together . . ." He rubbed her arm, but Jada could not feel it. "And I really care about you, but I'm about to have a kid. I have to be more responsible."

"What?"

"We both said this was just a hook-up in the first place. I'll admit that it became a little more than that." He lifted her hand and kissed the palm. She didn't feel that either.

"So, we're done, just like that?"

He looked at her longingly. "It has to be. I have a son."

"Not yet," she whispered. "It doesn't have to end yet."

Derek stood up, walked behind Jada, and kissed her neck. Gently, he lifted her from her chair. She let him. He wrapped his arms around her, and she leaned into him, feeling something like a tornado victim. Before her eyes, her home, her way of life, her being seemed to be uprooted, swirled in the air, and thrown somewhere she couldn't see. She grabbed Derek and held on so she wouldn't blow away too.

"Jada . . ." he whispered into her neck.

"No," she interrupted him, trying to halt the inevitable. To keep him from talking, she kissed him, not caring that they were at school and there was no lock on the door. Anyone could walk in: a student, another faculty member, the principal. But she didn't care. Jada needed to feel connected to Derek. She poured all of her emotions into him with her tongue. He kissed her back, communicating his own. Jada knew he didn't want to end this; he just felt obligated. She could respect his obligation, respect him for feeling it. But what they had was good. It shouldn't have to end because of a damn baby who wasn't even here yet. A thousand things could happen between now and then. There was no reason they could not be together until the baby was born, and when they got to that bridge, they could decide how to cross it. She tried to say all of this in her kiss because she had been a speechless fool when he was talking to her.

"Mmm, I'm going to miss this," he murmured, coming out of the kiss.

"You don't have to. We can keep this relationship going." She began unbuttoning his pants.

"Jada, I was serious. We have to end this." He halfheartedly attempted to move her hands from his zipper.

"Derek, you know this is what you want."

He shook his head as he silently watched her jerk down her pants and panties and pull his erect penis out of his boxers. Rolling his eyes upward in surrender, he pushed Jada against the cinder blocks behind her desk and entered her hard. Jada wrapped her arms around his neck and held on to him as he bounced her against the wall. She finally felt the connection. She closed her eyes and prayed that it would hold.

But it didn't. After Derek pulled up his pants, he promised her that would be the last time; he thought it best if they didn't even talk for a while.

The numb feeling reentered Jada's body and she walked through the rest of the day like a zombie. She didn't come alive again until Wednesday morning when Regina called her before work.

"The nurse just called. You better come over to Nana's. She

took a turn for the worse last night. The doctor's out here. They don't think she'll make it."

A flood of fear overran Jada's body. Just when she thought she had made it through Derek's tornado, a new disaster was aiming for her, threatening to drown her sanity if not her actual life. Nana could not die. What would she do without her?

At Nana's, Gina and the nurse were talking quietly in the kitchen. Jada barely acknowledged them as she practically ran to Nana's bedroom. She stopped at the doorway. Nana seemed even smaller than she had on Sunday. Thin, and transparent even, she looked like she was simply fading from existence. Her eyes were closed and the room was devoid of sound except the slow beeping of the heart monitor.

This can't be real, Jada thought. It was almost a wish, a prayer. "Nana," she called. She reached up and touched her necklace. Jada thought she saw the older woman's jaw twitch, but there was no other movement. She moved closer to the bed and threw herself on Nana's shoulder. "Nana, you have to stay here with us. You still have a lot to teach us hardheaded girls." When no response came, not even the jaw twitch, Jada grabbed Nana's hand and cried softly.

She didn't know how long she stayed like that. It seemed like hours, days, but it didn't matter. As long as she lay on Nana's shoulder and felt her warm hand, she knew she was alive.

But why was God punishing her? Why was God taking away all the people whom Jada loved? She was a good person; she loved her family; she worked hard for her students; she went to church. What more did God want from her? Didn't she deserve to be happy and loved? In this storm, she needed to be like those mothers in the tornadoes who lay atop their most precious ones and save them. Couldn't she save her world from total destruction? Wasn't she doing it now, lying atop her Nana to keep her from flying away?

But eventually Regina made her get up. Jada walked numbly over to the couch in the bedroom and lay down. She must have fallen asleep, because when she opened her eyes, it was dark outside and she knew what she had to do. Like a trickle of sunshine pushing a small space through a barrier of clouds, a light dawned on her. She did not have to be unhappy. She could fix this.

With a kiss on her grandmother's forehead and a quick prayer for her to keep living, Jada walked out of the house without saying a word to her sister or the nurse. She got in her car and drove the familiar trek up I-55 to Madison. She was going to Derek's house to do what had to be done.

This time, she did not park in the driveway next door. Instead, she parked on the street two houses down from Derek's. She knew on Wednesday nights he played tennis with some friends so he wouldn't be home. It would just be Jada and his wife. It would be quick and easy. Jada would ring the doorbell, *she* would come to the door and let Jada in after Jada told her she had important information about Derek. She would be shocked, but Jada would do it. She would stop the loss of everything dear to her.

It was spring and the sun was going down later and slower, it seemed. A faint glow painted the evening. Cars whirred by in the distance, but otherwise the neighborhood was oddly quiet, safely unaware of the storm of sounds gathering inside of Jada. She heard sobs and wails and pleas inside her head. She rang the doorbell, and for a brief moment the melody obscured the cries. But only for a brief moment. When *she* opened the door, smiling hospitably, they returned.

"You need to know something, Mrs. Ross." She spoke the

woman's name like a curse word. "Derek and I have been fucking for the past year."

Horror and disbelief wrestled across the woman's puffy, glowing face. Jada had to admit that pregnancy was agreeing with her; she looked less ordinary. But her new mom's glow did not dissuade Jada. Instead, it emboldened her. This woman and her baby were responsible for blowing down the walls of her happiness. That had to end. Tonight.

Quickly, she pulled her pistol from her purse. It seemed light as a pencil. Maybe because she couldn't feel anything on her person. She didn't even feel the cool release of the trigger. She may not have known she had actually shot the woman if Jada hadn't heard the loud *pop* and then another *pop*. Then a strange thing happened. All of her senses came back and she felt the gun, the warm mugginess of the night air against her back, and the hot splattering of blood across her bare arms and chest. *She* fell to the ground. Jada looked around, but no one was outside so she pushed the woman's lifeless body farther into the foyer, out of immediate sight. Then she turned and walked out of the house, pulling the door closed with her now-crimson hands. She rubbed Nana's necklace like a good luck stone.

But she had just made her own luck. She had eliminated the source of her problems. There was no baby to keep Derek tied to his wife. They could be together, and she didn't have to worry about losing him. It never occurred to her, even as she drove back to Nana's with blood covering her steering wheel and the pearly white of her necklace, that she had just lost herself.

MOST THINGS HAVEN'T WORKED OUT

BY WILLIAM BOYLE

Holly Springs

Back when I was fifteen there wasn't much Mississippi outside Holly Springs. I'd never hopped a train or even met someone from the coast. I'd been to a football game in Oxford with Phael once and to a doctor in Olive Branch when a roach got stuck in my ear. I stayed with Grandma Oliver because my mom was dead and so was my dad, though I never knew him. He was from Memphis and that was where he died. Shot by cops while robbing a liquor store. That was the story anyway. My mom smoked too much and got lung cancer and it spread everywhere and she went fast.

Grandma Oliver was taller than me and carried around an oxygen tank and smoked Pyramids and sometimes wore a Harley-Davidson bandanna across her forehead. I didn't get along great with her or her husband, who wasn't my real grandfather. His name was Jefferson, and he was Grandma Oliver's third husband. Her first one had died of a heart attack when he was thirty-two. Her second one, my real grandfather, had killed himself in the bathroom with a razor. You could still see darkness on the tiles around the tub. All the rooms at Grandma Oliver's had something like that. If it wasn't blood, it was a ghost feeling. The house was painted traffic-cone orange and it glowed like an electric burner. Kids made fun of me for that orange. When I wasn't in school, and even on some days when I was supposed to be in school, I spent all my time at the library. In the summer, I was at the library all day. I read books and watched a lot of movies. They had a little booth with a TV and headphones and you could watch a movie if no one was waiting. No one was ever waiting. Most people only came for the computers.

One day this lady came in and put on a presentation. It was right as I was getting to the naked part of *The Terminator*. The lady who did the presentation was called Miss Mary. She had this red curly hair and these freckles. She was maybe twenty-three or twenty-four. Her presentation was on birds. I saw it was going on out of the corner of my eye at first, but then I went over. Only two other kids were there for the presentation, and they were much younger than me. Miss Mary stopped what she was doing and smiled at me. "Welcome," she said. "What's your name?"

I told her it was Jalen.

"Jalen, you like birds?"

"I guess. Crows. Hummingbirds too. I've been to that Hummingbird Festival."

"That's where I work now, the place that holds the festival. The Audubon Center. I just moved here from New York."

I nodded and sat down on the floor and crossed my legs. I'd seen New York in movies. I wanted to live there. I wasn't thinking that New York was a big state. I was just thinking that she was from the city and that she rode in taxis and ate hot dogs on the street with a napkin balanced on her palm and that she took elevators up to the tops of tall buildings. I wanted to ask her why Mississippi, but she started showing us pictures of other birds. She leaned over, and I could see down her shirt. All that roundness. I wanted to kiss her freckles.

When she was done with the presentation and packing up, I asked her if I could help and she let me carry her box of binders out to the parking lot. Her car was yellow, the windshield webby with shatter. She had a red scrunchie on the rearview mirror and Obama bumper stickers. She thanked me for carrying the box and put it in the trunk. "It was nice meeting you," she said. "Someday you should come out to Audubon and I'll show you around. When the festival's not going on out there, it's so peaceful. We can watch the hummingbirds in the garden behind the Davis House. And I'll take you out on the Gator."

"Can we do that tomorrow?" I asked.

She didn't even hesitate. "Absolutely," she said. I was so glad to know that she'd meant it, that she hadn't just been saying it. I was so used to people just saying things.

"What time should I come there?"

"How's ten sound?"

I nodded. "Good. You miss New York?"

"I like it here."

"Will you stay?"

"I hope so."

"I'll see you tomorrow," I said, and I turned back to the library.

Miss Mary offered me a ride, but I told her I lived right up the block even though I lived almost two miles down Route 7 and had to walk all the way on the shoulder and would've killed for a ride. I just didn't want her to see Grandma Oliver's house. And Jefferson was always sitting out on the porch with a cooler of Bud and some scratch-offs. I didn't want her to see that either.

Holly Springs was full of sirens. Phael's great-uncle had been shot in his car the week before right off the square downtown and the cops seemed to be running around even more than usual. I walked home thinking about Miss Mary. I wondered where she stayed. I wondered what kind of food she ate. I pictured her reading at night in gym shorts with no top on.

Grandma Oliver was on me right when I walked in the door.

She wanted me to mow the lawn. I wanted to slam her head through the kitchen window. The way she spoke to me. Like I was a dumb slobbering dog. She didn't even know me. Didn't know I liked books and movies. I didn't say anything. Just took off my shirt and went out and pushed the mower around for two hours. I drank from the spigot near the old garden shed and cars honked as they passed on the road, not because they knew us, but because the orange of the house made people want to honk at it. I was sick of horns.

I ate a bologna sandwich with pickles when I was done and then went into my room and read a library copy of *Books of Blood* until I could feel my eyes getting weaker. I couldn't wait to be out at Audubon with Miss Mary. I wanted sleep to pass without actually having to sleep. I wanted the future.

The walk to Audubon was twice as long as the walk to the library. I had to go way out on 7 past Rust College and then make a left on 311. It was so hot the sweat had thickened all over me. I was wearing my red basketball shorts and a tank top, but I couldn't even feel the air on my skin. My socks squished in my sneakers. Across from Rust was an abandoned building. I stopped to drink a Great Value citrus soda I'd brought with me. I wiped my head with the back of my hand. A cop buzzed by with his windows open and gave me a long look from behind his dickhead sunglasses. I didn't wave. I knew that waving was the wrong thing. Phael taught me that. He told me they were just waiting for an excuse to shoot me.

The second part of the walk was the worst because the shoulder shriveled up on 311. Cars and trucks swerved out over the double-yellows to avoid me. Sweat stung my eyes. I'd finished my soda and hadn't brought any water. My lips stuck to my teeth.

When I finally made it to Audubon, it was almost eleven and

Miss Mary was waiting outside the visitor's center for me. "You walk all this way?" she said.

I nodded.

"You should've told me you needed a ride. Come in and have some water."

She brought me inside and put ice in a plastic cup from Corky's and filled it to the edge with tap water. I took it and drank half in one long slurp. Some of the water spilled out of the side of my mouth and down the front of my shirt. "I'm sorry," I said.

"You didn't bring any water?"

"Just a soda."

"Let's go out on the back porch," she said. "You rest awhile."

The back porch was screened in. We sat in reclining chairs at a long oak table with paint splashes on it. Eight feeders hung from the eaves of the roof right outside the screen. Hummingbirds skittered in to drink sugar water. Trees spread out in their greenness beyond the feeders. I drank more water and took a few deep breaths.

"Are you okay?" Miss Mary asked.

"Thank you, ma'am," I said. "I'm fine."

"Well, I'm glad you're here. I'll give you a ride home later, don't worry." Then she told me some things about hummingbirds, about their little hearts, about how fast their wings beat, about mixing the sugar and water and boiling it and letting it cool before putting it in the feeders.

"Beautiful, aren't they?" Miss Mary said.

I wanted to know how high they went. I wanted to know if no one put their feeders out what would happen. I wanted to know how they knew to come here to the festival. I wanted to put my hand on Miss Mary's leg. I just sat there and finished my water.

"Were you born in Holly Springs?" Miss Mary asked.

I said yes.

"I told you I'm from New York. People think New York and they think the city. But it's a huge state. I'm from the Hudson Valley. Everyone asks me if I have culture shock. I don't think so. I like it here."

"You got family back there?"

"My family's gone."

"My mom and dad are dead. I live with my grandma."

"Sweetie, I'm sorry."

"Your family dead?"

She paused and looked out at the fluttering hummingbirds. "My dad is. My mom's just gone."

"Is anyone else here today?" I asked.

"Three other people work here. Landry is the director. He's at a conference in Jackson. Willa is the native plant specialist, but she took the day off for a horse thing in Memphis. And then there's Jimmy, the groundskeeper-slash-maintenance guy. I think he's got jury duty." She stood up. "You bring lunch? I have a peanut butter and banana sandwich. We can split it."

"Ma'am, that's okay."

"You must be hungry." She disappeared into the kitchen and came back out with half a sandwich wrapped in a paper towel.

I unfolded the paper towel and looked at it. The crust on the bread was thick and the bread was flecked with seeds. The peanut butter was crunchy-looking. I was used to Great Value white bread and peanut butter, the same peanut butter Grandma Oliver put in the mousetraps. I took a bite.

Miss Mary started telling me other things about herself. She said she hadn't traveled much, but she'd spent some time in Florida. She had a distant cousin in Fort Myers who owned a bar. She said she was reading the *Game of Thrones* books and she wanted to go to France and she drove to Oxford last week to get milk at Brown's Dairy and had gotten interested in birds after college.

I didn't really have a life to tell her about. I wanted to make things up but that seemed like the wrong thing to do. I told her I liked whatever for music. I told her I watched movies at the library and that I liked horror books, but I didn't remember the names of the ones I'd read. I told her I went to Oxford once for a football game against LSU and I couldn't ever forget the people with chandeliers up in their tailgate tents.

She laughed and said, "Let's go out on the Gator."

We drove out to the far parts of the property on the Gator, and Miss Mary showed me an old sharecropper house where vultures tucked themselves into the darkness behind the broken windows. Across from that, down a scrubby dirt trail, was a slave cemetery that was really just a small patch of markers and mounds. The markers were thin stone slabs without any writing. Brightness settled on the graves from gaps in the nearby stand of trees. "It always makes me sad to think of what they must've gone through," Miss Mary said, patting me on the shoulder.

Next she took me to Sharecropper's Pond, where a beaver was trying to build a dam with a tree he'd gnawed down. She said they had a motion-detection camera set up on the other side of the pond to catch the beaver and the cranes and whatever else in action. One of her favorite things was to watch the footage when she came to work in the morning. "I didn't have anything like this in New York," she said.

"I went fishing with Phael once," I said.

"Who's Phael?"

"He's my friend. He's afraid of eating poison by mistake."

"Like getting poisoned?"

"Like eating something that no one knows is poisoned. We

didn't eat any of the fish we caught. We just left them with the hooks in their mouths on a picnic table."

"That's sad."

"I didn't hate those fish though. I liked them. I felt sorry about it."

Miss Mary was wearing a droopy backpack and she took out a canteen of water and a pair of binoculars. She shared the water with me; she really didn't mind my lips on the canteen. I liked having my mouth where her mouth had been. She showed me how to focus the binoculars and I looked up at the sky and the tops of trees. I saw some little birds she said were chimney swifts.

We sat down on the grass and passed the canteen back and forth.

When we were done, she screwed the cap back on and we took the Gator over to a blind where a telescope was set up. A boom box was chained to the wall and Miss Mary turned on the radio to a Memphis station.

I looked through the telescope and I saw everything close up through the glass. Birds and mud and flowers and bushes and dry things and the ground where the sun had baked it hard. I aimed the telescope at the sky and focused in on the brightness.

Probably about forty minutes passed, and I was still looking through the telescope. Miss Mary wasn't getting sick of it. She wasn't complaining. She was just sitting there, looking peaceful. Eventually I stepped away from the telescope and sat next to her. "I got lost looking," I said.

"You don't have to apologize," she said. "I was just taking in the day. It's beautiful, isn't it? I came from some bad things back in New York. I'm trying to be positive. I've been doing yoga. I've been trying not to let negative energy influence me."

"I wish I had a telescope or a pair of binoculars," I said. "I'd look at things all day."

Miss Mary opened up her backpack and took out the pair of binoculars she'd used at the pond. "Here. Take these."

"Ma'am, I couldn't."

"Take them. I got them cheap. I have another pair. Plus, we have about twenty pairs back at the visitor's center for camp."

I took the binoculars and hung them around my neck and then glassed the treeline beyond the trail we were near. "I see a bird with a red head," I said.

"That's a woodpecker."

I examined the woodpecker closely, the way he kissed the bark. "Why do you like me?" I asked. "I mean, why do you like hanging out with me?"

Miss Mary didn't look startled or anything. "I guess I see something in you. Something I recognize. Some loneliness. I think we're kindred spirits. I believe in that kind of thing, I do. Like maybe you were my son in another life. Like maybe I sang you to sleep."

The woodpecker flickered away and I let the binoculars fall around my neck. "I feel that way too, I think. Like you took care of me once and you're taking care of me again."

"See?" she said.

"Thank you for the binoculars," I said.

We went back to the visitor's center and Miss Mary made me a glass of iced tea with honey stirred into it and a piece of lemon wedged on the rim of the glass. It was the best iced tea I'd ever had, nothing like the mix Grandma Oliver made or the Arizonas I got at the Shell. We sat in the main room where there were taxidermied animals: a bear, a coyote, a fox, a squirrel, two hawks, a mallard, and an otter. Glass cases filled with skins and hides and bones lined the walls. Miss Mary said, "I hope you had a good time. Next time we'll pick blackberries."

"I did."

"I have to be here until four. Just wait for me, if you don't mind. I'll give you a ride."

"I don't mind."

Outside we heard tires crunching gravel in the parking lot.

"Looks like we have a visitor," Miss Mary said. "You can help me show them around. Maybe you want to volunteer here eventually? I can train you." She went over to the window and looked out.

I stood next to her. A van had parked behind her car, blocking it in. The van was red with gold stripes, and I could see the shape of a lady in the driver's seat. She was smoking a cigarette, and I thought she must be pretty old because she carried herself with a sharpness. Miss Mary's face had gone pale.

"Who is that?" I asked.

Miss Mary scrambled around and locked the doors and shut off the lights and took me in the back bathroom where we crouched down next to the toilet.

"What's going on?" I asked.

"Oh God," Miss Mary said.

"Ma'am?"

"It's Mother Edna."

We heard a tapping out on the front porch, like Mother Edna was nudging the ground with a stick. I didn't ask questions. Miss Mary was scared to her bones. Next we heard what sounded like one finger streaking down a window.

"Honey!" Mother Edna called out. Her voice was deep and smoke-grizzled. "I'll burn you out if I have to."

Miss Mary crumpled to her knees. "How'd she find me here? How'd she know about Mississippi?"

I stayed quiet.

"A nature *sanctuary?*" her mother said through the glass, drawing out the last word.

Miss Mary put her hand on mine and said, "I'm going to go out. You stay in here. Don't be afraid. Just stay put." She stood up and left the bathroom.

I felt alive. I pressed my ear against the door and tried to hear what Miss Mary was saying to her mother. All I heard was the low rumble of their voices. The sound of my heart racing filled the hot little bathroom. A mildewy towel was folded across a rack near the sink and the smell tickled the back of my throat. I opened the door and crawled out into the main room on my hands and knees, the binoculars still hanging from my neck. I tried to see out the window but couldn't without standing up, so I went to the back door, unlocked it, and tiptoed onto the porch where Miss Mary had given me water that morning. The hummers were buzzing at their feeders. I opened the screen door, careful not to let it slam shut, and ducked around the side of the house. I hid behind a picnic table and lifted the binoculars to my eyes. Miss Mary and her mother weren't that far off, and I could see way up close in the glass. The old lady had a cigarette in a cigarette holder and was exhaling smoke in big gusts. She was wearing thick heels and a red skirt that stopped at her knees. The skirt was unwrinkled. Her blouse was white and her sleeves were rolled up, as if she'd had to show somebody how to do something the proper way. She was old but not that old. Maybe fifty. And she was beautiful, with glassy eyes and the same long red hair as Miss Mary, except hers was a dye job and the red was closer to purple. Her nails were long and painted with clear polish, the half-moon cuticles dotted red. She was wearing a gold cross on a wispy chain around her neck. But it was her earrings that stopped me: little silver guns with diamond triggers.

I still couldn't hear what they were saying, but Miss Mary's shoulders were slumped as if she'd been scolded into submission. She was trembling.

The old lady, as if she could sense me, swung around and peered in my direction. I didn't have much cover. I tried to stay hidden behind the table. She didn't holler or charge. She removed the cigarette from the holder and then twisted it under her heel and walked calmly across the lot. I thought about running into the woods, but I didn't move.

"Come on out here," she said, sitting at the other end of the table and putting her elbows up on the splintered wood.

I let the binoculars fall to a dangle and stood.

"And who are you?" she said.

Miss Mary came running over. "He's just a kid who was visiting today. Let him go."

"*Just a kid*. I've heard that one before."

"He's got nothing to do with any of this."

Mother Edna laughed. "My daughter here," she said to me, "is a coward, pal. A bona fide coward." She paused and motioned to the bench. "Sit down."

I sat at the table.

"Never met such a subdued little shine," she said. And then: "Take those binoculars off."

I took the binoculars off and put them down on the table. I pressed my fingers against the lenses on the small side. I wanted to put them back on and look up at the birds in the trees and have Miss Mary whisper in my ear what they were. I looked at her and saw that she had changed in her face even more. No birds could brighten her.

"Everything will be okay, Jalen." Miss Mary sat down across from me and touched my hands over the binoculars.

Mother Edna didn't say anything. She just sat there and then she cracked her knuckles. They sounded like stomping on bubble wrap. Miss Mary tightened her grip on my hands as if the knuckle-cracking signaled the beginning of something terrible.

"I'm not scared," I said.

"You should be," Mother Edna said.

Mother Edna walked us over to the van and made us stand face-to-face. I was taller than Miss Mary by two or three inches, but she looked even smaller now. She looked like she'd lost about ten years. Mother Edna opened the back doors of the van and took out two pairs of red plastic ties and then she made us cross our arms and cuffed us left-to-left and right-to-right, cinching the ties with a tab that pinched my skin. Then she pushed us into the back of the van. The rear seats had been pulled out and we spilled across the floor like dead deer. Mother Edna slammed the doors and walked around to the driver's side. I was so close to Miss Mary I could feel her breath on my neck and smell her sweat. I couldn't fight off getting wood. I couldn't look at Miss Mary's face even though I knew my dick was the last thing she was worried about.

"She's not going to kill us," Miss Mary said. "She needs me." But the words caught in her throat and she stopped talking. I knew why. Mother Edna needed Miss Mary for whatever reason, but she didn't need me. She'd kill me if Miss Mary didn't give her what she wanted. I still didn't feel scared; I wanted the chance to kill Mother Edna. I wanted to kill her for Miss Mary. Maybe she'd love me for that.

Mother Edna got under the wheel. She reached across to the passenger seat, palmed something, and brought it up to her face. I twisted my head to see what it was. It was a plastic lion mask with an elastic strap that she'd pulled around the back of her head. The mask was well-worn, orange faded to rust, and the plastic was chipped and cracked around the edges. "You remember this, Audrey?"

Miss Mary shuddered against me.

"Audrey's her real name," Mother Edna said. "Audrey Rose

O'Brien. I used to wear this around the house to spook her when she was little."

She kept the mask on as she started the van. A hole was cut in the mouth. She put a cigarette in her holder and inserted the holder into the hole. She lit the cigarette and took a long pull and then exhaled smoke around the edges of the mask. "I'm waiting," she said.

"I don't know what you want from me," Miss Mary said.

"Tell me where to go."

Miss Mary had tears in her voice but held them back. "This is about the money I took?"

Mother Edna laughed.

"I don't know where it is," Miss Mary said.

"Try again."

"It's gone. I spent it all getting settled."

Mother Edna took off the mask and hung it from the rearview mirror. She climbed into the passenger seat and opened the glove box. A pair of wire cutters rested on top of a stack of road maps and a snuff container. Wire cutters in hand, she climbed into the back with us and kneeled over me, slipping the jaws of the wire cutter around my left pinky. "Every lie you tell, I snip off one of his fingers," Mother Edna said.

"Just let him go," Miss Mary said.

"Okay. Sorry, pal."

I felt the jaws digging into my skin and closed my eyes. Time slowed down. I tried to visualize the wire cutters tearing through my skin and bone, my little finger falling between me and Miss Mary, blood fountaining from the stump. Nothing happened.

"I buried it," Miss Mary said, kicking her feet around, trying to push her mother off me. "Most of it. I kept a few thousand at home. The rest is buried."

"Where?"

"Here. Out on the property."

"Let's go. You have a shovel?"

"There's a shovel over in the maintenance shed," Miss Mary said. "You have to promise to let Jalen go before I tell you where the money is."

"I'll let him go *after* I get my money."

"I don't trust you. Let him go first."

Mother Edna leaned over me again and put the jaws of the wire cutters back in place on my left pinky. She squeezed the handles together and I felt pressure first and then a bolt of pain spreading from my hand to my shoulder and I knew there was only air now where my little finger used to be. I looked up at Mother Edna. She was holding my pinky in her hand, dangling it like a slug. Miss Mary was screaming. Blood spread between us. A wave of nausea hit me and I passed out.

When I woke up, I was alone in the back of the van and the first thing I felt was the absence of my finger. I'd dreamed Miss Mary was kissing my neck. I'd dreamed all my teeth were gone and I was trying to kiss her back with a mouthful of slobber. Pain thumped through my body. My ankles were tied together but my hands weren't. A T-shirt had been wrapped around my left hand and duct-taped into something like a boxing glove. I sat up, drenched in sweat, and looked around. Out the windows all I saw were trees. I heard Miss Mary and Mother Edna talking. Their voices seemed distant at first but then I realized they were right out in front of the van.

"I should've killed you before Kingston," Mother Edna said.

"Just let me dig," Miss Mary said.

"You and your father, I should've fucking done you at the same time. I thought I could make something of you at least. Your father was nothing but that policy he took out."

I twisted around and made it up to my knees, the pain in my hand throbbing. I straightened my back and strained to see through the windshield. The van was parked on the dirt trail leading to the slave cemetery. Miss Mary was digging up one of the mounds. I couldn't see how deep the hole was. Mother Edna was standing with her back to me.

"Why do you care about the Tatarskys so goddamn much?" Mother Edna asked.

"You ruined their lives," Miss Mary said, tossing dirt to the side of her. "That old man killed himself. For what?"

"The money, sweetheart." Mother Edna shook her head. "I don't know what the fuck I did wrong raising you. Somehow I let you be weak. I guess that's from your father."

"Don't talk about him anymore." Miss Mary finally started crying, but she was still fighting it.

"He died because he was weak, and I need weak things out of my way." Mother Edna paused. "You're just lucky you got to the hospital that first time, that's all. Luck's just luck. It doesn't last. The things you thought took guts—like stealing my money—didn't take any guts. You don't know from guts."

Miss Mary stopped shoveling and wiped her eyes with the back of her hand.

"Get back to it," Mother Edna said.

Miss Mary didn't move.

"You need incentive? You, I'm gonna put in that hole, but the kid I'll turn loose once I have the money. My word's as good as you'll get."

Miss Mary started digging again.

I couldn't walk with the plastic ties around my ankles, but I knew I'd be able to hop. I scrambled to the back of the van and pulled the handle and then pushed the doors open with my feet. I was hoping for a quiet exit but the doors whined. I jumped to the ground, turned, and saw Mother Edna spinning to me. She didn't have a weapon that I could see. No gun hiding in an ankle holster either. She came at me, hands raised, and I bunny-hopped to the side, which made the pain in my hand even worse.

"Get back in the van," she said. "I'll let you go once I have my money."

Miss Mary was fast on Mother Edna's heels with the shovel. She swung it once, aiming for Mother Edna's back, and missed, slamming the blade into the hard earth.

Mother Edna, lucky for the whiff, turned to Miss Mary and scratched her face, breaking a few of her nails and drawing blood from her daughter's cheeks.

I hopped painfully past them and went to the hole that Miss Mary had been digging. One of the markers nearby had been loosened. I picked it up with my good hand and held it to my chest. It was an old stone tablet. Thin but sturdy. It looked like bone and felt like it too.

Miss Mary tried to swing the shovel again but she was too close to Mother Edna, who reached out and disarmed her. Mother Edna poked the handle end of the shovel into Miss Mary's stomach, knocking her to the ground. Then she pinned down her daughter with her foot and swatted her face with the flat end of the shovel blade. Miss Mary whimpered and brought her arms up to protect herself from another blow.

I hopped back to where they were, cradling the grave marker.

Mother Edna stepped back and pointed the shovel at me.

Miss Mary rolled around on the ground, holding her face. Mother Edna was only half-watching her, focusing on me now. Miss Mary was aiming to take out Mother Edna's legs, but she was off course. She drove Mother Edna closer to me.

I let out a breath.

Mother Edna swung the shovel, and I ducked it.

I hopped closer to her and lashed out with the grave marker, mashing it into the side of her head. The stone split in half. Mother Edna went down hard, landing on her elbows and then collapsing forward. Miss Mary stood, her face covered in blood and dirt, and picked up the shovel. She brought it down on the back of Mother Edna's head. Mother Edna screamed into the ground. Her blood misted across my legs. I wanted to spit on her.

It was still light out, the sun two hours away from setting. Birds in the trees squawked and sang. Miss Mary kept hitting Mother Edna in the back of the head with the shovel until her hands and feet twitched and she went limp. I noticed those earrings again, tiny guns that weren't worth shit.

"Ma'am, what are we gonna do?" I asked.

Miss Mary sat down on her mother, holding the shovel across her lap. "I'm so sorry you had to be part of this."

I leaned against the van, blood starting to soak through the T-shirt wrapped around my hand. "I'm glad she's dead. I didn't mind hurting her."

"She deserved it. Hitting her with that shovel felt good. I know that's wrong."

"You still feel the same about me, like I was your son in another life?"

Miss Mary stood up and hugged me. "Sure I do, Jalen. And you saved me like sons are supposed to. I can't tell you how much that means. I hope when I have a son he's just like you."

We stayed hugging for a while and then she kissed me on the mouth. Her lips fireworked against mine and the pain in my hand seemed to disappear. I could smell her freckles. I could smell down to her bones. It was a quick kiss, just lips, but I got wood again. This time I tucked it up in my waistband to deflate it.

"We'll bury her, I guess," Miss Mary said, pulling away.

"You have that money?"

She nodded. "It's buried where I said."

"I'm glad you got that."

She cut my legs free. I wondered what I smelled like. I sat back and watched as she dug out the money, which was in a brown suitcase covered in stickers. Then we rolled Mother Edna into the hole with the broken marker and filled it in. I hated to think about her buried with the bones of all those people who'd been done wrong. We tried to make her grave look like the rest of the cemetery, dry and hard, not freshly dug up. Miss Mary said no one would care that Mother Edna was missing and they wouldn't look here anyway.

We walked to Sharecropper's Pond. She tossed the shovel in and it sank down to the murky bottom. Miss Mary told me Mother Edna had tossed my pinky into the woods near the visitor's center. She said it was probably too late. I'd also lost the binoculars.

We left in the van, the money in the back. I threw Mother Edna's lion mask out the window when we turned onto 311. Miss Mary came up with a story that I'd been attacked by a stray dog. She dropped me at an urgent care clinic up the road in Collierville. I expected her to wait for me, but she said she couldn't, not with her face messed up and driving Mother Edna's van the way she was. She shook my good hand and said she'd come check on me. But I knew she'd disappear with that van, and I was right. No one else knew why she left like that, her car still parked at Audubon, her apartment paid up for the month.

I found out where Miss Mary's place was the next day and broke in. She'd been there and taken some stuff. I went through what was left. In the garbage I found a few pairs of underwear streaked from her period. I held them to my cheek and then balled them up and put them in a plastic bag. I took scrunchies off doorknobs and books from her bed stand and painted rocks she'd lined up on the windowsill. I drank the rest of her good milk and made peanut butter sandwiches. I took her toothbrush; I still use it.

Grandma Oliver was very aware of me from then on. I never slept anymore. I'd stand in the kitchen and bounce a rubber ball off the wall. One night she put her hand on me like I was a dog she was done taking care of, a Pyramid hanging from her mouth, her oxygen tank rattling at her hip. It's not hard to make someone who smokes on oxygen go away. Jefferson was passed out drunk when the fire ate them up.

These days I wake in a wormy sleeping bag and gnarl my way into unsteadiness. I'm etched with loss like some kind of crippled king. I'm twenty-four but I look twice that age. Miss Mary was it for me, with her smile and bright promise. My one shot. The hours I spent with her I knew all of life. Now I'm dirt. I ghost the town. Break in places for food. Steal from sheds and gardens. Cop cars spit gravel at me when I'm out walking. I'm the freak at the gas station missing a finger, the one who scrapes change for a short dog of wine, the one they say kills pets for food, the one whose eyes linger on your clean high school girl in her cheerleader skirt. Dirt. Even the Nation of Islam guys by the post office ignore me. I stay in a tent out in the woods near the slave cemetery. Sometimes I walk over there and I can hear the old bones singing about the meanness of the new bones and I know that's the same meanness that chased Miss Mary through life. Me, I got broken by being so close to kindness.

PART II

WAYWARD YOUTH

UPHILL

BY MARY MILLER

Biloxi

The RV park is nice and shady. The residents are mostly older and quiet, but the bugs are loud. There are all sorts of bugs and they are all so loud.

I'm sitting at the picnic table next to the trailer Jimmy has just bought, carefully avoiding the piles of bird crap while watching him fashion a wooden chute for the sewer hook-up. He's impressed with himself, using nails he's found on the ground and wood from a scrap pile. Every few minutes he stops to regard his work.

"Our shit travels uphill," he says, looking at it admiringly.

"That's amazing."

He sits across from me and I watch him dig around in his box full of small tools.

Before the trailer he lived on his uncle's boat, but he sunk it, and before that he lived in a van in his boss's garage. When I get drunk, I yell at him and call him homeless and we don't talk for weeks but then I find myself with him again—just a cup of coffee, just as friends—and the cycle repeats itself. We're at the beginning of the cycle now.

"So I got this call earlier," Jimmy says. His voice has the high, strained quality it takes on when he's lying or asking to borrow money. "This friend who lives in Hawaii wants me to drive to Biloxi to take a picture of a lady."

"A picture of a lady?"

"I haven't talked to this guy in a long time."

"Who is he?"

"He sells dope," he says. "He's a bad guy."

A lot of his friends sell dope, but I've never heard him call any of them bad guys before. "He sells weed?" I ask.

"Huge quantities of high-grade stuff. Mostly legal."

"That sounds like a bad idea."

"Yeah, it's probably a bad idea," he says.

I'm surprised to hear him agree with me. He stops digging around in his box. I turn a page in my magazine. "How much did he offer to pay you?"

"He said to name my price. I was thinking a thousand."

"A thousand? If someone tells you to name your price, you don't say a thousand. Did you tell him you couldn't do it?"

"I said I'd call him back."

"Why didn't you tell him you couldn't do it?" If I wasn't here, or we were in a fight, he would already be on his way down there.

"I'm not gonna do it."

"They're going to kill that woman," I say, because I want to hear what it sounds like. I want him to say, *No, they're not,* but he doesn't. There she is—eating a tuna fish sandwich or watching a game show on TV, not knowing she will soon be dead. It's kind of thrilling. I wonder what she looks like, if she's pretty.

"I'll call him right now with you sitting there and tell him I can't do it. I'm going to have to make some stuff up."

"Of course, make some stuff up. I don't care." I flip another page in my magazine, a *Cosmopolitan* from November 2002. I found a whole stack of them in his laundromat. "Wait," I say. "Hold on a second."

"What?"

"Let's think about this for another minute." This is not my life, or it is not the life I'm supposed to be living, and so I can pretend that it is. I don't consider the actuality of my situation, which is that every day I live this life it becomes more and more mine, the real one, and the one I'm supposed to be living falls further away; eventually it will be gone forever. "Whether or not you take the picture, somebody's going to do it and the woman'll be dead, right?"

"That's right," he says.

"So either way she's dead and all he wants you to do is take a picture. And you're broke."

"I'm not broke."

He takes a sip of his beer, the beer I bought. I know exactly how much money he has because he empties his pockets out on the counter as soon as he gets home, balled-up ones and fives, sometimes a couple of twenties. He never has more than fifty dollars on him.

"People take my picture all the time," I say. "Every time I go through a toll road my picture gets taken."

"Not really the same thing. And when are you going through toll roads?"

"Are you sure he doesn't want you to do anything else?"

"No, just the picture."

"Your child support's late," I say, though we don't talk about his children, who live in Oregon—a state he is not allowed to enter for a reason that remains unclear—or his child support. I can just assume he hasn't paid it. He has no bank account. When someone writes him a check, I have to cash it for him because he lost his ID, sunk to the bottom of the lake along with the boat.

"You think I should do it?" he says. "I can't believe you think I should do it."

"For two thousand."

"Are you serious?"

"You'd do it if I wasn't here."

"No I wouldn't."

"Then why didn't you tell him no right off?"

"Because he's my friend—I was going to think about it first. I owe him that much."

"Well, call him back and tell him you'll do it. And I get to come."

"No, babe. I'm not involving you in that kind of stuff."

"I'm coming," I say, "and that's final." He seems pleased and I wonder if this is what he wanted all along, if I'm stupid. We stay together, I tell myself, because the sex is so good; if the sex weren't so good, I would have broken this cycle a long time ago.

He calls the guy back and makes affirmative-sounding noises while I watch him pace. So many of my boyfriends have been pacers—it must make them feel important. He says, "Fifteen," and gestures for a pen. I hand him one and he scrawls an upside-down address on my magazine, a phone number, and the name *Susan Lacey*. I went to school with some identical twins named Lacey. They were of average intelligence and attractiveness so no one seemed to know what to do with them.

I gather my stuff and climb the two steps into the trailer. I'm still not used to the dimensions—the narrowness of the doors, how small everything is. There are booby traps everywhere, sharp edges that need to be filed down, cabinets that fall open when you walk by. Only in the bed do I feel my normal size.

I open the closet and a light comes on; it's his favorite feature. I shove my clothes back into my overnight bag, my toothbrush and toothpaste and foaming facial cleanser. We'll have to go by my apartment to get my camera because he doesn't have one. I wish he had his own damn camera and find myself getting angry about all the things he doesn't have and how he assumes I will provide them. I sit on the bed with its ugly pilled comforter that probably came with the trailer and look at my arms, the finger-shaped bruises. *I'm going to be involved in a murder*, I think. There is no voice that tells me to stop, that says what I am doing is wrong. I can't remember if there ever was a voice. I don't remember a voice.

I refuse to let him take my car so we clean out the truck he uses for work, which belongs to his boss. There's a situation with a headlight that is an illegal blue color; the cops have already pulled him over twice and told him to get it fixed. We pour two beers into giant McDonald's cups and he rolls a joint for the road. All of this is worrisome but he says he would die before he went back to prison and I believe him—he says it with such conviction—and he's been out for five or six years and has never been back for even a night.

We pass a group of men near the entrance and Jimmy rolls down his window. They are born-again bikers, men with lots of tattoos and angry faces, but they don't drink or do drugs or get into fights; they show up at trials to support children who have been abused, stand in the back of the courtroom with their arms crossed. They're biker angels, he tells me, making fun of them, but I think it's what they call themselves.

At my apartment, he waits in the truck while I walk the three flights upstairs. I get my camera and a pair of shorts and a bikini; the bottoms can double as panties. I wander the rooms wondering what else I might need, if I should just lock the door, put on my pajamas, and get in bed. It looks so comfortable, the sheets newly changed, sage green—such a pleasant color. I grab a pack of cigarettes and a Clif bar and then we're on the highway, headed south. I haven't been to Biloxi since I broke up with Richard. I have so many old boyfriends now, spread out all over, and so many things remind me of them. I'll pass a Wendy's and remember the one who would only eat plain hamburgers. There we are, sitting under the yellow light with our trays in front of us, eating one french fry at a time. Nearly every movie, every song and TV show and food item, reminds me of someone and it is a horrible way to live.

I flip down the visor to look at myself. My hair's in a ratty ponytail and I don't have any makeup on and I'm too old to be going around barefaced, my mother says. I wish I'd showered before we left his trailer but it's so small and the water runs everywhere and I can't turn around without the curtain touching my arms or legs, which is the same curtain that touched the arms and legs of some stranger.

"I brought my swimsuit in case there's a pool at our hotel," I say. He puts a hand on my knee. "I need a new one—this one's from three summers ago and it's all worn on the butt."

"I'll get you a new one," he says. "I'll get you a white bikini so I can see your nipples." The word *bikini* doesn't sound right in his mouth. He hardly ever buys me anything, though it is always his pot we smoke and I've never once bought condoms. Condoms are expensive, he tells me, especially the way we go through them. He has never suggested we don't use them, though, which is nice of him.

"Do you want me to drive?" I ask.

"I'm fine."

"I haven't had as much to drink."

"I'm fine," he says again.

"Did the guy say what he wanted the pictures for?"

"We know why he wants them."

"I know, but did he say it?"

"No."

"'Cause that's not how it works."

"Right," he says. He turns the radio up. We both like country music. We also like rap. No one knows where I am. When I'm with Jimmy, I don't return my friends' text messages or answer my mother's phone calls unless she calls twice in a row. I fall down a Jimmy rabbit hole.

It's not a bad drive down 49. There are plenty of places to stop, which I appreciate, and lots of antique malls made out of connecting storage units. My mother used to make me go to them with her back when I was too young to refuse, but I don't remember her ever buying anything. I wonder what she was looking for. There's a catfish house shaped like an igloo and another one in a massive barn, only about five miles apart. I like the men on the side of the highway selling sweet potatoes, nice-looking men in overalls, real country people. We live in Mississippi and almost everyone we know is from Mississippi but we don't know any real country people.

"I have to pee," I say, "just stop wherever, whenever it's convenient." He tells me I pee too much, and it's true, I do pee a lot. I close my eyes and think about the woman, Susan Lacey. I imagine her in a shapeless housedress and heavy shoes with rubber soles like a nurse, eating ice cream from a gallon container. And then I imagine a younger Susan Lacey, her hair long and dark, eyes full of life. She's on the street, carrying a recyclable bag full of organic fruits and vegetables, flowers sticking out the top of it. The picture will capture her midstride, head turning to look for cars as she crosses the street. It's a picture I've seen so many times on the crime shows I watch, the photograph snapping the color out of everything.

"Can I smoke?" I ask.

"I don't care."

"No, the joint."

"Let's wait till after," he says.

I say okay but *after* feels like forever. I wish I'd grabbed a book from my apartment; all I have is the *Cosmo* with the address and number on it and I've already read it from cover to cover. I reread an interview with Cameron Diaz. *Cosmo* asks her what the secret is to being an effective flirt: "Is it 'flipping your goddamn hair,' like Lucy Liu advised you to do in *Angels?*" And Cameron Diaz says, "Yes, flip the goddamn hair [laughs]. I think the secret is trying to be charming. I always try to make a man laugh, and usually, it's by making fun of myself." I wonder if her answer would be different in 2013, if she would say something so embarrassing and unfeminist-like. I light a cigarette and try to focus on the trees, the way the light filters through them, but there's Susan Lacey again—she is definitely the younger, dark-haired one. Perhaps she's even beautiful, but that isn't going to save her.

Three hours later, we're in Biloxi. Jimmy pulls into a gas station and I slip my card into the slot before he can ask and then I go inside, buy a sixteen-ounce beer and a king-size Twix.

He's still pumping when I come back out, talking on his cell phone. I get in the truck and take off my flip-flops—my toenails bright red, so pretty.

He hands me a receipt, which I let fall to the floor without looking at it. I type the address into my phone, direct him through the city. For some reason the sound isn't working and I can't get it to work even though the volume is turned all the way up.

"Don't you have a boyfriend that lives here?" he asks. He knows I have an ex-boyfriend that lives here. He lives in a high-rise apartment and drives a black Mercedes with a personalized license plate that means *supreme ruler* in some Asian language. He is a horrible person who made me go to church with him on Sundays, a pretentious guy full of pretensions, a Californian, a former Marine, a drunk. I have no idea where I find these people.

"No," I say.

He looks at me.

"That was like three years ago."

"When's the last time you talked to him?"

"Not since we broke up," I say. "Richard."

"Dick," he says, "that's right, good old *Dick*."

"Let's talk about your ex-girlfriends. Were they all ugly? Make a left at the next light."

"I don't date ugly chicks."

"You know I've met a lot of the girls you dated, right?"

He sighs because I'm right—they were all weirdly tall or hook-nosed or something. One of them had so many tattoos she looked deranged. "How much further?" he asks.

"Farther."

"Okay," he says, "Jesus Christ. How much farther?"

"Three miles. If he has her address, why's he need a picture? Why doesn't he just send somebody there to kill her?"

"We're going to her job," he says, and then, "Hey, babe? Could you just stop talking for a minute?"

We pull into the parking lot of an Office Depot. "Is this it?" he asks.

"This is the address you wrote down."

Office Depots depress me and I refuse to get out. I open my bag and hand him the camera, turn it on and off. "This button here," I say. "I hope she's in there and we can get this over with. I want to go swimming, and maybe gamble. I love to gamble." I've decided I'll definitely rent a room at a casino, a nice one, and order room service and drink overpriced drinks at the hotel bar and fuck him in a huge bed with too many pillows.

I watch his back as he walks into the store: stocky and bald-headed, tattoos covering his thick arms. He's not attractive in the conventional way but he makes beautiful babies. I'll never have a baby with him but I like the idea of it, having a small version of him that I could control, who would listen to me and obey me and tell me every thought that popped into his head. The doors slide open and he's gone, disappeared into the sadness of Office Depot forever. The turn of events deflates me.

Ten minutes later, he gets back in the truck.

"So?"

"No Suzie."

"What took you so long?"

"I bought some envelopes," he says, and tosses the bag to the floor. He hands me the camera and I immediately check to see if he took any pictures; he didn't. I turn it off.

"What now?"

"I don't know. Let me think for a minute."

"Drive us to a nice hotel and I'll rent a room and we can pretend we're on a stakeout. Set up a command center."

"This isn't a game," he says, pulling out of the lot. "It's not a game."

He drives in an angry silence. When someone is mad at me, I don't know what to do except be mad back. He drives fast, like he knows where he's going, and I don't ask. When he decides to talk to me, I won't be ready to talk to him, I tell myself, and it makes me feel better, but then I start thinking about all the things I want to say. Every one of them is a question. I look out the window as he drives and I have no idea where he's going or what we're doing. I want to be inside his head for one minute, just one minute so I can get ahead of him, or at least not feel so behind. We could be here to kill Susan Lacey, for all I know, though I don't think he would do that for fifteen hundred dollars, but maybe it's fifteen thousand and then I'd go to prison as an accessory because they wouldn't believe me, they never do. I'd get five years, at least, even if all my people pooled their money to get me the best lawyer.

I tell him I have to pee again and he pulls into a gas station, throws the truck into park so fast it lurches. In the bathroom, I wash my hands, my face. I look at myself in the mirror and think, *Fuck you. Fuck you, you fuck-up.* I think all my problems might be solved if I could look in the mirror and see my ugliness reflected back at me.

As I'm purchasing a six-pack, my phone rings and I know it's my mother so I don't answer. I don't even look. She'll call again in twenty minutes or half an hour and ask what I'm doing, if I'm okay. She always wants to know if I'm okay, if I'm happy, which makes it impossible to talk to her.

"Where are we going?" I ask, as coldly as possible.

"I'm dropping you off at my father's house," he says. "You can spend the night there."

"Oh no, I'm not going there. I don't know your father."

"You'll be fine," he says. "It's safe there."

"Why? What's going on?"

"I have to find this woman."

"I know, that's why we're here. We have to find her so let's find her."

"You don't understand," he says.

"You're right, I don't, so explain it to me."

I open a beer and he takes it out of my hand. I open another. I tell him I am not, under any circumstances, going to sit and watch TV with some old man I don't know. An old man he hates and doesn't talk to. I had forgotten that his father even lived here. I tell him to take me to a hotel but he doesn't take me to his father's house or to a hotel. He takes me to a bar. We get out and I follow him inside. It's not the kind of place we frequent—a fancy wine bar with too many mirrors, where I feel underdressed and greasy. The Office Depot girl wouldn't be here.

I sit next to him on a barstool and he orders his usual: a Budweiser and a shot of Jameson. I order a gin martini, dirty. The olives are pierced with a long wooden stick, dangerous, and I eat them carefully, one at a time, and remember that there are pleasures in life; sometimes they're so small they shouldn't compensate for all of the shit, but they do. They really do. Once the olives are gone, I look up hotel reviews on my phone even though I know where I want to stay: the Hard Rock. There are young, good-looking people there and they let people bring their dogs.

"Hey, babe," he says. "Hey, love." I don't look at him. Other women may do their best to be nice and accommodating, but I try to be as unlikable as possible, test men too soon and expect them to love me for it. The right one will, I imagine, though I've been through enough to know that the right one doesn't exist, this perfect man who will be whole yet malleable, who will allow me to be as ugly as I want.

Twenty minutes later, I'm in a hotel room by myself: two beds, a large bathroom with an array of soaps and lotions, everything perfectly beige. It's on the fourteenth floor overlooking the Gulf and I stand in the window and try to make out the barrier islands: Cat Island, Ship, Horn, some other one I forget. In '69, Camille split Ship Island in two: east and west. I used to go to West Ship with another of my exes.

It's not the first time I've waited for Jimmy in a hotel room. I've given up so much to be with him and some of these things are for the best. He has taught me sex without love, a Buddhist's degree of unattachment. He's taught me that I can only rely on myself and it's a good lesson, one I needed to learn. He also taught me to drive a stick shift and put cream cheese on sand-wiches, an appreciation of Westerns. Everyone leaves something behind; there are so many things I wouldn't have if I hadn't had all of them, every one.

I know Jimmy'll show up in the morning when it's time to check out and it'll be done: the picture taken, cash in hand, an inexplicably large amount unaccounted for. I call room service and order a bacon cheeseburger with fries and a vanilla milk-shake and eat everything including most of the condiments in their fat little jars. Then I lie in bed and watch the most boring thing I can find on TV—old women selling garish jewelry and elastic-waist pantsuits—and the longer I watch, the more I begin to imagine a world in which these things might appeal to me.

I call my mother; I can't help it. She always answers, even if she's with her priest or in the movie theater.

"Hello?" she says. "Who's this?"

"Mom? Are you there?"

"I was asleep," she says. "I fell asleep. What time is it?"

"Eight o'clock." I don't know why I called her but I do it con-stantly, against my will. More often even than she calls me. I call her because she is there, because she loves me, and because one day she'll die and I won't know how to live in a world without her in it. I don't even know how to live in this one.

When we hang up, I look at my phone: three minutes and twenty-seven seconds. It seemed like so much longer.

Sometime during the night, he comes in. I pretend to sleep as he takes off his clothes and gets into bed. He puts a cold hand under my shirt, pinches my nipple.

"Tell me," I say, swatting his hand. "What happened?"

"I got it."

"Where's my camera?"

"On the dresser."

"What'd you do?"

"It was nothing," he says. "It was easy."

"Okay, but what'd you do? What happened?" I ask, knowing I'll never know what happened. I'll never know what he does when I'm not with him. When I'm alone I don't do anything the least bit interesting. He tugs at my panties and I help him, kick them to the end of the bed. I run my hand over his prickly head because it's what I like best about him. But once I'm safe inside my apartment, I won't answer his calls or listen to his voice mails. I'll watch him through the peephole until he goes away and if he acts crazy I'll document his behavior and get a restraining order. I'll tell Farrell, the apartment manager, to keep a lookout and she'll be happy to be given this assignment—she loves a purpose, someone she might yell at as she hobbles around the parking lot on her crutches. I'll even move if I have to, to Texas or North Carolina, somewhere far enough away that he won't bother to find me unless a bad man calls and offers him money, and he's the only bad man I can say for sure I know because this is not my life. It isn't the one, I tell myself, as I wrap my legs around him as tightly as possible.

BOY AND GIRL GAMES LIKE COUPLING

BY JAMIE PAIGE
Lauderdale County

Glen meets me at the overpass over Pine Forest Road, just after sunset. She's wearing a pink tank top and a pair of jeans. I'm sitting on top of a cinder block by the guardrail. There's one for her too. She puts her handbag down and sits next to me.

We've been together for six months. I didn't know we were together, but she says so, and it's too much trouble to fuss. I had known of Glen since second grade, but we had never talked. Then one day she and her boyfriend Terry got into a fight in homeroom. I watched the whole thing from my desk in the back of the room. Glen broke up with Terry and spent the rest of the day crying. That afternoon, I saw her walking home from school, about a mile from her parents' house. I knew that Terry usually drove her home, so I pulled my truck next to her on the shoulder and rolled down the window. Her cheeks were flushed, and she was panting.

"Want a ride?" I said to her. She spent a minute looking me over like she was trying to place me, then she opened the door and climbed in.

"Thanks," she said.

"I could have run you over just as easy," I said.

She laughed.

Things are pretty good most of the time. Fucking? Oh yeah.

And she brings me food home from her job. Sometimes she gives me money for weed, but she doesn't know it. She really needs to be more careful with her purse.

Lately she's been acting strange, talking about wanting me to meet her family, wondering why I spend so much time here at the overpass. It was her idea to come along. We're way up high. I stand and look over the rail. I'm straining through the dark for something, anything. Glen is talking about her family again, and I can't think.

"When you meet Mama, you'll understand," she says. "I'm not saying I want you to hate her, but I don't see how you couldn't at first. Don't get me wrong. I want you to like everyone if you can, but I can't see how."

The wind is cold. I put my jacket around Glen's shoulders. I'm shivering and leaning closer against the rail now. The rail is still warm from the evening sun. I grit my teeth.

"You don't have to meet them all at once," she's saying. "I know how you are about people."

We're quiet for a while. I'm glad. Glen knows everything, and she's always telling you about it.

"I just don't understand why you like it up here so much," she says. "It's so lonely."

"It's peaceful," I say. "Usually."

"Don't you wish you were doing something else?"

"Nothing else to do."

"You could call me," she says.

She calls me at all hours of the night. I hold the phone up to my ear and let her talk. She goes on for hours. "I get so lonely sometimes," she told me once. "I feel like I don't have nobody at all sometimes, except you. Why don't you ever call me?"

I never liked phones. And knowing Glen is like falling into the middle of something all the time.

"My dad would like you, I think," she says. "He's got his quiet ways too. Loves to shoot. He says he'll take you hunting when you meet him. He can't believe you've never been."

I don't say anything. I feel her eyes on me. I feel her hand on my shoulder. She moves closer, puts her arm around my waist. Her breath is warm against my ear.

"I tell him you're too gentle. Baby, I just know my family's gonna love you," she says.

"Sure." I put my arm around her. I hear nothing but her breathing, my breathing.

Soon there are headlights cresting the hill far off, and I say, "Just a minute," and pull away from Glen. I'm leaning over the rail again, looking out. The lights are growing, haloed. It's a pickup truck, I think, going thirty-five, maybe forty.

"Baby, is something wrong?" she says.

I don't say anything. I back off the rail. I'm stooping now, feeling around in the darkness. I hook my fingers through the holes in my cinder block, and I'm lifting it, pushing up with my legs.

"We're going so soon?" she says.

"Something like that," I say, and I wobble closer to the rail. I balance the cinder block along the edge. I'm reckoning time. The truck comes closer. I turn. "We better hurry up and get yours lifted. It won't be much longer now."

Glen is just looking at me.

"Let's go," I say. "You can push this one."

"Quit playing around," she says.

"Who's playing?"

"Have you lost your fucking mind?"

"Something like that," I say. I look back down the road. Glen is screaming now and reaching around me, trying to grab the cinder block. She gets a grip, but I pry her fingers loose and push the cinder block over the edge. I hear the screech of tires. I hear my cinder block crash and break against the pavement. I hear the crunch of gravel as the truck veers onto the shoulder.

Glen is staring at me, again not saying anything. I grin, and she backs away.

"What's wrong, baby?" I say to her. "Don't you understand?"

She says nothing.

"I bet you were right," I say. "Your folks would love me. I'm so gentle. I'm so sweet."

"Stop it," she says, her voice just above a whisper.

"Let's get married. Let's have babies and drop them off this overpass."

She's crying. "Please, just stop."

I'm laughing now. "You've gotta love the whole of the man," I say. "Gotta love him all the way."

Then I hear footsteps crunching through the high grass leading up to the overpass. I hear two men's voices, angry voices. One of them pumps a shotgun, and they keep coming, creeping their way up the slope. I turn and run, from what exactly I'm not sure anymore, but I'm laughing harder all the time. The soles of my tennis shoes go slapping across the pavement, then I run deep into the woods, cutting down the old dirt road toward the fish camp. Glen is right behind me all the way. Running like hell.

OXFORD GIRL

BY MEGAN ABBOTT

Oxford

> *I fell in love with an Oxford girl*
> *With dark and darling eyes.*
> *I asked her if she'd marry me,*
> *And me she nothing denied.**

Two a.m., you slid one of your Kappa Sig T-shirts over my head, fluorescent green XXL with a bleach stain on the right shoulder blade, soft and smelling like old sheets.

I feigned sleep, your big brother Keith snoring lustily across the room, and you, arms clutched about me until the sun started to squeak behind the Rebels pennant across the window. Watching the hump of your Adam's apple, I tried to will you to wake up.

But I couldn't wait forever, due for first shift at the Inn. Who else would stir those big tanks of grits for the game-weekend early arrivals, parents and grandparents, all manner of snowy-haired alumni in searing red swarming into the café for their continental-plus, six thirty sharp?

So I left you, your head sunk deep in your pillow, and ducked out still wearing your shirt. Wore it hustling across the Grove, my legs bare and goosy in last night's party skirt, the zipper stuck.

---

* *"The Oxford Girl" is an English ballad with multiple lyrical variations dating back at least to the 1820s and possibly as far as the seventeenth century. This version comes from the John Quincy Wolf Folklore Collection at Lyon College.*

I wore your shirt, frat boy, because it was stiff and warm and smelled like you, your bed, you.

I wore it all day Friday, to my midterm and to gen chem lab and to Walgreens and Holli's Sweet Tooth to pick up the cookies for tomorrow's tailgate.

That evening, head in my calc text, I fell asleep at my desk still wearing it, page crease on my cheek.

So of course I was still wearing it when you woke me up, coming on eleven o'clock, you drunk and heated up on something, everything.

You had a funny look in your eye I'd not seen before and I thought, *Does he know?* But you couldn't have.

I'd only learned myself a few hours before, the Walgreens bag hidden in my trash.

The baby inside me was far smaller than a pinhead, the Internet told me.

Did you feel it, though, somehow—can boys?—when you hoisted me on the sinktop in the Kappa Sig bathroom the night before, your hands on my belly? Your fingers were five thumbs like hot dogs but you were strong, strong as my dad swinging a bat in our backyard in Batesville, saying, *My girl, my girl, she's going to the U, all. That's my pride and joy. She aims proud and true.*

Someone as strong as you couldn't feel something as small as a pinhead, could you?

But is that why you did me, because of the baby you put inside me?

It wasn't even a baby yet, except maybe to God.

Didn't you know I would fix it. I had dreams too.

Bigger dreams than you, frat.

෨

The first time I saw you was at church, and it was fate because I hadn't been since Easter. Your face stuck out among all the others. It was like I knew you, girl.

It wasn't until later I figured out where I'd seen you before: in the painting hanging on the wall of my grandmother's house. A smudgy rendering of a petticoated country girl feeding a baby calf with a bottle. It was on her wall my whole life, right above the table with the phone you had to dial, and the girl was so beautiful, with light on her face.

You had that light on your face.

The next day, I saw you again. You were gliding up the library steps at seven a.m., just as I was slouching home. One of those mornings I'd been sneaking fast through some girl's pink-foiled door—the entire door covered in wrapping paper, that's a thing some girls do, the door also dripping with things, Mardi Gras beads, a message board with a frilly pen hanging from it. So many things, so that when you snuck out just as the sky was shaking night off you couldn't help but wake that girl, the cinnamon blast of last night's fireball from her open sleep-mouth.

Even after I escaped the sweet cream whip of a bed, wriggling free by sliding out from her arm hooked around my neck, wrist pinned to my thigh, that booby-trapped door still told on me. The clatter-click shimmy-slap of that gimcrack door, waking all the girls on the hall, their topknots sliding from sleeping heads.

These girls, they were all like candy, sweet 'n' sour.

My mouth, my gut, coated with it. With them.

But you were different. I could tell.

Your heart, pure as a girl in a dream—that's what I knew, just from looking at you. You in the faded pasteled picture in my grandma's house, that baby calf near purring with delight, head nestled on your soft bosoms.

Your heart pure and your body barely touched, never said a curse and bet you ironed your bedsheets just like my grandma too. She told me that boys were meant to misbehave and it was for a good girl to save us boys, each and every one.

You were that girl.

&

"Don't drink anything served out of a trash can."

That's what my big sisters told me before the party.

"Which will be a change from Batesville," one of them added, winking mean at me.

I was the only Batesville Chi O. Mom had the plan long ago, all those weekends I spent babysitting for her boss at South Panola Veterinary, Dr. JoAnn Kitts, who also happened to be president of the local Chi O alum chapter.

Once she knows you, Mom said, *she will love you, everyone does, and then you'll get your bid and you'll live in that big house white as coconut cake with such grand pillars.*

After I pledged she had me take pictures of her standing on the porch wearing her *Proud Chi O Mom* sweatshirt, waving and waving under the sky-high pillars.

At the party, there was no trash can I could see, only the sunshine punch in the plastic bowl made to look like crystal.

Do you know it was you who served us first, me and my Chi O sister Briane, giving us two plastic cups apiece, saying to me, *Pretty gals shouldn't have to wait twice?*

The music was shaking through us and the punch tasted like Country Time, but I saw the jugs of Everclear behind you.

Soon, we were dancing. Time shook us free and our bodies leapt and writhed for hours.

Chi-O, my ho, it's off to bed we go, some of you boys were singing. Were you one of them?

Midnight struck with Briane puking great golden gushes on my shoes in the bathroom.

In the tight stall, she cried hot shudders against me and told me all about you. *Did you see the boy who gave us the cups?* she sobbed, sputtering. Then saying she couldn't believe you didn't recognize her because you had loved her one weekend last spring. How she met you in this very house for a boots-and-bowties mixer and after many vodka sodas you took her on the roof and persuaded her with such honeyed words to dip her dainty duckling neck into your lap and gave you everything her little motor mouth could. Later, she passed out in your room and in the morning you were gone but left her a half-full bottle of Gatorade and an empty trash can in case.

Which she thought was sweet.

But she was a Jackson girl, and what did she know of love?

Her breath sweet and rank in my ear, she confided that, the next day and the next, she texted you and texted you—dirty things she thought you might like, and romantic thoughts too because you'd told her the night you two met, her head resting wearily in your lap after her task, her mouth suffused with your love: *You are my girl, aren't you?* you'd said. *Ah, you are, hot thing.*

You never texted her back, not even when she sent you that picture of her *Chi-O-My!* thong twirled around one sparkly fingernail.

When Monday came—or so she told me, her gritty teeth clicking in postvomit chill—she walked into the student union, the air thick with the sour yeast from the Subway's ovens gusting through the pipes, and saw you sprawled across one of the crusted lounge sofas with a ponytailed girl in shearling boots and the shortest of MissBehavin pom shorts and probably hailing from Texas. Oh, how she wriggled and cuddled against your Kappa Sig shirt, the same one against which Briane had pressed her cheek two days before, doing your business for you in your frat boy lap.

That was all there really was to Briane's sad story except for a dry heave or two. So I cleaned her face with a paper towel and tried to winch her upright, but there was no doing. I would have to call for backup.

I waited on your staircase steps, Briane huddled at my feet. That was when I saw you again and you were so drunk you tried to hand me another cup of that selfsame party punch that had been splashed on my ankles as Briane had relayed her tale of woe.

I said a foul thing to you, but you didn't seem to hear.

But what you said, frat—do you remember? You said, *I've seen you so many times. Like, my whole life.*

And I didn't know what it meant, but it moved me.

Well, I never cared much for Briane anyway, or any of the Jackson girls with their pearls and buttery purses.

Me, I hold my heart with great care. I do not tender it lightly, over soft words.

~

I called at her sister's house
About eight o'clock one night.
I asked her, would she walk with me,
And we'd name our wedding day.

The party after the LSU game, and there you were, in my own house.

You were holding that stubby Chi O's hair back as she heaved SoCo punch down the front of herself like a little girl spilling lemonade on her Sunday dress.

The church, the library, and now here: I guess it came to seem you were always doing honorable things: praying, studying, helping people.

Later, after king's cup and the glass leg of beer, I looked for you. I hunted the house for you, calling your name, bawling it, shantying it. I sought to conjure you, but you had gone.

It never would have happened if you hadn't left the party. In that way, it was your fault, in part.

Searching on the sagging back porch, so heavy with red-faced partiers it seemed to undulate, a ship on a stormy sea, I came to see that Sigma Nu derelict (oh, I knew his kind, played against them in high school, those tufthunters from Jackson Prep). He was swinging high his solo cup and shouting for all to hear, his arm flailing back and swatting that little white-blond girl, who collapsed like my grandma's lung.

I had to hit him, you see. I had to hit him every time I did. All those times.

I did not have to kick his head on the porch floor, his body curled S-like, like the snake he was. But it felt at the time that I did.

It turned out the white-blond girl had only been bent over laughing, her beer cup knocked from her hand by that Sigma Nu in a way that made her laugh.

But when she saw what had happened—the guy, the dude, the date-raper-type miscreant lying there on the planks, his face swirled red—she stopped laughing, her hand to her once-loud mouth. She did not even have the words to thank me.

There was the feeling that I should leave, and Keith put his baller hands on me and made it so.

His bros will be here soon, he said. *They will hunt you, dude. They will take you down and bury your bones in the Walk of Champions.*

I wasn't afraid.

I took a long stroll and fell asleep a while on a sofa in the student union. When I returned, everyone was gone. My shirt had red dots all over the front and I tore it off, hulk-like, and hid it in the dumpster behind the house.

The dude was fine. Mr. Sigma Nothing. I saw him in accounting on Monday.

The blood collecting under his cheekbone, well, it looked impressive. Like a Purple Heart.

≈

Two days later, there you were, frat, sitting two tables away at the library Starbucks. You came over, hot chocolate for you, skinny mocha for me.

Is that what we all drink? I said. And I told you I'd heard some things about you that I did not care for.

You said it was probably all true. Regrets, misdeeds, bad temper, and careless love. But you weren't like that anymore, everything was changing inside you.

Then, like in a bad song lyric, you fingered a heart in my foam.

I rolled my eyes, but still: I felt a shiver on me. Inside, I was afraid. Because it seemed to me you didn't know yourself at all. Like others, my brother, my loudmouth dad.

But just like that, your finger there, your eyes lowered, I knew I likely loved you anyway. Because we were meant to cross paths, boy, just like I knew what was coming.

I could feel the blood pushing at my temple.

≈

I knew you would taste like the inside of a sweet apple.

I talked you into following me up two sets of library stairs, among the humming copiers, the chug of the vending machines, whispering students, keys clicking.

Then I talked you into taking my hand as I led you between two rolling stacks in a far corner where books on things like tax incidence and the fishery industry sit.

My boy Keith spotted us and summoned a young pledge to wind the handle on one of the moving stacks, pressing us two together.

We could feel everything about each other. I wasn't even embarrassed. We were crushed.

You reached out for my hand. In that moment, I would've married you. If only you—

&

The next night, we took that walk in Bailey Woods, beers poured into camelbacks, and the sky went gold, then black, and we got lost, even though it's less than a mile deep. Sweet gum trees overhead, kissing long and slow at the juniper stump, our fingers poking into its dark pockets. Then we saw that dead dog and said a prayer over him because we both have Jesus sneaking in our hearts somewhere. We went back to the Kappa Sig house and to your mold-furry room and your roommate gone, and I couldn't get my jeans off fast enough.

You owned my heart, frat boy.

So fast the feeling, I didn't care what was coming.

I think it wasn't what we did in your dirty-sheet twin bed that mattered. After all, it only lasted as long as it takes to walk across the square. I think it was the way you looked at me, the moon coming through the Reb pennant hanging in the window, pink on your boy face.

How you looked at me. Your eyes all crazy, like you saw something I've never seen in myself before, never seen ever.

There's a universe out there, little girl is what I came to know through each of those soft explosions I felt after I showed you what to do with your hand, that trick of the wrist.

You had a surprising way of shivering through intimacies, which you did each of the twelve times we did it before I died.

&

My legs shaking, like a little bare-balled virgin.

I'd forgotten to put in my contacts and during it everything was blurry and flashtastic and I couldn't see much of you in the dark except the dark inside of your mouth, open when you felt the shock of love, or pretended to.

There's been so many girls, and they are all in some way one girl, tan and sparkle-lashed, like my sisters' dolls arrayed on the circle carpet, hair stretched radical to center.

But you.

It was only after that I saw the tear in the condom. Which is on me, baby, it is. It always is.

Would you believe me if I said it wasn't like the other times?

I swear I didn't feel it rip, didn't feel anything but you, your monumental fucking beauty and the little sounds from your throat, and the way your thighs, like smoothed sticks, held me so.

You were in the bathroom for so long after, and I was glad because my legs were still shaking and I didn't want you to see.

The longer I waited, having slung the split condom from thumb to trash can, I started to wonder a little at how quick you had laid down for me.

But I swear, girl, getting you so easy didn't make me love you any less. Just wonder, a little.

࿏

It was only when in the bathroom after, the boy bathroom so thick with mildew you could feel it fuzzing your mouth, that I found the piece of latex inside me.

My brother had told me once, and older girls too. *They always know when it happens*, they told me, *and they should stop.*

But it had broken and part of it was inside me now.

Oh no, I cursed myself. *I have let myself be fooled and misled. I am such a girl. A weak, weak girl.*

Except still, I didn't know I cared, my hands trembling, shaking with that speckle of powdery latex on my fingertips.

Part of you was inside me now.

And you asked me to stay over. And you talked in your sleep, your face in my hair, your hands on my excitable hips.

You said I was your country girl even though I told you I was from Batesville. I guess you were still drunk.

❧

You came back from the bathroom, scrubbed and smelling like our soap-on-a-rope. Your shyness made my blood hotten again, but I couldn't make it work, the heavy of the beers pinning me down.

We slept.

I dreamed all night of scaling skyscrapers and sailing the high seas. Of pirate ship masts and spaceships. And I was king in all these worlds.

I didn't even care to find I'd slunk so strangely in the bed that my head was resting against your chest, your tiny tits still in their bra, me too drunk to flick the hook.

There would be time enough.

I have to go, you said, before I could. *I have my kitchen shift at six thirty.*

No, I said, *because, look . . .*

> *We walked along and talked along*
> *Till we came to level ground.*
> *Then I picked up a hedgewood stick*
> *And knocked this fair maid down.*

Standing in the cold and big kitchen of the Inn at Ole Miss, I could still feel you the whole three hours. In front of the industrial dishwasher, scooping stuck-corn pudding and biscuit-gravy skim into the disposal trough, I could feel you inside, and slipping from me.

Is this the one? I wondered. Even as I knew it was.

You see, you were foretold, frat boy.

Sun beating down, the railroad festival in Amory when I was

ten years old, a man in a shabby hat was giving out fortunes from his slanting card table. Staked between the heat-pressed T-shirts and the frozen cheesecake on a stick, he sat in that folding chair, the little sign before him, corrugated cardboard, that read: *Fates Disclosed. Paths Foretold. I See You, and All.*

My brother was far ahead, wending through tents and bouncy castles to catch up with some girls in snug shorts, and I could tell the shabby-hat man had me in his sights.

Pointing one horny finger, he said: *I'll tell anyone but yours. You're too pretty to have your heart broke.* That yellowing finger seeming to hypnotize me closer.

Tell it! said a passing lady, large of body with a hat shaped like a steam engine and evil eyes. *Tell the little girl! Tell her what she must know!*

And bringing me close, hand on my arm, the leather twists of his pinched finger skin, the man told. *He will come with nectar on his tongue,* he said, tears in his eyes, I swear. *But he will send your head spinning, seal you up in silver. Swallow you whole.*

Standing there, still in his clutches, I felt my heart cut loose inside me. *Is this to be my fate?*

Suddenly, my brother's hand fell fast upon my shoulder, tugging me backward. *Don't you know not to talk to the tatty hobos?*

Quickly, we were stumbling through the grass of Frisco Park, the sparkle from all the hanging goods, the sparkling purses and glad rags for ladies who'd venture through the festival, looking for objects to wear to entice boys and men.

⁓

Listen: I told you I had once been a bad young man, a fool and coward. And I told you I'd changed, and I had. You were my change, and I thought about you days and nights, in accounting and business communication, and porch-drinking at the house with Keith and the boys. Just like a girl, I held my phone tight, and when it pulsed with you, it felt like a church thing.

I didn't sleep with anyone else, all those three weeks.

> *She fell upon her bended knees;*
> *"Oh, Willie," she did cry.*
> *"Oh, Willie, dear, don't murder me;*
> *I'm not prepared to die."*

And so, October fell to November and that Friday came, the one where I came to be sneaking from your bed at dawn in your XXL shirt, green as a glow stick, as play slime, as a jellyfish under a microscope.

Did I know that would be the day? No.

But I had a special stitch of worry over my brow anyway.

Checking my underwear between every class. I was only five days late, but I had not forgotten the latex clot found via my fingertip three weeks prior, and I could not wait any longer.

പ

In our three weeks together, you always came to my room, so I decided that night to come to you. I wanted to see your room, and your tits so extrasoft the night before, I got crazy just thinking about them.

Dusk falling, I stepped through the Tara pillars and into Chi O.

Your door (spare, unfoiled) was open, but you weren't there.

Sitting on your bed, I waited, smelling your powder-fresh smells and looking through your underwear drawers filled with such neon-colored beauty I felt sick from it. Honey and strawberry butter, the sheets smelled just like you.

You don't remember me, the girl in the doorway said.

And I said, *Sure I do.* Because I did. From the party where I met you. And how that puke bib she wore and her weakness to drink had taken you away from me.

She said she had something to show me and outstretched her hand, palm up. At first I thought it was a blowpop stick, or a thermometer, its tip blue.

But it wasn't either. It was scepter. A sword into the center of my heart. Because in its little window there was a +, like a tiny blue cross.

She said you had shown it to her, confided. *I just thought you should know,* the girl said. *Being as you're a good guy.* Adding, *She's my sister, but she's a sly kitty.*

৵

I saw you buy the kit, Briane said, standing outside the bathroom stall. *I saw you today at the Walgreens.*

Briane always had eyes on all sides of her bobbly head.

It's okay, sis, she said. *It's okay.*

I opened the door, my—your—neon shirt like a flag, a flare, staring her down.

That's right, I said, *it is okay. Because I'm not.* Which was a lie, at least for now.

Maybe I should have taken the blue stick with me. Hidden it in the dumpster behind the kitchen, somewhere. You could never hide things in the house. The sisters were always watching. But I buried the stick under all the blister-foil laxative strips and seeping old tampons in the stall bin.

Briane couldn't ever have found it. She wouldn't have put her Jackson-girl fingers into that bin, mingling with all our girl blood and shame.

৵

The Chi O girl wouldn't stop talking to me, saying she wants her an Oxford boy or Jackson or Houston oil. Country club golf and fine china on the Grove, a house with white pillars. None of this had to do with me, my dad in a divorced-man's condo in Atlanta for work, my mom the pharmacist at Kroger.

But the girl kept talking, and I had to leave, sickened suddenly by all the ugliness and the girls's pink-papered doors and sweet vanilla smells that are meant to keep you there forever, to choke you.

The Grove was dark but neck high in girls, all with their mouths open, teeth glowing. Or so it seemed.

But I wished I hadn't started drinking.

If only you'd texted me back right away. I said I needed to see you. Even if you were in some lab, or something.

But you didn't text back, at least not right away, and soon I stopped looking at my phone like a girl, because I found Keith, staking the spot for tomorrow's game, and we started drinking from that bottle of Aristocrat tucked under his arm like a baby doll.

We couldn't put up the tent till nine so we were tossing those loose tentpoles like batons, like girls swinging batons. We were swinging them like baseball bats. The ping of the fiberglass on cement, on everything.

Everything was like a bright, spangled blur. My blood was pounding. Like I said, I wished I hadn't started drinking right then.

❧

At my desk, trying for concentration, I wasn't thinking that much about the blue stick exactly, my palm touching once, twice, my stomach.

WHERE R U, your text said.

I texted you back, but you never replied.

This won't happen, I said to myself, but I wasn't even sure what it meant.

I knew I wouldn't have that baby. But I wasn't sure the way it would play out.

Until you came calling.

๛

Prowling the campus, Keith loud in my ear beside me, I kept talking about you. About how I'd seen you in church and you were just like the country lass nursing the baby calf who was like my grandma and all good women everywhere, and now I'd defiled you and myself in the eyes of God and all that. Except hadn't she said it was for the girl to save us boys? I couldn't make all the pieces fit.

Keith would have none of it anyway, and never liked church talk. He shoved me hard and told me to stop being a pussy. Then he told me how he saw you sneak out of our room that very morning wearing my shirt like you owned me, or some such badge of domination.

My shirt, I said, because I hadn't realized.

And that's how I came to thinking I hadn't defiled you, you had defiled yourself, your jeans off so fast our first date, and this dawn striding out of my room in my shirt, my own shirt.

And for that, you must be taught a lesson.

Well, that is how I thought.

> But I paid no attention to the piteous appeal,
> But I beat her more and more,
> Till all around where the poor girl lay
> Was in a bloody gore.

I had it in my mind that I would retrieve you and we would walk once more in Bailey Woods, like we had that magic night three weeks before when you sealed your fate with me, girl.

But I had no other plan, on account of I could barely walk

and had lost Keith some time ago, left him in the shadow of Vaught-Hem knocking out parking-lot lights with his tentpole.

That last pole he struck, it looked like something surged through him.

When he fell onto the cement, his knees knocked together, like a cartoon. On the ground, stuttering, he was a slug-struck bird.

So I pushed on. I couldn't remember at first which house was yours, even though I'd been there mere hours before.

They all had white pillars, you see.

But I still had that tentpole, it felt like a saber.

Show me your blue stick, I'll raise you a saber.

❧

It was so late. I'd fallen asleep, my arm still stuck in my phys sci textbook.

You can't hide, you said, standing in my doorway. And I thought it was a joke, you with the tentpole in your hand, the way you grasped it, caveman, club.

I didn't tell you no when you asked me to come with you. But I did not yet know what was in your heart.

We didn't walk far, you intent on mad circles, swinging that tentpole into trash cans, trees, whatever came in your way.

You said, *I know I'm drunk, but I wanna show you something.*

And I thought, *Is this going to be it? Will this be how it goes?*

When we came under one of the streetlamps, you looked at me, your face shadowed. You said, *Is that my shirt, girl?*

❧

You were more beautiful than ever that night. Your face angel-lit under all the streetlamps.

That's why it happened, if you want to know.

We tramped across campus, all the sculptures and statues of important men. You didn't seem afraid of me, despite all the noise that came from me, my mouth uncontrollable, and my arms too.

Watching you take that errant tentpole from my hand and twirl it like a baton, like you were a twirler, and weren't you? The way you wielded your weapons, after all. Blue stick, love's arrow, that warm spot between your legs.

And where did we end up anyway, roaming the campus near and far, the great bronze hands of the mentor instructing her flock in the rose garden?

Finally landing back where we began, at the foot of Sorority Row long after midnight.

All those white pillars, there must've been a hundred of them, all gleaming in the moon, and on the pond that lay there, silver and shimmery like a mirror laid flat.

Oh God, don't you see I had no choice?

☙

When I took the pole from you, everything turned. But I had to, don't you see?

Return my sword, girly, you said, your voice gone high and strange. And you yanked it so hard, I fell back.

You may ask me how I knew you were going to raise high that tentpole. But I never *didn't* know.

Except I do wish I could have stopped you.

☙

It was the two things at once, you see. It was you holding the pole and you wearing the shirt.

You could spin and flip it in ways that seemed miraculous. All while wearing my shirt, fluorescent-green and too big for you by half, dragged over your head like you owned it. Or me.

Under the shirt, your belly, the thing inside it—well, I thought of that too.

I know you! I said, shouting now. *I know your kind!* Because you'd pretended to be a country girl who never heard a word of sin, a girl who would make me—make me—behave. And be good.

I never met a country girl, and it turned out you were from Batesville.

My, oh, that tentpole in my hand felt like it swung itself, swinging with such a whirring sound and the terrible, suctiony *thunk* as it hit your pretty, perfect head.

Oh, my girl, my girl.

The swirl-slap of the alcohol, gallons of it, suddenly cleared away, like the seas parting and receding like the old, bright-colored movie I watched with Gran every Easter my whole life till she died last year.

I saw it then. I saw it. Like everything else fell away and you were praying in church, by the tallest window.

Alas, it was now too late.

&

This is it, I thought.

Yet I felt no danger.

High above your head, that pole glinted under the streetlamp, swinging it like a mighty ax, a giant in a fairy tale.

I felt a crashing in my brain. I think I saw stars. And I was hearing something like beads shaking inside my head, like in the woods, my brother showing me how to shake the cocoon we found in the branch.

If the caterpillar is alive, it's heavy, you hear a thud.

If it's dead, it's light, and all you hear is a rattle.

I wonder what you heard when you shook me, frat boy. Oxford boy. My beloved.

Did you hear our baby rattle?

> *Then I picked her up by her little white hand,*
> *And I swung her body around.*

I took her down to the riverside
And threw her in to drown.

❧

Remember how you fell?

Landing on your knees with such an awful smack, the pond like a black hole behind you, the black hole spreading in my brain. Oh, how you looked up at me, your eyes shining.

Please don't, you said.

But I saw what the pole had done, your temple sunk deep as a cave and your eye bulging.

You didn't know it yet, but you were nearly gone.

❧

Your face, I watched you watch me, my head spinning so.

It was that face I knew from the twelve times in your darkened room. The face that told me you had big visions of life in your head, the way you were shivering, standing above me, that same lovely way of shivering you had each of the twelve times we did it before I died.

I don't remember falling, but the red covered my eyes and I could see nothing.

Someone was crying.

❧

They say the light goes out of the eyes when you pass, but it didn't with Gran at Baptist Memorial and so not with you, my country girl.

I saw the shining as I carried you from Sorority Row straight to the edge of Silver Pond.

I saw it as I dropped you in the water, and my sword too, which was nothing but a tentpole, bent upon itself.

I saw it long after you sunk to the shallow bottom, my shirt billowing, a bright lily pad, and your body making ring after ring after ring.

❧

I wasn't gone yet, but you were dragging me. Down that grassy slope I went, like a sleigh ride, the leaves curling and cutting my legs.

I grabbed at you, clawing at your ankles, nails sunk deep, but you have near a hundred pounds and a foot of monster blood and bone on me.

My hair knotted in your hand, I looked up at you and my head kept knock-knock-knocking on the ground, the blood coming wet and soft from the open hole in my head.

He will come with nectar on his tongue.

I guess I always knew that shabby-hatted man would prove true one day.

But he will send your head spinning, seal you up in silver. Swallow you whole.

☙

You were well under.

There was stirring briefly, glugging bubbles. Once, your head came up, your eyes glassy, arms grabbing, wanly, the surface of the water. Then your head tilting backward, disappearing.

Finally, you stopped.

Then I went home.

> *But I rolled and I tossed upon my bed,*
> *And no rest could I find,*
> *For the flames of Hell seemed all 'round me,*
> *And in my eyes would shine.*

I did find my bed, my ankles and shins slimed up from the pond, and my face speckled red as Raggedy Andy.

I showered at three, no one heard. Then back to bed, a heave and horror in me, where I commenced crying.

Before that, I'd never even noticed Silver Pond. But the next day, and the next, Silver Pond was all I could see, from wherever I stood.

As there was no escaping it, I sought it out.

I even lingered at your house, hand on one of the pillars, like a wedding cake, wondering, missing you.

☙

In the water, I sunk. I felt the thing blooming at the top of my chest, spreading down and in. The thing was the darkness of you, and what we shared.

My lungs swimming inside me, my heart growing small and raisin-like, I thought how it came to be.

Might I have shrunk from my fate?

But one can't ponder such things too long.

☙

> *Her sister threw my life away*
> *Without a thought of doubt.*
> *Her sister swore I was the man*
> *Who led her sister out.*

I might've got caught anyway, but your sister sealed the deal.

He saw the stick and then he left the house filled with rage. That's what the Briane girl told the police, as if she'd played no part.

They were a fiery pair, she said, her voice excited, *and now their fire has swallowed them both.*

What did she know of us, girl?

For ours was a tender thing, deep down.

> *But I would not mind dying*
> *If I thought t'would bring me rest*
> *From this burning, burning, burning hell*
> *That keeps burning in my breast.*

They talked about how I smiled when they put the cuffs on to take me to county and that's not true.

But I did tell them how I pictured you up there in heaven, halo fired up, having sweet tea with my grandma.

How she said: *A good girl to save us boys, each and every one.*

&

Here comes that grapple hook again, swinging slow for me.

I can hide among the floating ferns and duckweed.

I won't leave until it has me.

From here I can see the white pillars.

My, how they shine.

DIGITS

BY MICHAEL KARDOS

Winston County

The Monday after fall break, I welcome everybody back and ask if anyone went anyplace interesting. (Winston County isn't so far from New Orleans to the southwest and the Alabama beaches to the southeast.) That's when I notice Britney, in her usual seat, end of the second row, with a heap of gauze taped to her pinky. Or to where her pinky ought to be.

"My family almost went to Dollywood but didn't," says Jason, my talker in the front row.

"Britney?" I say.

"Yes, sir?" she says.

Britney is pretty in the predictable way that my students depict pretty in their short stories: blond hair, blue eyes, hell of a smile. Except nobody writes *hell*.

"My God—what happened?"

She looks around at her classmates, then back at me. "I had an accident over the weekend." She could be explaining a rip in her knapsack. No wet eyes, no anything.

She's either being tough or is still in shock, so I let it go and start in on Ernest Hemingway's short story "Hills Like White Elephants." This is a fiction-writing class, but I assign plenty of literature too, so they'll have something to imitate besides stories about vampires. I can take or leave "Hills Like White Elephants," probably I've just read it too many times, but it's a useful story to teach setting and subtext, and I figure they ought know at least one Hemingway.

As I explain how the conversation about beer in the story keys us in to a broader power struggle between the man and girl, I keep stealing glances at Britney. At that finger. At the absence of that finger. When class ends, I consider keeping her after, but what am I going to say? So I pack up and drive home, where my wife will be counting the seconds until she can steal a moment of peace. We have a three-month-old.

The rest of the week passes predictably: too little sleep, always running behind. Some laundry gets done. The baby becomes a week farther away from the moment of his birth, when he was just a squishy stranger. You can't use a phrase like "squishy stranger" in Mississippi to describe your newborn, I've found. You can't joke to your neighbors about the old dog crate in the garage alleviating your need for a babysitter. Not unless you don't want any more casseroles.

The following Monday, the start of week seven of the semester, two more students walk into class missing their pinkies.

"What the hell?" I ask, and they all look at me critically.

"Accident," says Jeremy, from the back row.

"What about you?" I ask Brian, who sits front and center. His first writing assignment, in which the students described a farm from the perspective of a man whose wife had just died (but they weren't allowed to mention the spouse or death), included a detail about the peeling paint on the barn's walls. I knew right away he'd be one of my better writers. Specificity is everything.

"One of those weird things," he says.

Outside our windows, huge pine trees with their million

green needles are set against a sky as bright and blue as my son's Fisher-Price whale bathtub. Back in New Jersey everything has stopped growing by now and the air is raw, but here the sun is finally a warm kiss instead of a branding iron, and winter is still a lifetime away.

"Guys," I say—because y'*all* sounds inauthentic coming from my lips even after five years—"are you okay? I mean, talk to me." Half of them stare down at their desks. The other half look at me as if I'm overreacting. But I'm teaching three other classes this semester (two freshman comp, one intro-to-literature), and in all of them the number of fingers corresponds exactly to ten times the number of students. "Just do me a favor," I tell them. "Promise me you'll all be extra careful, okay?"

They smile. "Sure thing, Dr. P.," one of them says from the middle row. Baseball cap. College T-shirt. Brandon? Austin? Halfway into the semester, and I still confuse my baseball-cap wearers.

There's a similar look that many of them have. A way of dressing, a way of talking and moving through their days.

My students at Winston State, I have found, are almost uniformly gentle, kind, and Christian. Many are the first in their families to attend college. Most hail from tiny, tight-knit rural communities. They are totally secure in their beliefs about God and man and would rather not question the reassuring narratives that have gotten them this far. They have little use for nuance, don't like to consider that Atticus Finch's stubborn and naive refusal to see anything but the goodness in his dark-hearted neighbors nearly got his children murdered. Atticus Finch, flawed? Boy, they sure don't like to consider that.

So I push, but not too hard. Fifteen weeks is enough to open eyes but rarely very wide. Anyway, my objective is to make them better writers, not to muck with their lives or how they make sense of it. Yet writing isn't ever divorced from life, and how someone can become more attuned to the possibilities of literature without becoming more attuned to the world itself, I have no idea.

On the first day of the first class I ever taught—this was at Penn State—I was fishing for a text we'd all read before, something to forge a fast literary bond. I was working toward my PhD in twentieth-century American literature at the time, and in my class sat twenty-four freshman comp students who would rather have been anywhere else.

Most of them had been assigned *The Great Gatsby* in high school, and some had even read it. I confessed to them that I'd once had my own Daisy Buchanan problem back when I was an undergrad. The young woman and I had dated all sophomore year, and then I went to England for a semester abroad. When I came back to the States, she was seeing a guy on the lacrosse team. It'd wrecked me for a while, until I started to understand that Jessica had represented beauty and love and lightness to my twenty-year-old self more than she'd ever actually embodied those things. "Does that make any sense?" I asked my class of freshman comp students. "Do you see what I'm saying?"

Nobody said anything, until finally a student in the back row asked, "Which one was Daisy?"

I don't have a Daisy Buchanan problem anymore. I have Beth, my wife, who shares my bed and my life. I have a job where every day is, if not an adventure, at least interesting. I'm not rich, far from it, but I don't need to be. Don't want to be. I have a family. A career. Through the books I read, I can visit any place or any time, and, to paraphrase my pal Atticus, I'm able to step into an infinite number of other people's shoes.

Week nine and we're down two more fingers. Week ten and it's two more, making seven fingers total. Five are pinkies. One's a ring finger. Britney is missing the middle finger on her right hand now, in addition to the pinky on her left. I've started pretending not to notice, because there's no profit in calling attention to something that everyone with eyes can plainly see. We drag our chairs into a circle, as we always do when it's time to workshop their stories, and discuss two student manuscripts. One chronicles spring break aboard a cruise ship. Most of the story depicts a beer-pong tournament. The story ends with the sentence, *It was the best spring break ever!*

"Does anyone else feel that ping-pong maybe isn't enough conflict?" asks Brian.

"I agree," Britney says. She lowers her voice and says to the writer, "You're sort of wasting our time here."

"Now hold on," I say. Britney is right, of course, but this isn't the diplomatic workshop environment I've been fostering. I look around at my group of gauze-wearers and fight back a moment of nausea. "We should at least consider the possibility that Bruce has minimized conflict for some larger narrative purpose."

"No," Bruce jumps in, "I just wrote it for fun." He's a business major, one of the ten-fingered. I shoot him a look, because the author isn't supposed to talk during his own workshop. It's a cardinal rule. "It doesn't have any deep meaning or anything," he continues, ignoring my glance and further undercutting my pedagogical position. "I'm not trying to be Hemingway."

"Well, that's obvious," Britney says. "I mean—" She catches my eye and stops talking. For the next ten minutes, we discuss the story's descriptions of the ship's stateroom, the swimming pool, the grand atrium, the food served at the buffet, the vast sea.

In the second story, a fourteen-year-old girl living in a strict household with deeply religious parents lies to her mother about kissing a boy, and when her mother finds out, she has the girl's favorite backyard tree cut down branch by branch. Sap spills everywhere. The story is a big hit. The word *symbol* gets said a lot in our discussion. It isn't lost on me that only a handful of weeks ago, these same students refused to admit that the beer in Hemingway's story could symbolize anything.

Everyone has lots to say, and class nearly runs over. This is exactly the sort of student-centered learning that a teacher is supposed to dream about, but as I watch my students file out of the room, still chatting, I wonder just what it is that's being learned.

What I didn't tell my class at Penn State all those years ago, what I've never told anyone, is that Jessica, my college girlfriend, had been eight weeks pregnant when I left America. It was cowardly of me—I knew it then, know it now—but I was a college junior, just twenty years old, and practically a kid myself. I left her some money and refused to talk to her until it was done.

And it really was an awfully simple operation.

In bed that night, I tell Beth about the growing finger tally. She only knew about the first one. Between the postpartum hormones and lack of sleep, she didn't need anything else upsetting her.

"Where do you think they all are?" she asks.

"What—the fingers?" The lights are off. It's eleven p.m. Through the baby monitor, ocean waves crash softly onto shore. "I really don't know." I rub the base of her neck awhile in the dark. "I want my students to develop a deeper understanding of the human condition. But not at the expense of their fingers."

Pillow talk is rare these days. One of us will be up with Twain before long, and most nights Beth and I race toward sleep as if the first one to get there wins a night alone in a motel with free HBO.

"Do you remember that movie?" she says. "The one where the eccentric but devoted English professor gives his blasé students a renewed zest for life?" When we first started dating, we watched movies together all the time in theaters and on sofas.

"Are you talking about *all* movies?" I ask.

She yawns. "Exactly. It's a cinematic conceit."

Beth and I first met the year I moved to Mississippi. She's literally a sexy librarian. She said she was drawn to my tattoos and my shaved head. She liked that I didn't look like some crusty old professor. I feigned humility and told her I had no idea what she meant.

She's originally from Maben and graduated from Mississippi State before going on for a master's degree in library science at Vanderbilt. She stuck around Nashville for a few years afterward, working at Belmont University before coming home when her mother became ill. She and I had only been dating a couple of months when her mother passed, but instead of returning to her life in Nashville she decided to stick around. I'll always be grateful to her for that. A tenure-track job in my field is hard to come by, and I can't just pick up and move. Now she's a reference librarian here on campus—a good job in her field—and is halfway through the six months of unpaid leave that the college granted her.

"I need some adults-only time," she tells me the next morning. There are dark circles under our eyes. Twain was up every hour overnight. This has been happening too often lately—I thought we were past all that. But he won't fall asleep unless he's wrapped in a swaddle, and then he breaks out of the swaddle and goes nuts until he's wrapped back in it. But he hates being in it. Over and over again, all night long. I can imagine Twain years from now, a middle-aged man still breaking out of his swaddle ten times a night.

I e-mail my student Latoya to see if she'll come to the house on Saturday so that Beth and I can put on fresh clothes and cologne and have a date. It will be our first time out together, just the two of us, since Twain was born. Latoya is one of the last ten-fingereds in my fiction-writing class. She's an honor student double-majoring in English and French and strikes me as especially responsible. She arrives at the house missing a thumb, eager to tell me about the new story she's working on.

"Sort of O'Connor-esque," she says, looking around our living room. It's been overrun with the baby swing, baby mat, piles of laundry we haven't had time to put away, all the books we read to Twain even though he can't follow along yet. "It isn't very redemptive, though," she says. "I hope—"

"Sweetie," my wife says, "what happened to your thumb?"

Latoya glances at me, then back at Beth. "It was a dumb accident, ma'am. Totally my fault." She doesn't elaborate until Beth is doing a last makeup check in the bathroom.

"You know, the other kids are stupid," Latoya whispers to me.

I'm holding Twain, who finished nursing before Latoya arrived, and gently patting his back. "How do you mean?" I ask.

She raises an eyebrow as if I'm being intentionally obtuse. "Fingers are pretty necessary. But two thumbs and only one space bar?" She shrugs. "You do the math."

I do the math. The math tells me I'd better start thinking about deans and tenure committees, about campus police, about uprooting my family and trying to find another academic job in a recession. The math tells me to believe that Latoya's injury is the accident she says it is, and to tell her to eat whatever's in the fridge and that we'll be home by nine thirty for the baby's next feeding.

I hand Twain over to Latoya.

"You have spit-up on your shirt, Dr. P.," she tells me.

But it's only a little spit-up, not worth the time it takes to dig through the laundry basket for another shirt. For bank robbers and new parents, every second counts.

For the next two weeks, Beth and I talk about our two hours of chips and margaritas at the Rio Mexicana as if it were the daring adventure of a lifetime. It felt like it was.

The class before Thanksgiving, we're discussing Britney's second story. Her first one, workshopped early in the semester, was about a recent college grad who leaves Mississippi and struggles to find work in New York City. The main character carries around some kind of vague guilt because she left her steady boyfriend back home, and at the end of the story, she decides to leave New York, which she finds cold and unfriendly, and returns to him. Every semester I receive one or two of these stories, always written by bright young women who are far more ambivalent about breaking free of their families' limited expectations of them than they'd ever acknowledge. These students want to convince the class, and therefore themselves, that their white-gown, hometown endings are happy and redemptive, not realizing that their stories are actually the tragic tales of unreliable narrators. Britney's first story concluded with the words *kiss the bride*.

Her second story, turned in eleven weeks later, is set in a German concentration camp during World War II. When the Jews die, they become zombies that eat the flesh of the Nazi soldiers, who in turn become zombies that eat more Nazis, until there are no Nazis left—only a lot of zombies and a few very dazed Jews. In my five years at this college, it's by far the most compelling story I've received. Her sentences dazzle. Her scenes bring her monstrous milieu to life. You can smell the flesh rotting. You can feel the hunger, the urgency of insatiable revenge. Rarely have I read horror that rang so true, and never in a student manuscript.

"I thought it was just awful," says Jenna, who is generally quiet and always pleasant.

"*Jenna,*" I say.

"But we're supposed to be writing *realistic* fiction." She looks at me. "Isn't that right, Dr. P.?"

Jenna is right. It says so on page two of the syllabus. *Our mode is literary realism.*

I'm thinking about the proper response—something about knowing when to break the rules, or maybe quoting Flannery O'Connor, how writers are free to do anything they want as long as they can get away with it—when Jeremy, who's down to eight fingers, laughs and shakes his head. "She's earned the right, Jenna." He's looking at her perfect hands.

On the last day of the semester, we hold a class reading—always a nice, celebratory way for my students to hear a sampling of one another's revisions. I bring doughnuts and apple juice to class. I know I should be feeling drained and bewildered because of all the missing fingers, but the truth is I'm elated, because Twain slept for five consecutive hours between one and six a.m. We think he's finally worked out his swaddle problem.

There's time for each student to read two pages. Today we leave our desks in rows, and students go to the front of the room to read. I sit amongst the students in the third row, and listening to these introductory students read their own sentences, I find myself becoming misty-eyed. They've worked hard. They're invested. Even Jenna, my realism cop. She stands at the front of the room holding the pages of her story with trembling hands, her eight fingers really gripping the page, her voice quavering . . . well, it isn't great prose—she'll never be a writer—but there are a couple of moments where surprising language and emotional intelligence meet, and everyone in the room sits up a little straighter.

When class is nearly done, I return to the front of the room and tell everyone that I've enjoyed teaching them this semester, and I wish them all a happy and safe winter break. They file out of the room smiling and chatting with one another about travel plans and finals exams and end-of-semester parties. A couple of the baseball-cap guys come over to shake my hand, but our hands don't fit together well.

I've driven past this apartment complex on the way to the dentist. Four two-story brick buildings, small windows, Soviet aesthetic. Even the holly bushes lining the foundation look utilitarian. On the stoop outside apartment 3 sit two guys with cigarettes in their fingers and beer cans at their feet. They both wear knit, button-down shirts, blue jeans, and leather shoes I wish I owned. They tilt their heads up at me as I approach the door and step between them.

"Hey," I say.

"Yes, sir," one of them says.

My torn jeans and black T-shirt, chosen to make me look youthful, only flag me as out-of-shape and underdressed. I often run my choice of outfits by Beth, but when I was leaving the house tonight, Twain was asleep in his crib and Beth had seized the opportunity to shower. She was humming to herself, some melody I didn't recognize, and I left her alone.

Now, I try to remember why I decided to come. Other than the portfolios I still have to grade, the semester is over. I don't owe anybody anything. But after five years, this invitation is the first concrete bit of evidence that maybe I've had a lasting impact on my students. The first indication that despite our differences in age and geography and personal histories, we all expanded our sense of what it means to be a writer in the pursuit of truth and original expression.

Or maybe this: parenting a newborn is a lonely business, and it's nice to be invited to a party.

I open the door, step inside, and scan the crowd. Undergrad parties haven't changed much: too many people crammed into too small a space, a keg sitting in a barrel of ice, those oversized red plastic cups. Even the posters are the same as when I was in college—Bob Marley, Robert Plant—though the posters don't match the music, with its electronic beats and autotuned vocals.

A few kids eye me and turn away. Then Gina, who lives here, spots me, and her eyes widen. She shouts across the room—"Dr. P.!"—and weaves through the crowd to greet me, laying her hand on my arm. "You made it!"

I smile. "Of course I did."

"What?"

I have to lean in and talk directly into her ear. "Of course I did!" Her hair smells sweet and smoky, and I suppress a surge of jealousy toward every last person in the room.

She takes a step back and sizes me up. "Hard to believe this is . . . you."

"How do you mean?"

"You look really—cool!"

"I feel like an idiot. I like your bandanna." It's tie-dye, and covers her hair. She has some kind of flowery hippie shirt on.

Her smile returns, and she grabs my hand. Hers is warm. "Get a beer and come on. A bunch of us are in the bedroom."

She leads me to the keg, then pulls me through the apartment, past the kitchen, and into a short hallway. Just as I'm becoming a little nervous—young woman, bedroom—she opens the door. More than a dozen people are in the room, drinking and talking. Gina announces to the room: "See? I told you he'd make it!"

Then she's gone again.

"Dr. P.!" Brandon comes over, all smiles. He was one of the few kids who said almost nothing in class all semester, but here he seems relaxed and magnanimous. If I were his age, I'd want to be his friend. "We're glad you came." He clicks his plastic cup against mine, and the beer is cold and watery and wonderful. I haven't had anything to drink since those two margaritas several weeks back, and the first sip of beer slides down my throat and shoots out to every part of my body.

Gina reenters the room with three more of my students. Nearly the whole class is here now in this small bedroom. I'm touched. Wendy, not the best writer but a serious, earnest student with perfect mechanics, emerges from the hall bathroom. She totters—clearly drunk—into the bedroom behind the other students. She grins. "Hi, Dr. P." The cup of beer is to my lips when I notice the gauze on her hand. It's dark, blood-soaked. In her other hand she holds a large ball of tissues.

"Wendy—" I begin, but she cuts me off.

"It hurts," she says, "but not as much as you want." Another grin. "Are you going to do it tonight too?"

Gina shuts the bedroom door, dampening the music, and I whirl around to face my class.

"You're a really good teacher, Dr. P.," Brandon says. "You got us thinking." The others nod. "Don't you think it's your turn now?"

Gina steps over to the closet and reaches up to the top shelf. She pulls down a large black trash bag, from which she removes a stack of gauze, a roll of tape, a tube of antibiotic cream, and a branch lopper—same brand I use to prune the crape myrtles in my front yard.

"The semester's almost over," she says, and smiles warmly. She returns to the closet, pushes aside some dresses and pants on hangers, and carefully drags out something heavy. It's one of those capped glass urns you use to make sun tea. The urn is full of what looks like a streaming red ocean populated with little submarines.

I turn and catch Britney's dazzling blue gaze. Her blond hair is salon-perfect. She sits on the bed, legs crossed at the ankles. She's wearing an off-the-shoulder black sweater and dark blue jeans with pink high heels. Her toenails are the same color as her shoes. Her hands rest on her lap. She has three fingers on her left hand and two on her right. "Just think of it as your final exam," she says, smiling.

The beer feels heavy and sour in my stomach. "You don't understand," I tell everyone. "I don't need this."

"You mean because you once went to *England?* Because you have *tattoos?*" Britney shakes her head. "Come on, Dr. P.—you need it more than anyone."

"No, that isn't—" My class is watching me, rapt. I try to put words together as beer sloshes over the edge of my cup, soaking my wrist. "It's just . . . I have everything already."

A few of them are smiling the way you smile at an elderly relative who says the most darling things. Britney takes my beer cup from me and sets it gently on the bedside table.

"Sure you do, Dr. P.," she says.

The edges of my vision start to darken and my legs go weak beneath me, so I sit down on the bed beside Britney and look up at the ceiling, which has little glow-in-the-dark stars stuck to the paint in various constellations.

I stay there for maybe a dozen seconds, not looking at a single one of my students, refusing to be seduced into acquiescence or numbness or acceptance. "Dr. P.?" a couple of them say, but

I focus on taking breaths and letting them out. When I think my legs will support me again, I stand up, and then I leave the bedroom, still avoiding their faces, which will hold only disappointment, and I'm out of the apartment and hurrying home to my family, to my life of confident narratives and lucid exposition, my life of the mind and of ten fingers and of the next semester, and the next, and the next.

PART III

BLOODLINES

MOONFACE

BY Andrew Paul

Thief

When I was young I didn't know real hurt, but was still somehow capable of inflicting real hurt on those around me. It's cruel how often that sort of thing happens, but it happens, and I was one of hurt's propagators, a child thirteen years vicious. And I think it was this viciousness, in part, that killed Yitzhak Cohen.

It's important to know that he wasn't Yitzhak to us then, he was Moonface. Moonface got his name from his scars—great, circular layers of pink and violet tissue covering his entire body. Not so much a disfigurement as it was an extra layer splashed across him.

After the Six Million, some of the more unfortunate Jews gave up on their European ruins and crossed over to America, trickling down as far south as Thief, Mississippi. Some of them started businesses, worked in the First National Bank of Thief, but many simply made ends meet at the edge of town near the river, quarantined from any sense of the real world. This is where Yitzhak, where Moonface, wound up with a handful of others.

Moonface worked in the Jefferson Davis District School cafeteria, ladling out gruel to the pubescent. The first day on the job, Moonface wore a greasy T-shirt and slacks under his standard-issue apron, but we didn't gawk at his scars. Instead, we stood on our toes over the glass buffet barrier to see the tattoo. Most of us had never even seen ink in person yet, thinking it was reserved for gangs and brawlers and other lowlife idols.

"What're those numbers for?" my buddy John asked Moonface.

"Keep track of all women I stuck it in," Moonface said in broken English, handing John a tray of beef stroganoff. "Now go fuck you."

Their interchange spread through lunch before the next bell, and as we left for geometry, we saw Principal James career out of his office toward the kitchens. Moonface wore sleeves from there on out, and kept mostly quiet, but the number was already etched into our memory as clearly as it was on his forearm.

"Nobody could fuck that many girls," John reassured himself later that day on our walk home after school. "Their pecker would fall off."

As the fall semester dragged on, our theories on Moonface became more and more elaborate, increasingly grisly in their details. We became obsessed with the camps and their industrial murder. I suggested that he survived the worst Nazi death internments.

"It was a secret pit that JFK still won't even talk about because it's so shocking. The place where only the really threatening Jews were sent. Like Asswitz times one thousand," I whispered to John over our pizza.

"They only fed them slimy pizza once a week, but served on those crackers they like so much just to taunt them," John added.

"Why would they serve them on something they actually liked, dipshit?" I asked.

"Psychological warfare," he replied knowingly. "The worst of tortures."

"Do you know why he only works up front here?" I asked, my voice dropping even softer than before.

"Why?" John said, suppressing his metallic, wiry grin.

"'Cause of the ovens. How do you think Moonface got those scars? He was too mean for gas chambers, so they decided to throw him in a furnace, but the furnace just spit him right out."

We stopped talking, feeling we were approaching a truth we hadn't meant to near. Behind the serving line, Moonface looked toward us from across the room. Even then I knew it was too loud in the cafeteria for him to hear anything I said, but I worried he felt us encroaching on that same truth. We were quiet the rest of lunch.

There was a girl in all this, of course. Nicole. Four years our senior, and pretty much what you'd expect. Cheerleader. Straight-A student. Gold irises, I swear. Beautiful and sad and tired of all the rest of us, and with good reason. Her suitors were a series of rotten, pawing Goliaths, the last of whom roughed her up enough to get himself sent to a cellblock for a few months. Her mother was gone. Her father, Richmond, was a leering mess of a patriarch for the remaining household. I never heard stories about beatings or late-night sessions, but I was as much out of the loop then as I am now, so who knows.

I only saw Nicole and her father interact once, and that was enough for me. Enough for a predetermined image of her in my mind, anyway. The county bus dropped us off too early for school every day, so John and I spent about half an hour each morning shooting the shit near the steps until they opened the doors for state-issued breakfast biscuits and prayer.

One particularly swamp-fogged morning, Richmond pulled up in his rattling slag-heap car with Nicole in the passenger seat. The pair shrieked at each other from inside the cab, but were drowned out by the sputtering of the exhaust, as though their volumes were turned all the way down. I nudged John, and the two of us watched their muted shouting match from the safety of the yard. After about ten minutes of this, they were both maroon from bellowing, and Richmond raised his hand to slap her. She looked at him without flinching, waiting for the blow, as he froze in place, then lowered his arm and said something quietly.

The wind changed direction briefly, causing the burnt-oil smoke to billow around the car instead of rising behind it. Nicole opened her door as the plume surrounded her, and I heard Richmond say, "You don't burn quite as bright as you think." By the time she made it out of the exhaust, Nicole composed herself anew, like nothing happened.

In my ignorance, I found it arousing how she bottled her distaste so well, how she let it twist into something which fueled her successes, and I somehow hoped it could one day propel her out of the groping pull of her life and into mine.

I thought I was made for Nicole, given these adolescent rationalizations of her pain. The one time I tried to slap her ass in the hallway she spun around, as if with some sexual harassment sixth sense, and just fried me with her eyes.

"Go ahead," she said in front of John and me, turning back around while arching her butt toward us. "Do it."

I had never been so terrifyingly hard in my life, and I dropped my open palm to cover my crotch.

"Yep," she said, and walked to class.

I was late to Mississippi history for whacking off in a bathroom stall, and never spoke to her again.

Moonface talked to her, which infuriated us. Nicole talked back, which infuriated us even further. What was more, they seemed to *enjoy* talking to each other, like it was something they looked forward to every day. The lunch line halted whenever she caught up with Moonface.

"How goes your day?" he would ask.

"My day goes fine," she would answer, then make some joke

about the food, or try to convince him to see her cheer at the next home game. This continued for a number of weeks until I couldn't stand the injustice any longer.

"Get ze move on, Juden," I finally shouted one day in my best German accent. Everyone around me giggled.

"Ah, sprechen Sie Deutsch?" Moonface said to me over Nicole's shoulder.

"What?" I said, sensing my classmates stepping aside, separating me from the pack.

"Deutsch. Sprechen Sie es?"

I backed against the wall behind me.

"You speak German like natural. Like some of men I knew back there," Moonface explained, leaning forward while reaching up to rest his arm over the heated buffet lamp.

Part of his right sleeve caught on his forearm so that the last few digits on his tattoo showed. Since the state consistently denied budgetary increase requests, we were annually warned to take our trays from under the scalding metal, not over it. Now, Moonface rested his scars on top of the heater, not taking his eyes off me.

"I didn't say anything German," I muttered.

"Did you not say Juden? Jew?" he asked.

Nicole glanced back at me before walking toward the tables. Only then did Moonface momentarily break his gaze.

"I don't think so," I said.

"You don't think so?" Moonface said, returning to me, his eyes widening in mock surprise. "Could have fool me."

His arm still lay across the heater, and my eyes began to water from imagining the sensation. Kids started to snicker again.

"Well. Double serving for you who fool me," he announced, doling out with his left hand extra portions of oily spaghetti onto a tray.

"I'm not hungry," I said.

"I'll keep tray warm for you in case you change mind," Moonface offered, and I heard his skin unglue sickeningly from the lamp covering as I rushed to my usual seat next to John.

"We're getting rid of Moonface," I declared.

My weekends were dull since I wasn't allowed to see my father anymore. The previous summer, my mother convinced a court to keep me to herself. I only saw him a handful of times after that, and would continue to do so until he died two winters later on his own birthday. Mostly, I entertained myself from then on with solitary things—comic books and masturbation and walks near the Thief River.

On a Friday in October, after I finished both my comics and myself, I followed the riverbank south, tossing stones toward birds and water bugs, until I reached the tiny Jewish settlement outside of town, comprising mostly single-wides and leaky houseboats. It was strangely quiet to me, so I crept behind the treeline until I arrived at the lean-to homes, as if expecting some Maccabean ambush. I knew one of those places belonged to Moonface.

I stayed crouched behind a line of bushes, waiting while the sun set in pastel brushstrokes behind a small grove to my right. Even in my coat, I shivered, felt my breath leave my body with each exhale, and I sat back on my hands to keep them warm. One by one, pairs of candles began to glow through the windows of the homes, every residence except one.

I made my way to the lightless, sagging trailer and peeked through its rear window, only making out vague silhouettes of furniture through the curtains. A nine-stemmed candleholder balanced on the inside windowsill directly in front of me. I heard movement, and ducked down to peek around the corner.

There was a creak as the porch door opened, then Moonface walked outside, staring at his overly polished shoes while heading for his truck. He paused, noticing the candles glinting from his neighbors' homes, then spat on the ground and got in his ride. I watched him turn the ignition, straighten his shirt collar in the rearview mirror, and head down the gravel road toward town.

The window above me was cracked slightly to let in the slight breeze, and I edged it further open to part the curtains and peek into the vacant room. Without thinking, I hopped one leg over the sill, slowly easing myself into the quiet house, careful not to knock over the candleholder.

One glance around Moonface's living room was enough to take everything in—there was a fold-out sofa bed, a couple of box-crate nightstands, and a small bookshelf near me at the back window. A large radio stood by a hallway which led into both his kitchenette and bathroom, and that was it. I couldn't think of anything else to do, so I went to use the toilet.

After pissing, I turned on the light and opened the mirrored medicine cabinet, finding only a couple bottles of Darvon, a toothbrush, and some toothpaste. The kitchenette proved equally anticlimactic, revealing nothing except a few bits of clutter on the sink's countertop near the gas stove and a TV tray littered with sealed mason jars full of clear liquid. I walked—really, only a couple steps—across the room, kneeling down eye level with the collection. A thin layer of sediment rested at the bottom of each, and I picked one up, shaking the mixture into an opaque potion while heading back toward the living room.

I kicked my feet up on the couch, and looked out the window into the bruised dusk, then worked at unscrewing the mason jar's seal. After a brief struggle, grunting alone in the living room, I managed to open the lid, and instantly recoiled at what smelled like a combination of black licorice and turpentine and my father. The first sip nearly ruined me, and I winced to keep from retching onto Moonface's carpet. As I cleared the water from my eyes, I noticed a small picture frame sitting on top of the radio set across the room. I set the drink on one of the crate tables, then went over to examine the photograph.

It was almost too dark to see by that point, but by angling the frame toward the remaining trace of sunlight, I realized it was a picture of a large family posing for the camera. An attractive couple stood behind their two sons and three daughters, all wearing what I assumed were their best clothes, at least what looked to be much better than the thin, itchy threads I wore for class portraits. The three daughters had the same crooked grin of their father while the sons' eyes pinched at the corners as they smiled, like their mother. None of the children could have been older than me.

I choked down a couple more gulps, and tried to figure out which was Moonface, but nightfall soon made it impossible to examine the photo any longer. I took another swig, sputtered, then closed the jar to place it in my jacket pocket. My brain began to congeal, and I leaned back into the couch, staring out the window at the faint candlelight across the road from the other families' homes.

The sound of tires crushing dirt and stone jolted me awake, and I saw a pair of headlights coming down the way. I jumped up and nearly fell to one side, then remembered the concoction in my pocket. I staggered toward the radio and placed the photograph back in its place as I heard Moonface's truck creakily decelerate toward his home. When his high beams crept into the room, I fell to my hands and knees and slithered toward the back window, quickly leaping out the way I came, and eased the sill near shut like I found it.

The front door opened and slammed, and I found myself unable to leave just yet. Despite my lightweight drunkenness, I wobbled up enough to peer through the window once more. Moonface turned on the overhead light, and I saw his right eye was swollen closed. Small flecks of blood dotted his clothing. He ripped off his dress shirt while making his way to the kitchen, and I bent a little lower. I looked toward the ground and noticed the candelabra laying in the dirt—I must have knocked it out during the escape. I heard footsteps again, and knew it was too late to try to put it back.

Moonface sat on his couch with a small sandwich bag of ice held to his brow and a full mason jar in his other hand. It wasn't long before I heard another vehicle approach from the road. It parked, and its driver hurried up the steps and threw open the front door.

"What the hell were you thinking?" Nicole said.

"I was try to help," Moonface explained, taking a sip from his glass.

"That wasn't *help*. What do you suppose is going to happen now?" she said. She wore her cheerleading outfit.

"It was good game, though. You perform well. And we won," he said, smiling.

I staggered slightly as the drink worked its way through me, and I bumped against the wall. Moonface and Nicole looked toward the window, and I turned my back toward them, sliding down and pressing as close against the house as I could while staring into the woods ahead of me. For some reason beyond me now, I thought if I couldn't see them, maybe they wouldn't be able to see me. I've lived most the rest of my life that way.

Even so, I waited for the window to open, for Moonface to grab me by my hair and pull me into his home as it transformed into some dark, Shylockian lair lined with weights and scales and knives for pounds of flesh, but nothing happened. I turned around and peeked in once more, and saw Nicole straddling Moonface on the sofa, kissing him as he let his drink fall to the ground.

"Moonface is fucking Nicole," I told John between heaving breaths, cold sweat dripping from my arms and neck.

He looked behind him into his house, saw that his stepfather was passed out on the couch, and closed the door as he stepped outside to meet me.

"Bullshit," he whispered.

I tried to say, *It's true*, but only got the first word out before vomiting near his front steps.

"What the fuck is wrong with you?" John nearly shouted, leaping aside from my spew.

I finished as quietly as I could, then withdrew the mason jar from my inner coat pocket and wiped my hand on my sleeve. John snatched the glass from my hand, opened the lid, and winced in gleeful disgust.

"So you found some of your old man's brew stashed away in a closet. That explains it," he said.

I reached into my pockets once more, taking out the small menorah and handing it to John. His eyes opened wider, then he took a sip of the liquor and struggled to maintain a straight face.

"So, Moonface makes moonshine," he rasped. "I guess we know how Nicole pays him for the stuff."

I led John back toward the village as we passed the mason jar back and forth, drinking the bare minimum to appear like men. It was a clear night, the kind that feels like the stars are spotlights trained on you and everything you do. Now I realize it's always like that, even when you can't see them, but back then I thought

I could lose their sights, so I made John follow me into the trees until we reached Moonface's home.

A few minutes later John said, "I guess you didn't hear what happened at the game tonight, now that I think about it."

"No," I replied too quickly, somewhat sore at my ignorance.

"Well, I tried to invite you to come, but I guess you were out on your little Peeping Tom mission already. Moonface got in a fight near the end of the match."

"What?" I said, remembering his black eye.

"Yep. He was sitting on the front-row bleacher nearest Nicole, not being shy at all about why he was there. But she wasn't being too shy about it neither."

"What's new?" I said.

"Yeah yeah. But then her dad caught on to what was happening, and he wasn't having it."

"Huh."

"He must of been on something like this stuff you got here, because as soon as the time ran out on the clock and everyone stood up to cheer, he hopped down from his bench a few rows up and clocked Moonface upside the head."

"Shit," I said.

"It was a pretty good hit. For a sucker punch, I mean. It took everyone a minute to realize what was going on, but then everyone stepped aside and it was just Moonface and Richmond going at it in front of Nicole and the whole lot of them."

"What happened then?" I asked, seeing the village lights through the pines.

"Well, people were trying to pull them apart, and Richmond called him a *kite* or something. Moonface just let go of his collar, then took off for his truck and left before anyone could stop him."

By this point we neared the edge of the trees, and quietly made our way over to Moonface's shack. We took spots behind the back window, and leaned in as close we comfortably could.

Oh my God, John mouthed.

Nicole stood naked by the radio holding the picture frame, illuminated only by two recently lit white candles nearby. The flickering glow washed over her so that no one part was ever fully revealed, like an apparition.

"Which one is you?" she asked Moonface, still examining the photograph. He lay on the sofa, naked as well. His scars patterned his whole body.

"Which do you think?" he answered, the edges of his eyes creasing.

She squinted and held the picture closer to her face, then half-smiled as if figuring out some small puzzle.

"You were very beautiful," she said.

There was a squeal of tires and a roar of gears shifting too quickly. Everyone looked in the direction of the incoming din.

"You should go," Moonface said, standing up and grabbing his clothes.

Nicole didn't say anything, only put the photo down. Headlights raised into view.

"No," she finally said.

"Stay inside. They will see you," Moonface said slowly, briefly eyeing the window.

"I don't care. That's all they do. They just see me," she told him offhand, walking toward the pile of her uniform.

I motioned back toward the woods to John, but he shook his head.

"Are you crazy?" he whispered, still trained on Nicole's body.

A pair of beat-up, jangling cars rushed toward the house, their doors opening before they fully parked. Four men leaped out of the vehicles, a couple of them clutching bats. A roughed-up man near the front cocked a pistol.

"Cohen, you kike, get your ugly ass out here!" he shouted.

A couple lights turned on in neighboring houses. Moonface looked at Nicole one more time, his eyes crinkling again as she slipped on her skirt, and he walked outside. I tugged at John's shoulder and dragged him into the woods, and we huddled behind a tree trunk.

"Shalom," Moonface said, exiting his home.

"Where is she?" Richmond demanded.

"Inside," Moonface said.

A small breeze passed through the trees, around us, through the village. Richmond swayed slightly, as if he were only a pine sapling.

"What's she doing in there?" Richmond said.

"Celebrating our win," Moonface said. "Go team."

"Fuck you," Richmond spat, advancing toward him. The group followed, and I saw John's stepfather was among the posse. I couldn't bring myself to look to John next to me.

I realized I still held the near-empty mason jar. Years later I am unsure of my logic, I hope that it was for the right reason, although a part of my mind croaks otherwise, but I threw the glass through the woods at the window. It crashed through the pane, knocking over the two candles nearby, and rolled out of sight. John patted me on the shoulder like I accomplished something heroic, but there was something distant in his gaze, as if he had seen into me, farther into myself than I could see on my own, and it worried him.

The men out front jumped at the noise. Nicole peered through the window into the woods, directly toward us, but we were in the forest, and the sky didn't shine on us, so we were hidden. Moonface took the distraction to swing at Richmond, connecting with his jaw and causing him to drop his pistol while, behind them, a trace of smoke twirled out the window near the curtains. Nicole glanced to her side and withdrew from the window, and I never saw her again.

A couple of the men went at Moonface with their bats, and he was able to dodge the first few swings. The fire inside his house fanned across the room, up the drapes, accelerated by the liquor-soaked carpets. Moonface heard the roar and whipped around. John's stepdad saw it as an opportunity to bring his bat across his back. It made a sound like striking a mattress, and Moonface groaned as he fell to one knee.

"Nicole!" her father shouted.

Moonface managed to roll over, and kicked John's stepfather in the shins. He let out a yelp and fell backward as Moonface scrambled up toward the flames that seeped out the front door. Richmond felt around in the dirt like he'd lost a pair of glasses while the other men stepped backward slowly.

Two things happened near simultaneously; John and I still disagree on the exact order. He remembers Richmond finding his pistol and shooting Moonface in the back, causing him to spin around and tumble into the burning trailer. But I know what I saw—you don't misremember when a moment burrows into your memory, they're always there to recall as they were preserved:

Richmond shot and missed, the bullet hitting the doorframe. Moonface did spin around, but only to look at Richmond one final time. The sides of his eyes furrowed as in his photograph, and he leaped inside.

I heard the distant cry of sirens while the neighboring families started racing toward the giant fire, although it was clear there was nothing else to be done. Richmond steadied himself on the hood of his car, repeating his daughter's name to no one. I remembered the remaining jars of moonshine in the kitchen, and was about to grab John when he beat me to it.

"We've got to get the fuck out of here," he said.

I nodded, and we raced through the trees back toward our homes. A few seconds later, I heard a great roar from the fire and, for a moment, our path shone brightly ahead of us before darkening again to a dull glow.

The next morning, I hid the menorah under the cinder-block risers of my house and feigned ignorance of the previous night's tragedy.

"That poor girl," my mother said after getting off the phone with her gossiping friends. "She was so pretty. It must have been terrible trapped in there with that monster of a man."

The story warped even more within the week, in part due to John's near-constant retelling of his account to our classmates, and soon, Richmond was fleshed out for the story. Richmond the brave, doting father, who tried to save his rebellious daughter from the leering, deformed cafeteria worker from foreign lands. He defended her honor at the homecoming football game, and Moonface—the name caught on—then kidnapped her at gunpoint, forcing her to drive them to his lair in a final, desperate attempt to have her. The two foes grappled outside the house, Richmond wrestling the gun from Moonface's hands and mortally wounding him before the creature fled into the house. He then torched the place from the inside. If he couldn't have her, then no one could. We were nowhere to be found in the story.

To solidify the legend, it was rumored that the emergency crews couldn't find any trace of bodies in the smoldering wreckage, as if Moonface and Nicole burnt away in the heat completely. Years later, when I finally could bring myself to investigate this bit of the story, I found information scarce, records lost, graves forgotten, and I couldn't confirm or deny this addition to Moonface's legacy.

* * *

I'm much older now, I've more or less kicked drinking, and I love a woman who loves me in kind, despite this story, the true one, which I have also told her. She is not as beautiful as Nicole, she quit school the same year I did, never cheered for a game in her life, but she is full of wonder, and that's almost the same. On many days, that's even better.

I am nothing like Moonface, but I wish I was. There is very little light from the night sky where we live now, it's all washed away in the muddy glow of the nearby city. Sometimes, while we make love to each other in the dark, I look down at my body to find it lit in patches from streetlamps through our window blinds. I imagine these illuminations are scars from my youth, from the things I am powerless to understand. I look at the menorah resting on my bookshelf while I imagine myself Moonface, and my hurt is not hidden like those around me. I never have to explain the past to anyone ever again. Everyone will see it etched into my skin, but they won't realize what it's doing to them until it's done.

GOD'S GONNA TROUBLE THE WATER

BY DOMINIQUA DICKEY

Grenada

I

Elnora Harden had just sat down on her back step to sort through a mess of mustard greens when the pounding started on her front door. Everybody in Boone Alley knew she kept the front bolted shut except for emergencies or business. Even then, she rarely answered it. With heavy, dark clouds rolling in, she wanted the greens cleaned, in the pot, and on the stove before the storm hit. This disturbance already had her on edge because it was interference. Dammit, Elnora hated interferences.

"All right, shit," she muttered under her breath.

She dropped a dishtowel over the sorted pot of greens and put both it and the dirty, unpicked batch on the back porch out of the way of the potential downfall. The noise at her door hadn't stopped by the time she reached it and her temper was beginning to match the tempo. She wiped her hands clean on her apron and yanked the door open. Curses waited on the tip of her tongue. They had to wait longer still because the front porch was empty.

Elnora stepped outside. The slamming of the screen door echoed, but she paid it no mind. A lone figure walked down the alley toward Lake Street. In the waning sunlight, she made out a womanly shape with long hair pulled back into a single braid.

Bits of white flapped at her waist while the rest of her outfit was dark green, similar to what the maids who worked at the big-time hotel on Main Street wore. The smart figure, shapely legs, and long braid—it didn't take more than a second or two for Elnora to put those pieces together.

"Cissy!" She cupped her hand to her mouth to give the shout extra power. "Cissy Shaw, get back here!"

"Cousin El?" The younger woman spun on her low-heel shoes and hurried up the gravel-covered road to meet Elnora halfway. Tears stained her cheeks. She reached for Elnora's hands. "I was so scared you weren't home!"

"You know better than anyone to come to the back." She would have pulled free, but Cissy's hold was strong. "Come on. They're all at the window now. Let's get inside 'fore it starts to pour and everybody gets wet trying to hear your business."

The trembling young woman let go once they were inside. Elnora claimed the rocking chair near the wood-burning stove. Cissy perched on the edge of the wrought-iron four-poster bed. The smell of dust and rain blew in through the open windows. Lace hand-me-down curtains fluttered, reminding Elnora that she was overdue for spring cleaning. She sighed. Yet another thing to break up her peace and quiet. Just like the quivering, sniffling mass on her bed.

"All right there, Cissy." Elnora took an unused handkerchief from her apron pocket and patted it into the other woman's hands. "Banging on my door like that, you must want something more than to cry like a baby—"

"That's it!" Cissy cried out suddenly amid hiccups. "The baby! Cousin El, you got to help me. I ain't got nobody else!"

"What about the baby?" Elnora's chest drew tight just putting the question to words. Cissy's baby was the prettiest the colored folk of Grenada had seen in a good number of years. Skin as smooth as caramel, eyes dove gray like her foolish pappy's, and chubby cheeks that made a body smile on their darkest day. At just a toddler, she was already everybody's darling.

"She gone!"

When fresh tears threatened to halt the conversation, Elnora snatched the handkerchief and grabbed Cissy's shoulders. "Dammit, girl! Stop this foolishness! Where is she?"

"I don't know where Hattie is." She started to squirm. "Ow, that hurts."

Elnora took her time letting go. "What you mean you don't know? You going to work or coming off shift?"

"Coming off—"

"Then you know where she is. Shit, Cissy." Elnora rose from the chair and began to pace. She muttered a few more curses to set her breathing back to normal. "Clara has that baby—"

"No, she ain't! That's what I'm telling—"

"You ain't tole me shit."

Cissy's hands balled into fists, but she didn't strike out. She moved to the open window and her fingers dug into the sill. "Aunty met me at the back steps of the Baldwin right after I clocked out. She and Hattie laid down for a nap. When she woke up, my baby was gone!"

"Lord Jesus." Elnora's pacing came to a standstill. "Well, did she check Lee Ella's? That woman can't keep her hands off babies—"

"Yes!"

"What about the rest of the alley? And over on Cherry? What about down on Union? Hattie ain't one for wanderin', but babies get curious. It wouldn't be her fault."

"They checked. Ain't nobody seen her. You got to help—"

"I got to?" Elnora met Cissy's pleading eyes with a hard stare. "Girl, what you really over here for?"

"My baby gone."

"I know that. What else?" Elnora asked. She followed with a truth that her instincts confirmed: "You know who got her."

Silence hung there for a moment. In the distance, thunder tumbled. The old saying of God moving his furniture made Elnora wonder if He was angry about the remodeling project. Although the sound was distant, only a fool would dismiss the power behind those rumbles. The rain would hit hard. She was sure the storm was coming from the east. For sure, Grenada was in its path. Maybe the Delta too.

"Cissy." Elnora's patience was near worn out.

"I know," the younger woman mumbled. Her gaze locked on the crooked pattern of the linoleum nailed to the floor. She began to trace the outlines of magnolia petals and leaves with her shoe until Elnora cleared her throat. This time, she spoke louder: "Yes'm, I know."

"Well, go get her back."

"I can't."

Elnora sought comfort in her rocking chair. She hoped for additional relief from a pinch of snuff then remembered she'd thrown out the last tin a month ago. It was making her teeth yellow and her breath stink. At thirty-six, she still had a few good years left. She wasn't about to let some damn tobacco age her and keep her from having fun.

"What you come over here for?"

"Help—"

"Stop," Elnora said, her willingness to listen to bullshit completely gone. "Truth, Cissy, or you can see yourself out the way you come in."

Cissy wasted no time returning to the wrought-iron bed where she'd spent a few nights in her youth. She looked ready to grab Elnora's hands again, but hesitated. In that hesitation, her hands hung there in the space between them. Then she began to use her slender, work-roughened hands to plead her case, waving them around and molding shapes, ghostly images that reminded Elnora of a past she couldn't escape.

"You good at fixin' things."

"Ain't nothin' I'm good at but fixin' hair and a mess of greens. I have a pot waitin' for me out back."

"Please, Cousin Elnora. Can't nobody else help me with this."

It was the pleading that got to her. That and the look of desperation in brown eyes that were so much like hers.

"Fine," Elnora said. "Why did that white boy take your baby this time?"

II

The story hadn't changed. At least not to Elnora's estimation. Cissy and Graham Lee Donner had thought theirs was the big secret romance that no one knew about, but this was not actually the case. The boy was sprung the minute he'd set eyes on her. He'd come in place of his uncle to collect the rent, and Cissy, fifteen and just starting to smell herself, had handed over the money with a coy smile. Halfway down Newsome Alley, Graham Lee kept looking back. Elnora had been there, so she knew it for fact. Cissy, being young and incorrigible or maybe too much like her mama, had been unable to resist. Having released the right to voice disapproval or otherwise, Elnora had no choice but to watch some elements of history repeat itself.

For five years, the two did the dance of push and pull. During that time, the baby came and Graham Lee wanted them under his roof, but he wasn't man enough to stand up to his family. In Grenada, where the hell would they go anyway? But that didn't stop the fool from snatching little Hattie every now and again, making sure his little gray-eyed twin knew her daddy and hoping Cissy would find a way to stay too. In the beginning, she'd stay a week or two, but since she started working at the Baldwin Hotel, Cissy didn't want to take the risk. Besides, her aunt's husband promised to put her and Hattie out if she missed paying her monthly share.

The telling sickened Elnora. Twenty years ago, she made a hasty decision based on fear and shame. She saw no cause for either child to pay another day for that mistake.

"You know you got a bed here," she said quietly. They now stood in the kitchen. Elnora had finished with the greens while Cissy told her tale and prepared a ham for the oven. "Ain't nobody here but me," Elnora continued. "We get Hattie back and y'all move in here. Leave Clara and Josiah to themselves."

"What about Ed?" Cissy set the ham inside the oven and wiped her hands on a dishtowel.

Ed Jenkins was a Pullman porter for the Illinois Central Railroad. He was seven years younger than Elnora and fine as a shiny copper penny, but—

"Ed don't pay for nothing here. I do. You can stay if you want. Plenty of room."

"If you sure—"

"Wouldn't have said it if I wasn't." Elnora stirred the greens around the cast-iron pot with a wooden spoon. The salt pork would season them real good. Later, she'd make a batch of hot water corn bread. "Tell me why you can't get the baby from Graham Lee. Why you want me to do it?"

"He said next time I come for her I ain't coming back."

Elnora tapped the spoon hard against the side of the pot. A bit more force would have snapped the spoon in two. "That white boy threaten you?"

"No'm," Cissy said. "Well . . . truth is, I don't know. He don't make it easy for me to come back and you know Hattie and me can't stay with him. It ain't gon' ever work out like that."

"He needs to stop acting a fool."

"I was hoping you could talk some sense into him. Maybe get his uncle to go with you."

Oh, Elnora thought. So now they'd come to the gist of it. Rayford Drew had installed indoor plumbing in her little three-room shotgun house and everybody had an idea how that had come about. Well, they were wrong. She'd spread her legs once for a white man, and despite his best attempts, that man wasn't Rayford Drew Donner.

"I don't know about that."

"He's scared of his uncle," she said quickly, "and Mr. Donner is just as tired of this going back and forth too."

"You shoulda gone to him then."

Cissy bowed her head. "I'm scared of him too."

"Lord Jesus."

Elnora stood at the back door and looked out. Her yard wasn't much. She had a small garden and a few chickens in a pen. The addition of the bathroom had rendered the outhouse unnecessary so it had been boarded up. When Ed came back through, she planned to ask him to take it down, lime up the hole, and sell the wood for parts. Her neighbors' yards didn't fare with fancier trimmings either. Outhouse, garden, a few scraps of this and that. That's how it was in the colored section of town.

When she had worked as a cook for the Tennant family over on Line Street, well, that had been a different story. Fancy linens, fancy furniture, fancy food. Fancy everything. Elnora shook off the unevenness of it with a toss of her head. It was 1936 and some progress had been made. She earned a living doing hair right there in the living room that would soon belong to her, and she only cooked for white folks when the pay was good, not because it was her daily job. Times were changing. People just had to have their eyes open to see it.

"Will you ask him?" Cissy had taken rest at the square wooden table in the center of the stuffy kitchen. "Please?"

"You ain't got to beg. I'll get your baby back." Elnora turned from the door to look Cissy square in the eye. "But you got to promise me something."

"What? Anything."

"You got to leave that white boy alone."

Cissy nodded. "I'm done with Graham Lee. That ain't a promise. It's a fact."

The sincerity and conviction couldn't be denied. Elnora had no choice but to believe her. So she had one question left.

"You sure Hattie's with her daddy?"

"Yeah, I'm sure." The question seemed to stun her. "Wouldn't nobody else want her."

III

Romano's was a few doors down from Grenada Hardware on the corner of 1st and Green, right off the square. The Italian family had owned a grocery store there for as long as Elnora remembered. Unlike many, their treatment of coloreds didn't set her teeth on edge. She knew better than to call the owner by his birth name in mixed company, but if they were conducting business one-on-one, the talk was between "Elnora" and "Salvatore" and not "Aunty" and "Mr. Sal" as dictated by society.

With the greens and ham still needing a few more hours, Elnora left Cissy in charge of supper and checked the first place she knew to look for Rayford Drew—in his upstairs office above the grocery. The ringing bell announced her entry and Sal waved.

"You're lucky. I was about to lock up."

"I'm not here to shop," she said. "Is he upstairs?"

Sal frowned. His whole body managed to tighten with the act, from his slick dark cap of hair through his stocky build down to his scuffed work shoes. Red darkened his forehead. "He's up there. I don't want any funny business."

She bit back a smile at the very idea. "No funny business. Is he drinking?"

"Maybe," Sal said. He locked the front doors and flipped the *Open* sign over to *Closed*. "I'll go up too."

"I can handle him."

"He could be drinking." Sal untied his white apron, tugged it free, and tossed it onto the counter. The fabric landed in a heap beside the register. "If he's sober, I'll leave. Come on."

Elnora and Sal had practically grown up as siblings. Their mothers had taken in wash together. With two strong-willed mothers, the children had no choice but to either get along or pretend. They never had a reason to pretend.

Since he'd locked the front door, taking the outside steps was not an option. He led her to the back storeroom where another staircase hid among canned goods and fresh produce waiting to be stocked for tomorrow's shoppers. Sal pulled a string. Light from a single bulb filled the space and the tight staircase. She followed him up.

To her surprise, Sal didn't bother knocking. He simply marched in. Rayford Drew sat behind a desk. The top three buttons of his shirt were undone and revealed a damp undershirt. Tendrils of silver curled along the edges of his hairline, disappearing into the sandy brown hair that framed his boyish face. At forty-five, only the wisps of gray and the wisdom in his eyes offered any hint of his age. A ledger was spread before him. An unopened bottle of shine was not too far from his right hand. A glass waited beside it. The whir of a metal fan stirred the air and lifted the pages of the ledger. Overall, the fan was no match against Mississippi humidity in April.

"See?" she said.

"Not yet," Sal muttered, then turned to Rayford. "Elnora is here for you."

Rayford Drew made a show of looking around Sal and taking in Elnora from head to toe. She was mindful not to be self-conscious of the pair of sensible black shoes on her feet or the lightweight blue cotton dress that failed to hide the curves of her hips, backside, and bosom. She was thankful that she'd kept her hair pulled up in a bun and hoped that would contain whatever wayward thoughts entered his mind. But judging by how his hazel eyes lit up and the faint smirk that rested on his mouth, she knew the matronly bun had failed her.

"I can see that she is," Rayford Drew said. "Thanks, Sal. We'll see you tomorrow."

Sal looked at Elnora. If she wanted him to stay, he would. She gave a slight shake of her head and he stomped to the door.

"I'll be right downstairs." Sal gave the other man a hard, meaningful look. "Cleaning up."

His heavy footsteps trailed down and away. Elnora lingered at the door. The office wasn't quite the mess it'd been on her last visit. A Corner Drugs calendar hung over a metal filing cabinet. Two wooden guest chairs were opposite his desk. One held a stack of papers, but the other was free of clutter. A gray pinstripe suit fresh from the cleaners hung on a hook and a pair of shiny black shoes was on the floor right below.

"Don't be shy." Rayford Drew held up the bottle. "Have a snort."

She shook her head.

"I made it myself." He laughed when she remained firm. "Come on. Sit down."

She chose the empty wooden chair and pulled it to a respectable distance, realizing that sitting down was a first, as was his offer for her to do so.

"How's that toilet working out?" The words came slow.

Elnora squeezed her hands together in her lap. Several days of strong humidity had already set her disposition on a wayward course. Then Cissy showed up at her door with her sorrowful tale. Holding her tongue in check for Rayford Drew and his penchant for insinuation would require more control than she was capable of.

"Graham Lee took the baby again."

"Well. Shit." He ran a hand over his face. "Here I thought this was a friendly visit."

"Help me get her back."

"That stupid sonuvabitch." He reached for the shine, but didn't open it. "I'm tired of this shit, Nora."

"I'm not keen on it either."

"Where's the gal?"

"Does it matter?" She folded her arms.

He stared at her for a moment. Whether or not he resented her defiance, she couldn't be sure. His eyes had darkened and were unreadable, as was his posture. Gone was the lustful man appreciating the form of a shapely woman. The calculating, decisive Donner sat there in his place. He closed the ledger, then took both it and the shine to the filing cabinet, which he locked.

"Let's go."

IV

The dark blue 1935 Pontiac coupe still carried the scent of leather on its seats. He handled the vehicle with ease even over the bumpy gravel road that led them off the highway and into the backwoods of Holcomb. Elnora had spent summers picking cotton out there and farther into the Delta. Sometimes the work even took her and the other children her age out of school. She'd hated the work and would never forget the oppressive humidity, relentless sun, and painful blisters that riddled her small fingers. Her twelfth summer found her working in the kitchen alongside a cousin at the country club. She hadn't been out to Holcomb since, but those memories remained.

"All this is Donner land," Rayford Drew said, puffed with pride. "From that marker all the way back beyond those trees. Has been for over a hundred years."

She didn't comment on who had worked their asses off to make it so.

He turned off at a mailbox. The bushes had hidden it from view. They continued on for half a mile. A cozy one-story cottage stood amidst a grove of pecan trees and honeysuckle bushes. A Dodge pickup was parked near the door. Rayford Drew pulled up beside it.

Other than the eerie quiet, Elnora noticed that the clouds didn't loom as dark out there. They hung back as if they were saving their full power for Grenada and beyond. If Graham Lee had the baby, she supposed she'd rather Hattie not have clouds hanging over her head.

Rayford Drew headed inside first, calling for his nephew as he trudged across the porch. The silence, other than the elder Donner's loud voice, unsettled Elnora. She sensed something was off before she crossed the threshold and discovered the front room in disarray. Rayford Drew's voice echoed as he searched the rooms.

Plates and drinking glasses lay broken and scattered on the hardwood floor. A cotton sheet was in a puddle near an overturned end table and stuffed chair. A slip of paper caught Elnora's attention. She stooped down and pulled it from underneath the sheet. It was half of a photograph. Someone had ripped the black-and-white image in two. Her unease turned to dread the longer she stared at the photo.

"What is it?" Rayford Drew asked.

She hadn't heard his return. Nor was she surprised when he took the photo from her. He stared for a moment before handing it back to her.

"Don't mean a thing."

"That's the three of them," she said. "Him, Cissy, and little Hattie."

"How do you know? Half of it's missing."

True, Graham Lee was torn off the photo, but his pale hand rested on Cissy's knee plain enough for Elnora's two eyes. Cissy was sitting up straight and pretty in that white lace dress she wore last Easter, a slight smile on her face. Hattie's dress matched her mama's and she was plump and happy, as a baby should be on her mother's lap; a toothless grin revealed that she had not one care in the world. Who would want to ruin an image as innocent as that?

"That's him in that picture," she stated. "Where is he?"

"He couldn't go far."

"Why you say that?"

Rayford Drew went to the window and pulled the curtain aside. "That's his truck. He's probably fishing with his cousins or something. Maybe he didn't take her."

Elnora wasn't sure about that. She stuffed the photo in her pocket and started to straighten the room. He stood at the door watching, neither protesting nor assisting. Inside the sheet, she felt a bundle and quickly shook it out. A little rag doll rolled to the floor. She recognized it immediately.

"That's Hattie's," she said.

"Well hell." Rayford Drew rubbed his neck. "He couldn't have gone far with her."

"Gone far?" She wondered if he was blind or just didn't want to see. "Look at this room. It's tore up! Something happened here."

V

Elnora didn't like trouble. Some people catered to it; they went out searching for it when things were too good and easy in their lives. Not Elnora May Harden. She avoided trouble like it was a black cat crossing to her left at midnight with a full moon shining bright in a cloudless sky. Omens were nothing more than bullshit, but she wasn't about to test anyone's theory. Still, trouble often had a way of finding her. Either whipping up a storm in her life or raising hell in the life of someone she loved. By now, she should have realized that trouble was as unavoidable as a hot Mississippi summer and a Baptist preacher who overstayed his welcome.

"Say something." Rayford Drew took his eyes from the highway long enough to glare at her.

Ahead of them, cloudy skies loomed over Grenada, but only sunshine glowed brightly in the country town they'd left behind. She resented the difference. It was unreasonable, but she didn't care.

"Nora—"

"I'm just thinking."

"More like ruminating," he said. "Worrying over nothing. He knew that gal would send somebody for him, so he took off with the baby. When he gets tired of playing daddy, he'll bring her back. You'll see."

"It's that simple."

He chuckled. "Graham Lee ain't complicated. He never has been. Just got too caught up with that gal—"

"That gal has a name," she said, maybe more forcefully than she intended. His lean hand's grip on the steering wheel tightened and she considered apologizing. But the words lodged in her chest. She'd done enough bowing, scraping, and apologizing for her daughter to last a lifetime. The best Elnora could do now was speak softly. "Her name is Cissy."

"They can't have a life together," he said.

"I know that. She does too."

"Problem is Graham Lee," he said. "He has a head like a brick. It doesn't come from the Donner side. No, that's his mama's family. Those stubborn Perkins. You can't tell them shit."

"Where could he take Hattie that folks wouldn't ask questions?" Elnora asked. "She's light, but she ain't light enough to pass."

"Stop your worrying. He's stubborn and fool-headed, but he won't let a thing happen to that little girl."

Rayford Drew dropped her off at the corner where Clay Street intersected Boone Alley. The short walk home felt like a miles-long journey without little Hattie in her arms or anything meaningful to report. With evening and the supper meal closing in, her neighbors were rounding up their children from their yards or trudging in from a long day at work. They waved and mumbled the usual greetings, but none of them had an inkling of the weight she bore. She wasn't about to confide her troubles. She needed to get home and talk things out with Cissy. It could be that Rayford Drew knew his nephew well and understood the inner workings of the younger man's mind. She hoped that was the case.

Anticipation gleamed in Cissy's eyes when she woke from her nap. About an hour earlier, Elnora had arrived to find the greens and the ham done. A plate of hot water corn bread sat warming in the oven. And Cissy was asleep on the bed in the front room. Instead of waking her, Elnora eased onto the rocking chair, pushed her shoes off, and just watched her sleep. It had been a long time since she'd had that privilege. She didn't often dwell on the past, but giving away her only child had been a grave mistake.

"You find her?"

"No," she said. "Rayford Drew took us out to Holcomb—"

"That's where he usually takes her. To that little house out there."

Elnora nodded. "That's where we went. No sign of her or Graham Lee. Except I found this."

She pulled the torn photo from her pocket. She watched Cissy closely as the younger woman gazed at the image and frowned.

"We took this in one of those photo booths. Up in Memphis."

"It's torn."

"I see," Cissy said. "Graham Lee is ripped clean off. Some don't like the thought of us together. Not even in a silly, stupid picture. But look at Hattie. Don't she look pretty?"

"Yes, she does."

Elnora went to her bedroom that separated the kitchen from the front room and took the little rag doll from where it rested on the pillows. Back with Cissy, she handed the doll over.

"This is Hattie's. This is the one you made for her."

Elnora pressed her lips together to keep from speaking out of turn or saying the wrong thing. If the torn photograph meant nothing, surely the little rag doll meant something. The sight of the doll wrapped in the sheet had put Elnora on edge. She didn't want to tell Cissy what she was thinking, how she was feeling. That something wasn't right. That the house had felt cold and empty. That she didn't know how to fix this.

Cissy looked at the doll as if she didn't know what else to make of it. Like it had no right to be in her hands when she was without her daughter. "Where he take her, Cousin El?" she asked, looking up with eyes that were lost and unbelieving. "What Mr. Donner say about that?"

"Nothing. He doesn't know."

Sudden anger hardened her soft features. "He know! He just don't want to say. He helped Graham Lee steal Hattie."

"I doubt that," Elnora said. "He ain't in on this with Graham Lee."

"He put in a toilet and you don't think straight—"

"Cissy, don't say shit to me about that damn toilet! That white man ain't about to help his nephew steal a little black baby even if that baby is kin!"

Cissy hugged the doll to her. "I don't know what to do. I can't make it without my little girl." She sniffed the doll's dress and yarn braids. "It smells just like her. She calls it Molly. Says Molly's her baby. She wouldn't just leave Molly. She's throwing the worst fit right now, I bet."

"I bet she is." Elnora brushed a few stray strands from Cissy's forehead. "Supper's getting cold."

VI

Thunder shook the wooden-frame house and rattled the windows, pulling Elnora awake. She had rested her eyes for a moment to ponder her findings—the ransacked cottage, the baby doll, and the ripped photograph—when she'd drifted off to sleep. Now she discovered that Cissy had left but the little rag doll rested on the pillow in her place. The photo was on the chifforobe. Accustomed to having a plan, Elnora didn't cotton to the troubling sensations that filled her gut. The sudden *rat-a-tat-tat* of rainfall hitting the tin roof made her jump. When the knocking started at her back door, she rubbed her arms and cursed her fears.

Glimmers of red shone through the back door window. That was enough to set her at ease. She knew what waited on the other side. A handsome young man in uniform with a red cap on top completed the picture. She opened the door and Ed swung her up into his arms. Romantic spectacles had never been their thing, but he had been away longer than usual. From the way he squeezed her close, he had missed her as much as she had him.

A little while later, they sat at the kitchen table. Elnora confided her concerns about baby Hattie while Ed finished his plate of greens, ham, and corn bread. All the while he chewed, a frown creased his forehead and he shook his head.

"You don't need to be riding 'round with Rayford Drew Donner," he muttered after he swallowed a sip of coffee. "Bad enough folks talking shit about that convenience he put in . . . What it look like, you riding in that coupe with him?"

"I told you we were looking for the baby!" She pushed away from the table. Her chair screeched along the linoleum floor, warring with the sounds of nature that were exploding outside. "What the hell I care what folks think about anyway? You should hear what they say about you creeping over here every time you come home."

"I ain't creeping. I ain't hiding shit." Ed stood. Tall and self-assured in his blue-and-white-striped boxer shorts and white T-shirt, he took his empty plate to the sink and washed it. "Everybody know you mine."

She held up her hand. "Ed—"

"Elnora May." He folded his arms across his chest.

"I don't belong to anybody. Not you or anybody else."

"I didn't mean it that way," he said quietly.

"I know what you meant."

Emptiness captured the moment, waiting for one of them to

speak or make a move. Elnora sensed the spark of opportunity, but she wanted no part of it. She and Ed had danced around this cakewalk before. He was young. Maybe if she was sure that he understood about her past and some of what she had sacrificed, maybe then she'd be willing to accept more than the good times he offered whenever Illinois Central dropped him off at the Grenada depot. But for now, all she knew for fact was that she felt better in his arms than she had in any other man's in quite some time. If that was all the Lord was willing to give for the troubles she'd laid at His gates, she'd take it and be glad for it. Later she might have regrets.

She found herself putting her clothes back on and securing her hair before she had time to consider a different option. Ed lingered in the door frame of the bedroom. His dark eyes watched her movements; he seemed more curious than upset. There was some relief in that.

"Where you going?"

"Out."

"It's storming. When we rolled in, they warned us to stay put," he said. "You don't want to go out there."

"This ain't about want. I *need* to."

"The baby's probably with her daddy," he said.

Elnora slid on a pair of black rain boots and grabbed her coat from a nail off the back of the door. "What about Cissy?"

"She's at work or at her folks' place."

She shook her head.

"What if Cissy took off with Graham Lee?" Ed said, reaching for his pants. He spoke as he dressed. "We're going out in hell and high water, and she's back with him and the baby."

"We don't know that," Elnora said, "and you don't have to go."

He buttoned his coat and said, "Yes, I do."

VII

Elnora thought once again about trouble. She wouldn't fault Cissy for seeking her help in getting the baby back, but damn this storm. The heavy rain and relentless wind proved to be formidable foes. Pushing back as she and Ed pressed forward. The weather was nothing but trouble, and Elnora had a strong suspicion that Grenada was only getting a small taste of what the storm had to offer. Again, she hoped that wherever the little one was, she was safe from this ruckus.

They reached the Baldwin Hotel soaked. In normal conditions, the walk was half an hour. It took them close to two. Clyde, one of the dishwashers, saw them at the back entrance. He gave them dishtowels and let them dry off in the pantry.

"Thanks, man," Ed said.

"Is Cissy back on shift?" Elnora asked.

Clyde shook his head. "She doesn't work overnight."

"You sure you haven't seen her?" Ed asked.

"She would've come back a little before the storm hit," she added.

"Yeah, she'd have to come through here and I haven't seen her since she clocked out," Clyde said. "Ain't nobody come this way but y'all. She ain't here."

Ed gave Elnora a look that she ignored. She thanked Clyde for the towels and moved back to the door.

"You don't have to go back out in that," the man said. "As long as you're quiet, won't nobody know you're here. It's bad out there."

"I have to find Cissy."

"She's a smart girl. She's fine."

Elnora only nodded while Ed and Clyde shook hands. Out under the awning, she paused on the back steps. Ed took her arm. The walk to the hotel took them out of the colored section. Heading back to that side of town would mean another hour or more in the rain. Their options were limited. Unless they went back uptown to the little office above Romano's. Rayford Drew kept late hours, and his stash of liquor made him more inclined to stay there than go home to his wife.

"It ain't letting up," Ed said.

He was referring to the storm, but those words meant more to Elnora. Finding Hattie and probably Cissy too had become like a nagging shrew that refused to give her peace. The weather could continue to wreak havoc on her search, but going home was not a choice she even considered. Hell, she wouldn't let up either.

"It ain't good when you're quiet," he said. "Where to next?"

"I wish you had a car."

"You ain't the only one," he muttered. He drew in a deep breath. She sensed the moment he understood her meaning. He stiffened tight like a whipcord. The hand that was holding her squeezed then let go.

"I can't do that. I can't ride in that man's car, knowing he—"

"He what?" she said softly. "Careful with it, Ed."

"With what?"

"You know what I told you," she said. "That's all there is to it."

"But the folks say—"

"You stand here and worry about what the folks say," she said, stepping out into the rain. "I don't have time for it."

VIII

Before Elnora reached the intersection of South and Main, a car braked beside her. The door skimmed her knees as it was flung open. "Get in," Rayford Drew barked from the driver's side.

The coupe seemed more confining than it had earlier that day. Or maybe the conversations with Ed and the driving storm made Elnora conscious of the space. The aroma of liquor and Listerine billowed with every agitated sigh or dissatisfied grunt that came from the driver. Streaks of lightning interrupted the darkness of the night and the interior of the Pontiac. She chanced a long look at him and was taken aback at the hard line of his mouth. In over twenty years, she couldn't recall that expression of resolute apprehension darkening his features. He was not always the most pleasant person, but there was a certain air about him. At that moment, she didn't know what to make of him.

"Where are we going?"

"Out a ways," he said. "Sit tight. I don't like driving in this shit."

It should have crossed her mind to worry. Their families were linked in ways that some folks in Grenada weren't ready to accept or admit. Ed's beef about riding in this car with this man had nothing to do with that. He was jealous. Any other time, Elnora might have enjoyed his discomfort. Maybe she would have played with it a little and had some fun. But not when she didn't know where her girls were.

After a couple of glances at Rayford Drew's drawn face and his tight grip on the steering wheel, she grew concerned. While he had flirted with her many times, he had never come close to making any demands. Something was different. She had seen many sides to him, but not this one.

Her hand closed around the door handle and she sat up straight. "Where did you say?"

"Settle down, Nora." He rubbed his left hand over his face. "I'm not taking you to meet your maker. Hell, He'd get us both, I 'spect."

"So I'm supposed to just sit here and not ask any questions."

"Most would," he mumbled.

She clenched her hands together in her lap. Keeping her mouth shut was not easy.

The landscape, what she could see of it, held her attention. They had left Grenada city limits and were headed south toward Tie Plant. Her uncle Joe had been a sharecropper out there before he died back in '25. His wife and kids left for Memphis soon after that. She heard one of the boys got a job at the Ford plant in Michigan. They had invited her to come along, but she couldn't bear the thought of leaving Cissy or the idea of telling her the truth. Looking back, Elnora wondered how different their lives would have been if she had accepted their offer, taken her daughter, and left Grenada for good.

"Do you know who lives out here?"

His sudden question broke the silence and startled her. Elnora needed a moment to give meaning to his words and to form a response. The deeper the coupe took them into the country, the more the water sloshed against the car's wheels. She used the noise to ease her tension.

"Some of your people."

"You don't come out here much, do you?" he asked.

"My feet only carry me so far."

"You need a car," he said. "Can you drive?"

"Yes," she answered.

"Yeah, you were driving that old Buick that Will Tennant had before he got the Ford," he said. "Did Will teach you how to drive that or was it Billy?"

"I knew how to drive before I started working for them."

He turned off the road onto gravel. The heavy rainfall forced him to work hard to keep the car from sputtering into a ditch and Elnora was glad for the distraction. She didn't like where his questions were headed. For the most part, she had few complaints about her time with the Tennant family. Like her time at the country club, working for them had been a job. The elder Tennant and his mother were nice but she received no special favors, nor did she offer any.

"This is it," Rayford Drew said, his tone solemn.

A two-story framed house loomed before them. Even in the midst of the downpour, Elnora noticed that the home's better days were behind it. The place was livable, but just that. Her three-room shotgun house in Boone Alley was better kept. Shutters hung from the windows and clattered against the building. A forgotten swing dangled lopsided from a chain at the far end of the porch. Gloom haunted the air. Light glimmered from inside, casting an eerie glow through the pouring rain and the swaying branches of the nearby weeping willow. If not for her mission, Elnora would have been content to just sit in the car.

IX

"What's waiting for me in there?"

"My brother called," Rayford Drew said. "Graham Lee brought the baby to them—"

"She's in there?"

"I don't know," he said.

"What are we doing here? Are we going in that house or not?"

He pulled the key from the ignition and twirled the key ring around his index finger. Elnora recognized hesitation, and she wondered why he hadn't moved.

"What's going on, Rayford Drew?" she asked.

"Graham Lee brought the baby to them, but his mama wouldn't take her. He begged and she told him to take the baby back where he got her from. It got ugly."

The more he talked, the less she wanted to hear. Elnora

wished this had been spoken during the drive instead of questions about the Tennant menfolk and their Buick. Her heart weighed heavy in her chest. She feared the worst; his explanations didn't help.

"I'm going in."

Elnora was out of the car and onto the porch as fast as the wind and rain would allow. Her coat, now soaked, was nothing more than a heavy second skin. She clutched the dripping fabric like it was a lifeline. Rayford Drew came up on her left side. Tall and lean, his shoulder and arm brushed against her and she knew it was no accident. This was the best support he could offer. Still, the dread boiling in her gut made her want to push him hard and force him to feel half the agony that was coursing through her.

He reached the door first. He beat hard once against it and then stormed inside. Shuddering both from cold and fear, Elnora followed.

"Oh my God," he said as he stopped short in the middle of the room.

Tired and angry, Elnora tried to sidestep him—but if he hadn't reached out and grabbed her, she would have stepped right on the sleeping toddler.

Curled on her side with a thumb in her mouth, little Hattie lay on a blanket fast asleep. Elnora scooped the child into her arms. Other than a murmur, the little girl remained oblivious to the storm, her surroundings, and the trembling woman who held her close.

X

The storm's fury kept them inside. Raw emotion pulsed within Elnora. The loud thunderclaps and the increasing downpour could not compare to the confounding mix of elation and frustration that made her unable to sit still. To her surprise, little Hattie slept through the worst of it. She only whimpered once and Elnora hummed until the baby went back to sleep. Rayford Drew paused to stare at them during his task of building a fire in the hearth. Once he managed to create a brilliant spectacle of blue and orange flames, he lit a small branch as a torch and left the main room. His heavy steps thudded on the hardwood floor. Elnora edged close to the fire. She hummed every lullaby she knew, thought about Cissy, and wondered what else Rayford Drew was hiding.

He returned with two wooden straight-back chairs that appeared to be in better shape than the ripped furniture littering the front room. Unlike their discovery in Holcomb, this home had lost its peace years ago. No one person or event had stripped it bare. The assault had occurred over time. As Elnora pulled her chair close enough to dry off but not catch fire, she was aware of Rayford Drew's studied silence and how he kept looking from her to the child in her arms.

"You won't dry if you keep the coat on," he said.

Elnora's first thought was to lie and say she was fine. Help often came with a price. She'd accepted more from him today than she wanted to admit to herself. Acknowledging that he had good advice was her limit.

"You'll catch cold." He extended his arms. "I'll hold her. It won't take but a minute."

"No need to trouble you more than I have."

She positioned Hattie across her lap. The wet coat clung to her, but she managed to tug free of it. She hooked it on the back of her chair and had Hattie back in the curve of her arms before the next streak of lightning.

"I had nothing to do with any of this."

Elnora shrugged. Who was she to expect a man like Rayford Drew Donner to owe her an explanation? Hattie was back safe and unharmed. Once the storm cleared, they'd head back to Grenada and everything would be set right again.

"I can't say that my brother wouldn't leave her out here alone," he said, "but I didn't know. Not that she was alone. He just told me to come to Tie Plant—"

"Please," she interrupted, unable to hear more. The words created unbearable images—a little two-year-old girl left alone in an abandoned house during the worst storm of the year. Discarded by family like she was yesterday's trash. The knowing hurt. Elnora didn't want him to speak another word.

"I told Graham Lee a thousand times that he and that gal wouldn't ever work."

Hattie began to stir. Elnora kissed her forehead and smoothed her hair from her cheek.

"Fool kid thought a baby would change things," Rayford Drew said. "His folks aren't ready for that kind of change. I told him to keep the baby away from them."

"Who left her here?"

The question demanded an answer, but silence was all he offered. When he finally parted his mouth to speak, Elnora recognized the tilt of his head wavering between a lie and the truth. She wondered how far he planned to go with either. Then a noise came from a distant room. Footsteps advanced toward them. Elnora clutched the baby to her chest. Rayford Drew moved toward the sound, his hands balled into fists at his sides.

"Who's there?" he called out.

"Us."

Graham Lee entered first, with Cissy close behind him. She still wore her maid uniform and he was a younger version of his uncle in a button-down shirt and slacks. Both looked worn, beaten to the brink of exhaustion. Elnora hugged Hattie close on instinct. Cissy stepped toward them, reaching for the baby, but Graham Lee pulled her back.

"Cissy?"

"I'm sorry, Cousin El—"

"We hope you'll look after her," Graham Lee spoke up. "I'll send money. You won't be put out at all."

"You have lost your mind." Rayford Drew backed away and stood at the front door. The thunder was beginning to taper off, but the rainfall continued to pour at a steady pace. He seemed more interested in the weather than the foolish ideas being revealed in the room.

"And then what?" Elnora asked. She couldn't stop herself. She had to know if they were both as naive and hopeful as the words tumbling from the young father's mouth.

"We'll come for her," Cissy said.

"What did you tell me just this afternoon?" Elnora needed Cissy to see reason. She couldn't let her make the mistake of walking away from her baby. "What did you say about Graham Lee?"

"I know what I said—"

"Say it again."

The two women stared. Then Cissy blurted out, "I was wrong! We're a family. That's all Graham Lee ever wanted. I want it too. Hattie should have her mama and her daddy."

"Stupid kids," Rayford Drew said.

"I take care of what's mine!" Graham Lee's cry woke Hattie. He wasted no time taking his child and holding her. "Hello there. Daddy's sorry. Daddy's gonna make it better. For you and for all of us." He fixed his dove-gray eyes on Elnora. "You'll help, won't you? My family . . . they don't understand. Cissy says you've always been good to her. Will you help us?"

"Why did you take the baby again?" she asked. "You scared her real bad."

"It was the only way she'd come to me." He looked at his child's mother and smiled. "You know I'd never do anything to hurt you."

"But tearing up the photo?"

"The photo? I didn't do that. My mama saw it and she . . ." He frowned. "Look, will you help us or not? We can take her, but it'll be easier to get on our feet without her. Least for a little while."

"Where are you going?" Rayford Drew turned from the rain to face them.

"You gonna tell your brother?"

The older man shook his head.

Graham Lee snorted. "I don't believe you. We're going someplace safe. That's all you need to know."

XI

Elnora had just set little Hattie down for a nap on the wrought-iron bed in the front room when Ed Jenkins stopped at her door. The storm had delayed the Illinois Central schedule so he was stranded in Grenada for a couple of days. With a baby to care for, resolving their disagreement failed to become a priority. He had left word that he was staying at his mama's over on Poplar Street and that was just fine with her.

His somber expression had her prepared for anything. The storm had left debris everywhere. A toddler's natural curiosity created mysteries and surprises where Elnora had never imagined. A simple task of cleaning up the backyard had become more involved with Hattie underfoot. One little girl had made Elnora's reflexes quicker, sharper. So, whatever Ed had for her, Elnora was certain she could handle it without a flinch.

He took his hat off as he crossed the threshold and pulled out a chair for her at the kitchen table. After she sat down, he did the same.

"If you're here to say goodbye—"

"I'm here about the flooding," he said. "Ain't nobody told you?"

"There was some flooding on the east side. I heard about that. It always floods there when we have a bad storm."

"That wasn't just a storm. Tupelo had a twister."

"A twister?" She reared back. "Anybody hurt?"

"Quite a few," he said. "Nobody told you?"

"I've been busy with Hattie—"

"Thank God." He sighed. The will that had been holding him together started to crumble. His mouth trembled. "I'm glad she was found."

"Ed, what it is? You dancing around your words. Just out with it."

"Two bodies were found in the Yalobusha River. Now that the rain's stopped, the river is starting to go back down—"

"The bodies." She glanced toward the room where the little girl slept. "Whose bodies?"

"They ain't identified them yet—"

"You wouldn't be here if you didn't know," she said. "You wouldn't tell me if it weren't fact."

He reached for her hands. "It's fact. My uncle helped pull them out."

"He's sure it was Cissy and Graham Lee."

"Yes."

Elnora wanted to feel something. Her daughter was dead. Drowned in the Yalobusha River. Cissy's baby would never get to know her mother. History would repeat itself. Life should have more to offer than the act of waiting for the next dose of trouble to arrive. Cissy and Graham Lee just wanted to go where they would be free to be a family. It was not right their dream would never be.

"What can I do?"

She shook her head. Hadn't enough been done? She tried to pull free of his hand, but he refused to let go.

"We can raise her together," Ed said. "She'll never have to know."

"I'll know."

Elnora recognized the strength in his touch and the promises of family that she had never been able to fulfill for Cissy and herself. Her daughter had died never knowing the truth about their blood ties. Elnora's breath caught at the possibility of more lies affecting her family. Hattie deserved better. Besides, Elnora knew for a fact that untruths had a way of troubling lives in unimaginable ways. She couldn't help but think the loss of Cissy and Graham Lee were testimony to that.

A faint murmur sounded from the front room. Ed released her hand, and she felt his steps close behind as she went to Hattie. The toddler's embrace and watery smile filled Elnora with the firm belief that raising Hattie as blood was right, but no more lies would darken their future. Cissy always said that Elnora was good at fixing things. Elnora aimed to hold true to those words.

MY DEAR, MY ONE TRUE LOVE

BY LEE DURKEE

Gulfport

They have the most beautiful eyes, crazy women do, differing tints and gleams, true, but always that pinprick of wilding incandescence, the swamp gas rising. Oh, I have known crazy women with winter's constellations in their eyes, with flying saucers, brooding lava fields, aurora borealis, and diaphanously pulsing fireflies I have chased with my kill jar across many a darkening field. To put it less romantically, I have fucked the bipolar crazy, the schizoid crazy, the posttraumatic crazy, the obsessive-compulsive crazy, the klepto crazy, the compulsive-liar crazy (especially the compulsive-lair crazy), and, on at least three separate occasions, the nymphomaniacal-multipersonality-sadistic crazy, and so on and so on (I promise); however—and this is important—it is not the madness that enchants but its symptomatic glow, that prick of purest torn-off wildly jagged piece of light I can detect now and then, never for long, usually toward dusk, like a different creature spying out from within the lover you thought you knew: this inner being furtive, crouched, wary, neither evil nor benign but uncomprehending, alien, dangerous with fear.

When a man tells you he has known crazy women he should be able to roll up his sleeves, lower his pants, and part his hairline to show you the accompanying scars. If there are no scars, or few, or faint, then he is not a true lover of crazy women. And he cannot claim to have been lucky in avoiding such fissures because crazy women invariably attack at your weakest moments, when you are vomiting into a plant or narcotized in a recliner or submerged chemically, emotionally, or otherwise into a bathtub. And the more fragile the crazy woman, the more likely she is to employ others to pummel, stab, strangle, and plunge. Crazy women can summon willing accomplices from Parchman prison, from graveyards, Ouija boards, and tarot decks. Streetlights flicker as they walk under. Oh, I have known crazy women.

We are all, of course, responsible for our own crazy lovers. Yes (as we've been lectured many times), it's our own damn fault. And it is. No one to blame but that morning mirror, however blood-speckled or webbed or slashed with obscene lipstick glyphs threatening to castrate you or throat-slit some foul bitch of the imagination you've supposedly been fucking on the side. We stare into these mirrors while touching the white seams of scars, remembering, remembering, at times even bringing the scar tissue to our tongues so as to taste that distant pain we apparently learned nothing from. And why do we refuse to learn? Why do we succumb to that lunar lure again and again? The sex, of course. Yes, sex with crazy women is a sleek, diabolical fairground ride rumored to have decapitated two teenagers just last week in Pascagoula. C'mon, we've all boarded that ride, haven't we? We've all knowingly taken home the insane, haven't we?—from the floating slot machines of Biloxi, from the C-scar strip bars lining our beaches? No? Well, then uncork, I say. Unless you are a small man or sleep very deeply then I highly recommend sex with crazy women because crazy-woman sex lasts forever. They embed themselves into your mind like earwigs so that decades later you will be able to savor vivid memories of crazy-woman sex, a montage of baffling rituals, sinister accoutrements, terrifying confessions, shattered furniture, and shocking cumcalls in which hitherto confined interior personalities emerge, one by one, like bats from an attic, and always, always, the unexplainable and indiscrete wounds. Oh, I have known crazy women.

However, when I say I have known crazy women, I do not mean to say that I have always known the extent of just how crazy they were (prior to their arrests, etc.). Quite the opposite, I have a long history of underestimating the craziness of crazy women, and because of this shortcoming, let us call it, I have had, many times over, to swear them off entirely, to go cold turkey on crazy women, but it appears I command an eerie capacity for denial, and of course on some level, more mundane, I must be crazy myself. After all, no man is completely sane after his fourth crazy woman. Crazy women lay eggs into your ears, and if you're not good at deciding whether women are crazy, or gauging how crazy they actually are, or if you're just game about giving murkily beautiful women the benefit of the doubt, then you end up considering some strange and spooky theories on life. Creaking doors open into pink bedrooms piled high with the predatory eyes of stuffed animals. Crazy women tend to describe these haunted bedrooms to you vividly. They entice you into having sex within the confines of these supposed realities, the domed ceiling painted lasciviously with hovering goddesses and guardian angels and wild-haired prophets, and for a while the two of you live together in that space-time vacuum conceived during some childhood trauma involving an unleashed adolescent brother or a drunken stepfather or so-called uncle. Inside this hallucinatory mansion, you throw a bunch of dishes at each other or murder one of the neighborhood dogs, you explain things to cops or thank them profusely, and life goes on in this manner until someone gets led away in handcuffs or we find ourselves late at night once again shoveling away under the Mississippi stars, my dear, my one true love.

HERO

BY MICHAEL FARRIS SMITH

Magnolia

Hero and his dog Spur stare down the tracks, mimics of one another in the summer sun. Hero's ribs can be counted from a block away and he's clotheless except for sneakers and cutoffs. Spur's thin face hangs on his neck and his coat is mud-colored and matted. Both underfed, both with hollow faces, four eyes staring down the tracks anxious for God knows what.

"Dumb-ass," Wayne grumbles as the Ford clatters past Hero. "He's got as much sense as a brick." Wayne turns right at the first street past the tracks. At the third house on the left he pulls into the dirt driveway. I live in the house next door.

Living on the tracks in Magnolia has never been that bad. I can deal with the rumbles and whistles that seem like some strange heartbeat of small-town south Mississippi. It's living *across* the tracks. Only the tax assessor's office and the mail-man acknowledge us. All the business buildings have that long-moved-out-of look, with boards nailed across busted windows and spiderwebs that look like nets swinging from the corners of abandoned entrances. The large wooden houses are grand but have paint chipping so bad that after a strong wind it looks like snow has fallen across the yards. Kids steal bikes because theirs were stolen. The neighborhood is filled with abandoned cars, teenage moms, dirt lawns, and makes people say, "I bet a long time ago this used to be such a nice neighborhood," as they ride by with their windows up and doors locked and air conditioners blowing.

"Son of a bitch," Wayne says as he gets out of the truck and slams the door shut. His muscles flex through the thin T-shirt he wears to work nearly every day. I get out and we stand there looking at Hero and the dog, still glaring down the railroad tracks as if the drive-in movie was on the other end. "Hero! Get the hell away from there, boy!"

"He's all right, Wayne. Won't be a train until later on," I say as I walk behind the truck on my way home.

"I ain't worried about no train. Wish one would hit his ass."

I keep walking, too tired to listen to any more of Wayne's rumblings. I've suffered ten hours of it already today. I feel heavy, drained from a day in the sun. I climb the concrete steps of my house and sit down on the porch in a recliner I picked up out of somebody's garbage one day, and watch Hero and Spur.

Nobody remembers the last time Hero talked. He's about eleven now, and he quit somewhere between five and six, though the date isn't certain because Wayne and Doris either didn't realize it or plain ignored it. There's Wayne's side of it, that Hero's dumb and born that way, and Doris says little more than that except she swears one day Hero will snap out of it. And I have my own notions, listening to the crashing and tumbling that goes on in the house next to mine, the walls so thin I hear Wayne's beer cans crush at night, and I grimace when he screams, "Goddamnit!" and Doris yells, "Wayne, stop it!" and the racket of a wrestling match follows complete with traveling furniture and flying pots.

Over my shoulder a timer clicks and a buzz begins, and in the window behind me a blue neon hand shines with red letters that read, *Darna's Psychic Readings*. The light comes on at six o'clock every evening and glows until midnight, signifying the doctor is in for the curious, confused, unoccupied minds of the city blocks surrounding us. The door opens and I know Darna's behind me.

"'Bout time. Where y'all been?" a slow, angry voice asks.

"Workin', Darna. Where else?" I say without turning around.

"*Where else* my ass. You and Wayne ain't been workin' all this time. I'm open now so don't sit on this porch long. I don't want you running off business." When she finishes she goes inside.

"Guess you heard that," a softer voice says.

I turn around and there's Haley. Her aqua tank top fits loose, race-car-red lipstick her only makeup. "Oh, hey. I didn't know you were there."

"I was trying to be quiet. Darna scares me too."

"She doesn't scare me. I just get tired of hearing it, that's all. I swear to God. One day I'm outta here."

"Yeah, right," Haley says. She's Darna's younger sister, but as different from Darna as a kitten from a bull. Her legs and arms show off a July brown and she's skinny like me.

"I am," I say again. "One day."

"And go where and do what? Maybe you can join the circus." She laughs and juggles imaginary bowling pins.

"Go ahead and make fun, Haley. Just like Darna does. Never takes me serious."

"Stop it. You know I'm not like Darna. Just relax. You want a beer?"

"Yeah, I guess."

"You've got until I get back to quit pouting." Haley goes inside and returns with Budweiser cans for each of us.

"C'mon. Sit down," I say, and get up to let her have the recliner. I unfold an aluminum chair that's leaning against the wall. "You want in on the checker match?"

"I might. Bet Hero puts it to you tonight."

"He's not bad. I used to let him win but I think it's the other way around now. What've y'all been doing all day?" I ask her as she leans back in the recliner.

"Nothin' hardly. Darna carried me over to Hudson's and I got some nail polish. Only ten cents a bottle. I got every color in the rainbow. See?" She holds her hands out and every fingernail is a different shade. "Wish I worked there instead of Rose's. Bet they get better discounts."

I look up and Hero and Spur are making their way toward the porch. Two squirrels scamper down the oak tree by the road and like wayward lightning bolts run quick circles around Hero's feet. Spur leaps back, but doesn't bark. Hero bends down and puts out his hand and one of the squirrels runs up his arm and sits on his shoulder. The other plays between the two of them.

"That is so weird," Haley whispers.

"A little Tarzan," I answer. The first squirrel jumps off Hero and they scurry off. Hero and Spur resume their walk toward us. "C'mon, Hero. Haley doesn't think I'm your checker equal."

Hero climbs the stairs and I grab a milk crate from the edge of the porch and place it between us. Under the crate is a box holding checkers and a board, more pink and gray than red and black. Hero folds his lanky legs Indian-style on one side of the crate and I sit in my aluminum chair on the other. Spur nestles next to Haley and she scratches the back of his neck.

We play into the twilight. Hero smiles shyly when he wins and I see words forming in him so clearly that I feel I could reach down his throat and pull them out. Haley cheers for Hero, poking fun at my bad moves and slapping Hero on the back whenever I'm forced to crown him. It's warm with Haley here—she laughs and flirts and I imagine this as our house, our porch.

"I told you he was good," she says whenever he gets me in a pinch. I laugh and tell Hero he's just lucky.

"Hero! Get your ass over here! Your momma's got supper ready," Wayne yells from next door. It's nearly dark now. Hero scampers to his feet and he and Spur rush home, kicking up dust along the way. Haley is the next to go.

"Do you want a ride? Darna would probably give me the keys to the car," I say as she starts to walk the four blocks to her duplex apartment.

"Nah. It's not so bad out tonight. Nice for a walk," she answers. Haley twists her brown hair with her finger and marks a line on the asphalt with her foot. I stand at the top of the steps, looking at her, then glancing back over my shoulder at the blue hand.

"When will you be back?" I ask.

"When do you want me back?"

I shrug my shoulders. "Don't you know the answer to that?"

Haley rolls her eyes and stuffs her hands into the pockets of her jeans. "Better see what your wife is doing," she teases, and turns and skips down the road.

I dread leaving the porch because there's nowhere to hide inside. In our small house Darna's squatty, wide frame sticks out from around every corner. I don't remember the last time she looked pleasantly in my direction, and even if she did I'm not sure I'd recognize it. Now what's left of her smiles and graces are reserved for the customers who sit and pay twenty dollars a session to listen to the good faith and promises of a white-trash psychic.

I walk into the kitchen. On the stove is a pot of macaroni and cheese cooked sometime in the afternoon. I take my dinner into the back room of the house and lay down on the floor. A twelve-inch black-and-white TV with rabbit ears is my companion during the psychic hours and I seem to have worn a spot in the wooden floorboard where my body stretches out each night in between boxes of garage-sale bargains—pots and pans, flower vases, ugly ties, pillows, and various volumes of encyclopedias. I rest my head on a pile of large-woman blouses.

The front door opens and closes periodically as Darna reads palms, tarot cards, the crystal ball, or anything else that might reveal to her exactly what it is the customers want to hear. She is a friendly fortune teller, promising the hope of wealth or love to the lonely souls living in houses like ours, living lives like ours. So little changes in this town that is nearly out of Mississippi, almost in Louisiana. We live in the perpetual in-between. But she sells what they want. Twenty dollars salvages hope for another day, until the mailman leaves a new stack of bills or the husband passes out on the porch or the fifteen-year-old daughter spends another night away from home. Darna fills the emptiness with bullshit, recycled every evening until midnight for a small, nonrefundable fee.

At six thirty in the morning, me and Wayne are waiting in the lobby of Labor Locators. The bald guy named Ed sits behind the glass and calls out job assignments to the early birds.

About twenty-five of us are there in the "labor hall," as Ed calls it. Mostly men but a handful of women. Black and white, young and old, big and little—a pot of blue-collar gumbo there for the picking, willing to work any job Ed can scare up. People are scattered, some sleeping, some pretending to read. Everyone has a Styrofoam cup of black coffee, the steam dancing up and away.

"I hope that asshole don't send us back to West," Wayne mumbles to me. "That shit is killin' me."

I nod in agreement because I too don't care to be sent back. For the past five days we've been hauling sheetrock on the trucks that deliver supplies to building sites. sheetrock is four foot by eight foot and weighs about three Darnas a sheet, but breaks easy. There's no other way to move it than putting one man on one end and one on the other and carrying it long-ways, then letting it fall gracefully into a neat stack. The works gets rough when there's 150 a load, and by the time you get down to the last thirty or so your body is so fatigued and cramped that it's all you can do to cup your hand and let the sheetrock rest there while you bend your body to support the weight and try not to drop your end, wasting somebody's good money. When it's over you wonder how you were able to survive until the bottom of the stack, drink a jug of water, then get in the truck and go get the next load.

Ed looks up and sees us. There's a grin on his face as he fingers us toward the window. "Back to West, boys," he says.

"Shit, Ed. Ain't you got nothin' else?" Wayne replies.

"You wanna work or not?"

"Fine," Wayne says, and swipes our time cards off the counter. He cusses all the way out the door, the whole ride to West, and up to the time we're on the interstate with the first load.

We come home about the same time as the day before, and as we get to the railroad, Hero and Spur are there again zeroed down the tracks. We bump over the rails and Wayne yells, "Get the hell away from there I said!" Hero never looks up. "Guess the son of a bitch is deaf now too."

We get out of the truck and Wayne says, "You think Darna would give me a free reading?" I'm surprised because Wayne has never before alluded to Darna's cosmic enterprise.

"I guess. I don't know. What for?"

"Nothin' really. How about asking her for me?"

I open the front door and hear Darna yelling at the television. "Kick his ass! C'mon!"

I say "Darna" three times before she answers, and she only does then because there's a commercial.

"Wayne wants to know if you'd give him a free reading."

"Ain't nothing free."

"Shit, Darna, him and Doris have been living over there forever," I say.

She rearranges herself on her Aunt Martha's hand-me-down love seat. Her nightgown rises and her fat legs are white like church candles.

"Hell, I guess," she answers, never taking her eyes off the television. "Tell him I ain't giving him more than ten minutes though."

I yell out the screen door for Wayne to come in. Darna turns off the television and goes into her "reading" room.

"In there," I direct Wayne.

Darna is lighting candles and closing blinds. In the center of the room is a card table covered with an orange tablecloth decorated with the silhouettes of black cats. Darna turns on a lamp in the corner that glows with a red lightbulb. I stand in the doorway curious, but she pushes me into the hallway and shuts the door in my face.

They talk quietly. I press my ear against the door but can translate nothing. Darna does most of the talking. Wayne offers one- or two-word sentences when she pauses. Though interested, I'm also tired, and go into the kitchen for a beer. Before I'm halfway finished, the door opens and Wayne leaves, and Darna sits down again in front of the television.

"So?" I say.

"So what?" she answers.

"What'd he want?"

"You know I can't tell that."

"C'mon, Darna. It's just Wayne."

"I don't care who it is. He's a client and I ain't telling," she says.

"Client-smient, Darna. It's *just* Wayne."

"Same for everybody," she says.

I give up and walk to the back room. I stretch my thin body as long as it will go, straight out across the hardwood, visions of sheetrock dancing in my head, as I feel their weight even in relaxation, heavy on my shoulders. The exchange with Darna is the only one of the night, and long before the late news I'm fast asleep.

The warning whistle and thunder roaring closer awaken me. It's the early a.m. and a tremor grows in the ground. I go into the kitchen for some water. My mouth is dry and as I bend over the sink and guzzle from the faucet, the train whistle blows ceaselessly. I make my way to the porch and the whistle continues to scream as if the train were frightened of its own tracks, the sound of the weight thumping stronger and teeming with the whistle to blare and roar like an approaching war. I see the reason for its loud arrival when I look ahead: standing almost on the tracks are two shadows. They are side by side, ornaments of black in the night, when the train light hits them, and there's Wayne with a firm grasp on the neck of Hero, Hero squirming up and down but being held in place by the strong, solid grip of his father.

The light whiter on their faces and the whistle stronger and louder, the train rushes toward them, but Wayne won't let them move. I yell but it's lost in the train's roar. It's too late for the train to slow as the light grows wide on the ground around Wayne and Hero, spotlighting the boy's struggle.

Off the porch and I'm running toward the tracks. The ground bounces and I use it to spring forward with each step. I dash into the growing light and snatch Hero away from Wayne as he never hears me coming in all the noise. Hero stumbles and falls when I whip him around, and in the train's light Wayne's eyes are scattered. The muscles in his neck are bulging and it appears as though there is so much pressure in his head that his hairs might start popping off one by one. An instant after I yank Hero away, the engine blows past.

The train light disappears from our faces but Wayne's crazy eyes still show. He takes a step toward me, raises both fists over his head. "What the hell are you doing!" he screams over the clicking of the rails.

"Jesus Christ! What am *I* doing?"

He drops his hands and turns away from me, stomping toward his house. I go after him and he stops at the road and jerks around. I take a step back. The train is quieter now that the engine is down the tracks.

"Goddamnit! What's wrong with you!" he screams. I can only shake my head back and forth. "Shit! I'm out here trying to get him to talk and you butt your ass in and screw it up!"

I stare at him.

He's so furious he's doing a little dance and his fists are balled up. "What do you think? Hero! I'm trying to scare something out of him! Anything!"

"My God, Wayne, it's not the hiccups. You can't get him to talk by making him think he's about to die."

"How do *you* know? Are you a doctor? He ain't never gonna say another word, your witch-ass wife said so!"

"What?"

Wayne raises his arm and points toward our house. "Today! I asked Darna if he was ever gonna talk again and she said no!"

"Wayne, you know that nothing she says is—"

"Just screw it. To hell with it all. I don't give a shit if he ever says another word. He don't do nothing but take up space," he says, then storms toward his house, throws open the front door, and slams it behind him.

I turn to look for Hero but he is gone, and in the lights of the street running parallel with the tracks is a skeleton kicking up its heels, trying to keep pace with the train. I walk back to my porch, sit in the recliner, and count cars passing by. I never get tired of the trains passing in the night.

When I come outside the next morning, the checkerboard is lying on the seat of the recliner. I pick it up and written across it in black magic marker is, *I am gone. Feed Spur.*

Wayne bursts through his front door and yells, "C'mon, let's go! If we get there early enough maybe we won't have to haul sheetrock."

I fold the checkerboard and slide it under the recliner.

For once, I'm happy to be assigned to sheetrock because it's too exhausting of a job to spend your time talking, giving me time to think about Hero—where is he, what he's doing, and what I'm going to do or say.

On the ride home Wayne asks if I've seen him.

"Not since last night," I answer.

"Little shit didn't come home. You sure he didn't sleep on your porch or something?"

"I'm sure. I sat out there until late and then was out early."

"Just like his momma. Never know where the hell he is."

I sit on the front porch all night watching for Hero. Nobody has visited Darna by eleven o'clock and she turns off the hand, relieving the neon strain on my eyes. The moon is hidden by the clouds and everything is extra black. No sign of Hero.

The next evening, Haley sits with me. Spur lies in the dirt next to the steps.

"Two nights now," I say.

"I know it. Sad, ain't it?"

"What pisses me off is if Hero were to walk up, he'd ring his neck and call it tough love. His problem is, all he wants is something to hate. Without Hero around he doesn't have a cause."

Haley gets up from the recliner and sits down with me on the edge of the porch. Our feet swing back and forth out of sync and our shoulders rub together.

"What's gonna happen to him?" Haley asks. Her voice is soft, like it arrived on a breeze. "You swear you don't know where he is?"

"All I know is what I showed you on the checkerboard. I swear. But my guess is, if he's really gone, he probably hopped on a train sometime during the night."

Wayne's front door opens and closes and he comes over to us. Spur shrinks when he walks up.

"Where's Darna?" he asks, and I point a finger toward the door. "Is she with somebody?"

"Not now," I answer.

He goes inside and I hear the door to the reading room close. Haley hops from her seat and stands in front of me. In the blue neon she looks ghoulish and strange.

"Why don't we do something?" she asks, face full of adventure.

"Like what?"

"Like getting up and going after Hero, that's what. A manhunt, the big chase, you know, something exciting."

"And do what if we find him, Haley? Bring him back here? Back here so Wayne can whip the shit out of him? Back here to this?" I say, holding my arms out wide, running my eyes across the landscape.

"You know," she says placing her hands on her hips, "*this* ain't so bad to some people."

"No. But it is to others. I'm not so sure he's worse off."

The excitement disappears from her face. "And what about you? Is this so bad to you?"

I look at her and shake my head. "Not always, I don't guess, but it seems it's bad more times than not. I mean, there's you.

There *was* Hero. And there are nights when I'm on the porch with a beer, alone and watching the things that go on in the dark—the bugs in the streetlight, the cats milling around. That's when I think things aren't so bad. But I look up and down those rails and imagine the places they run to and . . . I don't know. Don't you ever think about somewhere else?"

Crickets chirp softly, warming up for the night's performance. Shouts of "Touchdown!" come from kids playing football in the street a block away. Haley looks at her fingernails and makes the colors dance by wiggling her fingers. "I just thought it'd be fun to go look for him," she mumbles.

The front door bursts open and Wayne roars out. "I knew you knew where he was!"

I look around and Wayne pops me in the side of my head. I hop off the porch and he comes down and gets in my face.

"You'd better take me to him right now and I ain't joking around," he says, pointing a dirty finger at my nose.

"Christ, settle down."

"I ain't slowing down. Darna's cards said you know where Hero is, just like I thought."

I back up a step. "I don't know where he is any more than you do. Darna's cards are full of shit."

Wayne reaches out and grabs me by the arm, twisting and pinching my skin. "You're coming with me and we're going to get him."

"Wayne, he doesn't know where he is," Haley says.

"You shut the hell up. Y'all both probably know. I'm gonna kick the shit out of all y'all when we find him."

Haley runs up the stairs into the house, yelling for Darna. Spur is up and barking, scraping at the dirt with his front paws. I try to shake loose from Wayne but lose my feet, and he drags me by the arm to the truck.

"Get your ass up and get in."

"Wayne, I swear—"

"Goddamnit, get in. You know Hero would run like hell if he saw just me. And don't give me none of that *I don't know* bullshit."

We climb in, Wayne cranks the truck, and we spin out of the driveway. As we pass in front of my house, Haley runs out the door and yells, "Wait! Wait!" but he never slows and I know it's going to be a long night. He'll be watching and hoping for Hero, and so will I.

PART IV

SKIPPING TOWN

PIT STOP

BY JOHN M. FLOYD

State Highway 25

Anna McDowell stood looking out the front window of the roadside gas station/minimart at the empty fields across the highway and the stand of pines beyond. Adrift on a sea of memories, she moved not a muscle, said not a word. Her nine-year-old daughter Deborah, obviously weary of both the view through the window and the delay in their schedule, stood at her side. Deborah turned every few seconds to stare at the closed door of the men's room, which supposedly contained her five-year-old brother Charlie.

"You think he fell in?" she asked.

Anna said, her eyes still on the distant woods, "He's okay. Be patient."

Deborah peered up at her mother's face. "You look funny, Mom. What's the deal?"

"Nothing, honey. Just thinking."

"When are we supposed to get to Aunt Penny's?"

"Late this afternoon." Anna turned to her daughter and smiled. Both children adored her husband's sister, a fact that greatly pleased Anna, and every summer for the past few years Anna and the kids had driven up to Nashville (Franklin, actually) as soon as school was out, to spend a week at Penny's house. Unmarried and childless, Penny happily smothered her only niece and nephew with attention and affection. The one bad part was the seven-hour drive to get there.

Before Anna could say more, little Charlie McDowell emerged from the restroom and gave them both a *What are we waiting for?* look. Anna grabbed his still-soapy hand, gazed one last time at the trees across the road, and led her children back down past the shelves of candy bars and potato chips to the front door. Thirty seconds later the three of them were outside and headed for their minivan. The sky was overcast, the day breezy and blessedly cool for early June.

Anna had just taken her keys from her purse when a short, skinny, greasy-haired man appeared from behind a parked car. One of his hands was out of sight in his pocket; the other he clamped around her right arm.

"Open it," he growled, nodding to the van, "and get the kids in. *Now.*"

Stunned, Anna dropped her keys on the pavement. The man glared at her, said, "Pick 'em up," and turned to make sure they weren't being watched. Both the children were cowering against the side of the van.

Anna knelt to pick up the keys, and when the man turned to her again she did something she would never until this instant have dreamed of doing: she leaned to the left, wrapped her left hand around her right fist, and pistoned straight up from her kneeling position, her right elbow jabbing upward like a spear. As hard as she could, with all the strength of both legs and both arms behind the surge, she drove the point of her elbow up into the hollow underneath the short man's chin—it thunked like an axe being swung into an oak trunk. The man's head snapped back, all his muscles went limp, and for a second or two he stood there staring up at the gray sky with eyes that were already rolling back into his head. Then he collapsed like a rag doll and lay flat on the ground, all his limbs extended toward the four points of the compass. A revolver he had taken from his pocket clattered onto the concrete.

Trembling, Anna kicked the gun underneath a car, gathered her children to her like chicks, and steered them toward the store while she took out her cell phone and punched in 911. Behind her, the hapless carjacker twitched, gagged, and staggered to his feet. Bent almost double, he stumbled away with his eyes squeezed shut and his tongue out and both hands holding his throat. Anna, safely inside the store now, saw him blunder head-first into a parked truck and fall to his knees. Finally he disappeared around the corner of the building.

Half an hour later all the right questions had been asked and answered, and the police left with a bagged-and-tagged weapon, a detailed account of the incident, and an even more detailed description of the attacker. No one knew where he'd gone or how he'd gotten away, but Anna was repeatedly assured that they would find him. She didn't much care. Her family was safe, and that was all that mattered. She was walking for the second time to her minivan with her children when a newly arrived state trooper approached her.

"Ms. Langley?" he said. "Is that you?"

She looked up at him, frowning for a second before recognition kicked in. She smiled. "It's me. Last name's McDowell now. How you doing, Keller?"

He nodded. "So-so." He tilted his head toward the store behind them, where a second patrolman was speaking to the cashier. "I heard what happened. How in the world did you manage that?"

"I don't know. I was mad and scared, I guess. And I just finished a self-defense class."

"I think you got your money's worth."

She shrugged. "It worked only because he wasn't expecting it."

"He could've killed you, you know. The kids too."

"He might have, if I had let him get in the car with us."

The officer pondered that and nodded. "Probably right. Just glad you're okay."

"Thanks, Keller. It's good to see you again."

As she turned to leave, he said, "Guess this proves it, right?"

"Proves what?"

"Lightning *can* strike twice in the same place."

Anna thought about that a moment. "Compared to last time," she said, "this was easy."

An awkward silence passed.

"Maybe what happened before . . ." He paused for a beat. "Maybe it made you tough."

She nodded. "Maybe it did."

Moments later the three travelers were inside their van. "Help your brother buckle up," Anna told her daughter. "And hand me a Coke from the cooler before we get going."

Deborah, her face still a little pale, stared straight ahead. "Mom?"

"What, honey?"

"That man. Did he just want to steal our car? Or did he want to . . . hurt us?"

Anna shook her head, reached over, and smoothed her daughter's hair. "Doesn't matter, Deb. Everything's okay. He won't be doing either one."

"They'll get his fingerprints, right? Off the gun?"

"Yes. They'll catch him."

Deborah hesitated, frowning hard in thought. "What did that policeman mean, about lightning?"

Anna sighed. "Something happened here, years ago," she said. "Before you were born."

"Here at this store?"

"Yeah. In the woods over there, actually." She glanced again at the distant trees and, jutting above them, the old windmill she remembered so well. Even from this far away, she could see its blades turning lazily in the wind.

"What happened?" Deborah asked. "Something bad?"

This time it was the mother who hesitated. "Not really. Something good, in a way. Something that got rid of something bad."

"Tell me," Deborah said.

A long stare. "Maybe I will. Maybe it's time. But first hand me that Coke."

When everyone was strapped in and they had eased out of the gas station's parking lot and onto the road, Anna popped the top of the can and let out a long breath. She glanced over at Deborah. "You sure you really want to hear this?"

"I'm sure."

Charlie was already snoozing in his car seat, but that was okay, Anna thought. He was too young to understand what she was about to say. If she was able to say it, that is. She hadn't talked to anyone about this for a long, long time.

Anna took a pull on the Coke, set it in the cup holder, and clamped both hands on the wheel at the ten-till-two position.

"Years ago," she said, "two people left Jackson, south of here, to drive to a ball game in Starkville, over a hundred miles north. And to hike around for a bit, afterward. They were young and they were foolish and they were in love. The girl was Anna Langley—"

"That was you, right?"

"That's right. And the boy was named Woody. Woody Prestridge. He was tall and blond—"

—and Anna thought he was just about the best thing that had ever happened to her. She stood there on the sun-dappled sidewalk in front of her dorm at Millsaps College and watched as

Woody loaded her picnic basket and backpack into the trunk of his Toyota and slammed the lid.

"Done," he said. "Prepare for takeoff."

"How long will this game last?" Anna asked as she climbed in and buckled up. "I don't care to spend all Saturday afternoon watching a bunch of guys bash their brains out."

"We won't, I promise." Woody cranked up and headed across campus and out the gates and onto North State Street. "It isn't even a conference game. We'll leave early and hike around in the woods a little, on the way back."

She stayed quiet awhile, watching the grand old homes drift by on both sides of the road. "Heck of a thing," she said finally, "when you're probably safer out in the woods than sitting in your own car. Right?"

He didn't answer right away. Anna knew he didn't want to talk about the Night Stalker. She didn't either. She didn't even like the name, something the stupid media had come up with because all three incidents had happened after dark. They could have at least been original, she thought. That name reminded her of the old TV movie about vampires in Las Vegas.

But this modern Night Stalker was plenty scary enough. It had been all over the news the past couple weeks, and she was worried. *Everybody* was worried—especially those who had to drive Route 25. It was on that highway—a four-lane that cut a bending path across the upper-right center of the state—that all three killings had taken place, or least all three disappearances; no bodies had yet been recovered. But the cars of the three missing women had later been found parked on the side of the road. The consensus so far was that the killer/kidnapper could be posing as a police officer, and had pulled his victims over beforehand. Whatever the case, Anna was less than thrilled to be traveling that same road today.

"Why don't we take the interstate instead?" she asked him.

"That would add half an hour to the trip, Anna. We'll be fine."

"Why am I thinking, *Famous last words?*"

"Look," Woody said, "people can't let this nutcase dictate where they're going or how they're going to get there. That's like refusing to travel by air because someone might hijack the plane and fly it into a building."

"It's not the same thing," she said.

"Well, I really want to go today, and I think you do too. We'll be careful, okay?" Before she could respond, he crooked a finger to her and pointed to something below his right thigh. When she leaned over she saw, underneath the driver's seat, one of those padded, telescoping steel bars that can extend to two feet or so with one flick of the wrist. In its collapsed state, it was maybe ten inches long. Woody took it from under the seat and showed it to her. "Anybody comes along who looks suspicious, I'll crack his skull with this."

"I'm so reassured," she said, frowning.

Her doubts were still there fifteen minutes later, when they stopped for breakfast at a Wendy's on Lakeland Drive, on the way out of town.

The only highway patrolman Anna knew sat down at their table with a plateful of biscuits and gravy. Officer Jack Speerman had been Woody's roommate in college and teammate on the football team when Jack decided to drop out and apply at the Police Academy. Some admired him for it, but some said he was throwing away a great future—maybe even the NFL. Jack didn't care. He'd been determined to become a cop. Woody had once confided to Anna that he suspected part of the reason was that Jack's brother Stuart, a year or two older, had been in and out of jail most of his miserable life, and that Jack might be trying somehow to atone for the sins of the sibling. Whatever the reason, Jack Speerman had done well, and seemed happy in his job.

He asked them where they were headed, and Woody told him. When Anna restated her concerns, Jack shook his head. "I agree with Woody," he said. "Don't change your plans because of whoever this guy is. He's probably a thousand miles away by now anyway. Just be watchful." He dusted some salt onto his gravy. "It's the folks traveling alone that I worry about."

"What?" said Anna.

Jack pointed his plastic fork at a young lady placing her order at the counter. She was tall and attractive in a sixties-hippie kind of way—straight black hair, long skirt, no makeup. A cloth purse was slung over one shoulder. "Said she's looking for a ride to Kentucky."

"Why worry about her?" Woody asked, chewing his egg sandwich.

"What?"

"When she finds a ride," Woody said, "she won't be traveling alone."

The cop chuckled. "Problem is, she might not find one. I'm going that way myself when I finish up here, but I can't take her with me—that's strictly against the rules. And I don't have a good feeling about her standing beside the road with her thumb stuck out." Then he paused, looked at both Anna and Woody, and cocked an eyebrow. "Unless . . ."

"We're only going as far as Starkville," Anna said quickly.

"That's on her way. From there she could find a ride to Tupelo, then maybe catch the Trace up to Nashville and points north. Or stay on Highway 45 up to I-40 and—"

"Sure," Woody said. "We could take her to Starkville at least."

Anna was scowling.

"You don't want to?" Woody said.

She shrugged. "It's just—well . . ."

"Well what?"

Anna swallowed and lowered her voice. "Nobody knows who this killer is, Woody. We don't even know if it's a man or a woman."

"I doubt it's a woman," Jack said. "All three victims disappeared without a trace, or any sign of a struggle. For that to happen, there was probably some lifting and carrying of a body. Miss Flower Child over there's not big and strong enough for that kind of thing."

"He's right, Anna. There's no risk. We could at least help her out."

Anna sighed, thought it over, and nodded. Who knows, maybe three traveling together would be even safer than two. But she kept that thought to herself.

When they'd finished their breakfast, Woody threaded his way over to the girl's table—her name was Mary, she told him—and invited her to join them on their trip. *Our good deed for the week*, Anna thought. Mary gratefully accepted and, after they were introduced, gave Anna a smile that warmed her heart and made her ashamed of her doubts. The three of them waved a goodbye to the cop, left the restaurant, piled themselves and Mary's travel bag into the Toyota, and headed east into the morning sun. Four miles later the route curved northeast toward the towns of Carthage and Louisville and Starkville. Lakeland Drive, when the trees beside it started outnumbering the businesses, was better known as State Highway 25. Anna tried not to think about that.

Besides, it was a gorgeous day for traveling.

* * *

Mary and Anna exchanged some polite small talk for the next ten minutes or so. Mary revealed that her brother was moving from their hometown in Lexington, Kentucky, to Jackson later this year, to work for an engineering firm there, and they all agreed that it was indeed a small world. Mary herself was on her way back to Kentucky, returning from a visit to an old girlfriend in Baton Rouge. Her junk heap of a car had died on a back road on Highway 61 near the Mississippi/Louisiana line, and was now in a repair shop owned by a friend of a friend in Natchez. She'd retrieve it later, after her brother moved here and got settled in, she said, although she wasn't sure the car was worth retrieving. She traveled light, and despite the safety issues she didn't mind hitching rides.

"Pretty trusting of you," Anna said.

Mary smiled. "I'm a trustful person. It's a prerequisite for my job."

"Your job?"

"I'm a nun," Mary said.

Woody almost ran off the road, and even Anna gasped aloud. "You're kidding," they blurted at the same time.

"Strange but true," Mary said. "I'm Sister Mary Patrick. Or at least I will be, when I finish my training. St. Anthony's Convent in Elizabethtown."

"A nun," Woody said, as if tasting the word.

"Don't worry, I won't try to talk you into choir practice or bless your car or anything."

"Actually, my mother'll be pleased," Anna said. "She worries sometimes about the company I keep."

"I hope you're not referring to me," Woody said.

She leaned over to Mary and whispered, "I'm referring specifically to him." They both laughed.

Ignoring that, Woody said, "I couldn't help noticing your

jewelry." He nodded toward a bracelet of sparkling green stones Mary wore on her left wrist. "It doesn't look very nunlike."

She grinned at him. "It's not. It's way too expensive. But it was a gift, and I never take it off."

"Girls will be girls?" Anna said.

"I told you, I'm just a trainee."

As they made their way north, Anna filled Mary in on her background, her family, her plans to be a schoolteacher. She'd been raised not far from here, Anna said; they would even be able to stop tonight on the way back and say hello to one of her uncles, since he worked at a Walmart right beside the highway up in Winston County. Most of her relatives still lived in that area, and most were miffed that she hadn't chosen to attend the university in nearby Starkville. But the scholarship she'd gotten three years ago to Millsaps, in Jackson, had been too good to pass up.

"Did the two of you meet there?" Mary cut her eyes over to Woody, who seemed to have tuned them out and was focused on his driving.

"No, Mr. Cool over here went to Mississippi State. He graduated last year, I met him at a party that summer, and I've been trying to educate him ever since."

"I'm afraid I don't know much about the schools down here," Mary said.

"He doesn't either," Anna replied, grinning.

The subject eventually changed to the Night Stalker—even Mary had heard about it on the news—and Woody said he'd been able to see in Jack Speerman's face this morning the pressure he'd been under lately. Especially since most everyone knew about Jack's brother's errant ways and had never seemed entirely trustful toward him because of it. In Woody's opinion, the fact that Route 25 was Jack's assigned territory this past year or so, and the fact that all the killings had taken place along that high-way, was both good and bad. Bad for the obvious reasons, but good because if Jack could somehow help break the case, he'd be a hero.

"Forget the hero part," Anna said. "If I were him, I'd ask to get reassigned."

Woody shook his head. "That'd be hard, in more ways that one. This is the ideal work territory for him—he lives near here, and only about a hundred yards off the road. Besides, he's smart, and good at what he does. Hell, he really could—oops, excuse me, Sister Mary."

"It's okay," she said.

"—he really could be the one who solves all these killings."

"Wish he'd hurry up and do it, then," Anna said. She felt a chill ripple its way up her spine.

On that note they fell silent. The next half hour was smooth sailing: they cranked down the windows and cranked up the radio and occasionally hummed along with an oldies station, the autumn sun in their laps and the wind whipping their hair around. Anna was suddenly glad she'd agreed to the trip.

It was almost ten o'clock when Sister Mary Patrick asked Woody if they could stop at the gas station just ahead on their left—the last one, Anna knew, before a particularly long stretch of forest and pastureland. "Too much coffee back at Wendy's," Mary explained, and was the first one out the door when Woody pulled the little Toyota into the station. They parked beside a metal trash bin almost as big as the car.

"Think I'll make a pit stop too," Anna told Woody. She followed Mary into the minimart section of the building and waited in the hallway outside the restroom door until Mary was done. When Mary came out and they squeezed past each other, Anna said to her, "Tell Woody to amuse himself for a while—when I finish in here I'm gonna buy some snacks before we leave, to bring along with us."

Fifteen minutes later Anna Langley took an armload of purchases to the cashier, who looked to be about a hundred years old. They exchanged pleasantries about the fine weather and the guilty pleasures of fast food (but, thankfully, no comments about the Night Stalker), then she paid up and pushed through the door into the sunlight.

She was annoyed to find that Woody had left the car unlocked. She tossed most of her purchases inside—several bags of peanuts and chips and pastries—and stuffed a six-pack of Sprite into the cooler they had put on the backseat. Neither Woody nor Mary was anywhere to be seen. Mary's duffel bag and purse were gone as well. Anna hoped they hadn't been stolen. There was such a thing as being *too* trusting, she thought.

Anna locked the car, headed back inside, described her traveling companions to the cashier, and asked if he'd seen them. He told her he had spotted Woody through one of the east windows, walking across the highway toward a stand of pines awhile ago, and had seen the young lady heading out there after him a few minutes later. That made sense, Anna thought; Woody was a photography nut, and couldn't resist taking pictures of almost anything, and Mary had probably spotted him out there and followed him after visiting the restroom. But if so, where were her purse and duffel bag?

"If you go over there," the old-timer said, "tell 'em to be careful—there are some dry washes and open wells around here, and things like that would be hard to see underneath all the grass and bushes. Most of it's private property, but there ain't no fences to tell you so. I'd hate for your friends to drop off the face of the earth."

"I imagine they'd hate that too," Anna said. But she doubted Woody would have any problems there. He had grown up traipsing through the backwoods.

She thanked the cashier and walked back out into the sunshine. After crossing the road and trudging through a weed-choked field with a sharp eye on the ground ahead of her, she spotted Woody's blue windbreaker in the distance. Sure enough, he was snapping photos right and left. At the very edge of the trees was a tall, ancient windmill, its rusted blades turning in the breeze while accomplishing nothing at all. Something was rubbing against something, though, and with every rotation came a high-pitched noise: *eeee-urrr, eeee-urrr, eeee-urrr*. It was a metallic, irritating, and infinitely sad sound.

"Where's Mary?" Anna called.

Woody looked up. "She hopped on the tornado to Oz. Found a better ride."

"What?"

"An old couple, she said, on their way to Tupelo. Told me she met them in the parking lot. That'll get her farther than we're going, and besides, they had a bigger car." He frowned and pointed to a spot near her feet. "Watch out—fire ants."

Anna sidestepped to safe ground. "Probably the folks I saw inside, awhile ago," she said. "I'm surprised, though, that she didn't at least say goodbye."

"She wanted to, but her new traveling buddies were ready to leave. I walked over to help her load her stuff into their car and they took off."

"Didn't she come out here with you?"

"Nope. When she found her new chauffeurs, she waved and hollered at me till I noticed her, then I hiked back over there to see her off and came on back. I'm getting some good pictures." He looked at his watch. "You took awhile in there."

"I bought some more provisions. I thought there'd be three of us." Anna was a bit surprised to find herself sad that Mary had deserted them. "At least we swapped cell phone numbers."

"Sorry she left," Woody said, going back to his photos, "but it's her loss. Now we can have all the snacks to ourselves."

Anna looked around. The ground was damp, but grassy and covered in pine straw. "Why don't we just eat lunch out here? You hungry yet?"

He grinned. "I'm always hungry."

"Stay here and do your camera thing—I'll fetch the vittles. Give me your car keys."

"It's not locked."

"It is now," she said. "I locked it."

He dug his keys from his pocket and tossed them to her. "Just don't go over there," he added, pointing off to the south. "Poison ivy."

"There are worse things out here than poison ivy and fire ants." She told him about what the cashier had said to her about hidden wells and gullies.

"Danger," he announced, drawing an imaginary sword, "is my middle name."

Going back to the parking lot seemed a shorter trip than before. A good thing, since the temperature was steadily rising. When Anna arrived at the car she unlocked the driver's-side door, started to pop the trunk to get the picnic basket, and remembered she needed her sunglasses. She thought a moment, then recalled that she had tucked them into the glove compartment. She hopped in, leaned across the middle console, reached into the glove compartment for her glasses—and froze.

Right in front of her, perched there in the compartment on top of Woody's road maps and gas receipts and her sunglasses, was a bright green bracelet. Mary's bracelet. Anna stared at it a moment, her mind reeling, then blinked and glanced across the road. Woody was still taking pictures.

Anna shut the glove compartment and stared straight ahead through the windshield. Her pulse was hammering in her ears.

What the hell is Mary's bracelet doing here?

She decided she would ask Woody that question—but immediately changed her mind. Taking long breaths, she replayed the situation as Woody had described it. While Anna was in the bathroom Mary had come outside, spotted the other travelers, maybe spotted a Lee County license plate—Tupelo is its largest town (would she have known that?)—and decided to switch horses. Woody was supposedly already across the road, poking around in the pine forest. All that was understandable, and certainly possible. It could have happened. But none of it explained the bracelet in the glove compartment. *I never take it off*, Mary had said.

It also didn't explain the fact that the cashier had told Anna he'd seen Mary walk across the highway and field to join Woody, something that Woody told her didn't happen. Woody said Mary had remained on this side of the road, and had signaled to him when she was ready to load up the other car.

Anna swallowed, and forced her mind in another direction. A direction that terrified her.

What if Mary *hadn't* found another ride? What if she had come back out and instead noticed Woody over there in the trees and walked over to join him, as the cashier said she'd done? What if no one else was around to see what happened then? What if—

What if *she* had fallen into a well?

That, of course, hadn't happened. But . . .

Anna felt ice-cold fingers tickle her heart.

What if she'd been *thrown* into a well?

What if Woody had then lied about her catching the other ride?

Anna thought back to what Jack Speerman had said earlier: the killer was probably big, and powerful. Woody was six three, and more than two hundred pounds. A former football player. And what better place to hide bodies than in an abandoned well? Maybe she was in there with the three other victims, right at this moment.

What if Woody Prestridge is the killer everyone's searching for? My God, Anna, think about what you're suggesting here!

But could it be? Woody had been acting strange lately—she'd figured it was just the pressure of his new sales job—and he also spent a lot of time traveling the state. He obviously knew these stops along Highway 25. And Anna had been in the restroom and in the store buying goodies for a long time; there would've been plenty of opportunity for him to do away with Mary, steal her bracelet, hide it in the glove compartment, and then take her belongings from the Toyota and toss them into the metal trash bin. Or forget the trash bin: he could've tossed them into the hole after her. No one would've noticed. The old couple Anna had spotted earlier, inside the store, were the only people she'd seen since arriving, besides the cashier. Thinking about it now, she remembered that Mary had been the one to ask to take a break here—but if she hadn't, Anna wondered, would Woody have found another reason for them to stop?

On the one hand, this kind of thinking was crazy; she couldn't imagine Woody doing something like that. But the truth was, she couldn't imagine *anybody* doing it. And somebody *was*.

She looked again at the closed glove compartment, pictured the bracelet inside.

Suddenly Anna knew what she had to do. *Call me if you need anything*, Jack Speerman had told them, just before they'd left him at Wendy's. And she had written down his number.

Anna dug her phone and notepad from her purse and stepped around the far side of the building. No one was out there except a mangy dog sleeping in the shade. She punched in Jack's number and held her breath while she listened to the ringing.

"Speerman," a voice said.

"Jack, this is Anna Langley. Woody Prestridge's friend."

"Sure, Anna. What's up?"

She hesitated. So far this was just speculation, she reminded herself. Nobody had been accused, nobody had been hurt. But that was about to change.

"I think I might be in trouble," she said.

"What do you mean?"

She swallowed hard. "I'm at a gas station on Highway 25"—she gave him pinpoint directions—"and I think someone . . . someone here . . . might be the guy who's making these women disappear."

"*What?*"

"There's no time to tell you everything now, but I think . . ." She stopped, took some more breaths. "That girl who caught a ride with us? Mary? I found something of hers, something she would never have parted with. And she's vanished."

"What are you saying, Anna?"

"I don't know. I think I'm saying she might be dead."

The phone went silent.

"Jack? Are you there?"

"I'm here. And you know my next question."

She rubbed a hand over her face, forced her voice to stay calm. "You want to know who did it."

"Do *you* know?"

She started to tell him her suspicions, then stopped. He and Woody were old friends; he wouldn't believe her. Not on the phone. "No," she said. "Not for certain."

Another silence. Then: "Where's Woody, Anna? Is he okay?"

"His cell phone battery's dead," she lied. "He's here, though—he told me to call you."

"Anna, you think it could be *him*. Don't you?"

She paused. "I don't know."

"Okay. Okay, I'm on my way." She heard, in the phone, the sound of hurried footsteps.

"We're across the highway from the gas station. In the trees near an old windmill," she said. "How long will it take you?"

"To get there? Twenty minutes."

"Should I call somebody else too?" Now she could hear his car door opening, and then the roar of a motor.

"No, I'm coming. Keep an eye on him, okay?"

She disconnected and stuffed the phone into her pocket. Put both palms over her face and stayed that way a minute, then rubbed her eyes with her forefingers and stood up straight. Whatever would happen would happen, she told herself. She walked back to the car and took the picnic basket out of the trunk. The cooler and the goodies she left in the car for later, although she now wondered if there would be a later.

On an impulse, she opened the driver's door again and groped underneath the seat until she located the padded steel club Woody had shown her earlier. She tucked it into her left shirtsleeve and buttoned the cuff to hold it tight and hidden.

At least she had a weapon.

After several long, deep breaths, Anna got out of the car and lugged the picnic basket across the field to where Woody was waiting. Actually, to where he was still snapping photos. If he'd just killed someone he was being pretty nonchalant about it. Above their heads, the windmill turned, tireless and eternal: *eeee-urrr, eeee-urrr*. In other situations, the grating sound would probably have driven her crazy. As it was, she had more pressing issues to think about.

She put down the basket, wiped sweat from her forehead, took a look around—

And saw it. Not far past where Woody was standing. A brick-rimmed hole in the ground, about five feet across. Several rotten boards lay in the undergrowth to one side. From what little she could see, the brick walls were chipped and blackened and the opening was half-hidden by clumps of what looked like Virginia creeper. Five leaves each, not three like poison ivy. Not that it mattered. A little itch wouldn't matter much to someone falling down that pit.

Woody glanced at her, and followed her gaze. "Looks like you were right about the abandoned wells."

But this one wasn't totally abandoned, she noticed. There was a rough path leading east from the edge of the well, and what looked like a single narrow tire track rutted the muddy ground. Something had been hauled to the well, and recently. Her first thought was a body, but she had another idea, one that made a lot of sense. If there was in fact a body in the well—or more than one—it would be stinking to high heaven. Unless something had been dumped in on top of it. And for that task, what would work better than good old dirt, and what better to carry dirt in than a wheelbarrow? Because that's what had been used to make the single rut beside the well.

She raised her eyes and studied the rest of her surroundings. No other clues presented themselves. Off in the distance, in the same direction as the tire track, what looked like the gray-shingled roof of a house rose above the trees. No doubt it faced an unseen road, somewhere farther off to the east.

Woody's voice snapped Anna out of her musings. "Something wrong?"

She blinked, looked at him, and forced a smile. *If you only knew,* she thought. "Just wondering where to set up the feast."

"Here, I'll help you."

"Aren't you worried about being late for the game?"

"It won't start till two thirty," he said. "Plenty of time."

They chose a clearing twenty feet from the well, although Anna was much more aware of its presence than he seemed to be. After he'd spread out the blanket she unloaded the sandwiches and thermos bottles and sat with her back to the distant gas station, barely visible from here. She'd decided it was more important to watch Woody than to try to watch the parking lot for Jack's arrival. Woody insisted on taking a picture of her sitting on the blanket with the picnic gear spread out around her, then he sat down as well and dug into his lunch. Her stomach was doing backflips. She'd never been less hungry in her life.

She was trying to decide whether to try a sandwich, at least for appearance's sake, when Woody said, "Aren't you gonna eat anything?"

She felt her face heat up. "Guess I'm a little uncomfortable. What if we're trespassing?"

He looked amused. "We're not. I know the owner."

She blinked and glanced at the distant rooftop. "Of the house over there?"

"The land too. I should've told you—"

Suddenly her cell phone buzzed. She dug it out of her pocket and checked the display. No name was shown, and she didn't recognize the number. Keeping her eyes on Woody, she held the phone to her ear.

"Anna?" a voice said.

"Yes?"

"It's Mary. Mary Patrick."

Anna felt her heart leap in her chest. *Mary?*

"Sorry to call out of the blue like this. I sort of need a favor."

Anna was breathing hard. She couldn't believe it. *Sister Mary Patrick is alive.* "Where are you?" she managed to say.

"I'm at a McDonald's in Louisville"—she incorrectly pronounced it *Louie*ville, like Kentucky—"having lunch. The folks I'm riding with stopped here. Hope you don't mind that I cut out on you."

"No, that's fine," Anna said, trying to keep her voice steady. She pictured Louisville on the map in her head: Mary wasn't far away. "What favor do you need?"

Anna looked at Woody, who was happily eating his turkey sandwich. *He's innocent,* Anna thought, her eyes brimming with tears. *Thank God. Thank God I was wrong.* And she knew what Mary was going to say before she said it.

"Anna, I think I lost my bracelet, the green one, when I took my stuff out of the car. I remember snagging it on the door handle. I know it's a long shot, but I was wondering—"

"Woody found it," Anna said, loud enough for Woody to hear.

He looked up at her, his eyebrows raised. Anna pointed to her wrist and silently mouthed the words *Mary Patrick.* It took a second, then he understood and nodded and said, around a mouthful of turkey and cheese, "I found it after she left, put it in the glove compartment. Forgot to tell you."

Anna turned her attention back to the phone, and to Mary's gushing thanks. "You're most welcome," Anna said. "This is turning out to be a crazy day." As the thought struck her, she added, "Your address is on the card you gave me. I'll mail the bracelet to you soon as we get back."

"Great. I sure appreciate it, Anna. And hey—thanks again for the ride."

They exchanged goodbyes and Anna disconnected. She felt light enough to fly. One friend was alive and well, and another was innocent and exonerated. An incredible weight had been lifted from her shoulders.

Just as she was about to confess everything to Woody, including her ungrounded suspicions, she realized she should call off the reinforcements; after all, Jack Speerman was on his way here at this moment. Already feeling guilty about the false alarm, she picked up her phone and was about to punch in Jack's number when the phone buzzed in her hand. She checked the display and saw that it was Mary again.

"Anna? Sorry to be a pest, but I just remembered something. Could you just give that bracelet to Jack when he gets there? He can bring it to me."

Anna frowned. "Jack?"

"The patrolman. He's on his way there, right? He said he'd be back soon, and my ride says they'll be glad to wait, so—"

"Wait a minute," Anna cut in. "How'd you know he's coming here?"

"I overheard him talking to you on the phone awhile ago. He called your name when you phoned him about your car trouble."

Anna felt her head spinning. *Car trouble?*

"He stopped and was eating with us here at McDonald's when you called him," Mary said. A silence dragged out. "Anna? You still there?"

Anna's brain seemed to have gone numb. Her head was roaring.

She had told Jack she thought Mary had been killed—and yet Jack had been there with Mary at the time, while they were talking? He was sitting right there *with* her? *Why didn't he tell me that?*

There could be only one reason. Dazed, she peered up at Woody, who was still wolfing down sandwiches, and then looked past him, focusing as if for the first time on the roofline of the house just above the trees behind him. The house owned by someone Woody said he knew, someone who wouldn't mind their trespassing . . .

Oh my God.

Anna felt her stomach turn over. She lowered the phone and said to Woody, "That's Jack's house, isn't it?"

Woody had turned away and was digging around in the picnic basket. "What?"

But she knew it was true. Jack Speerman lived there—*about a hundred yards off the road*, Woody had said. He lived there—here—and the well was on his land. The well with the wheelbarrow ruts running toward it from the direction of the house. Anna's thoughts were flying now, zinging around in her head.

And then she heard something behind her. She whirled around—

And stared straight into Jack's face. Anna yelped and clapped a hand over her mouth.

Woody heard her and turned. "Jack?" he said. "What are *you* doing here?"

She just kept staring. This wasn't the mild, friendly Jack Speerman they'd seen at Wendy's. This face was drawn and flushed with anger—but also with something else. Frustration? Guilt? Regret?

Anna was breathing in ragged gasps, trying to think. Had Jack heard enough of the phone conversation just now to know she was talking to Mary? "Jack," she said, panting. "Thank God you're here." She leaned closer and whispered, "I haven't said anything to Woody about all this. In fact, I think I might've been wrong. I was just about to call you back and—"

Vaguely, as if from a distance, she could hear Mary's voice in the phone she held in her hand: "Anna? Are you there?" Anna looked dumbly down at it, knowing that Jack had heard it too, but before she could say or do anything more, the phone was suddenly gone, slapped out of her hand and onto the ground six feet away. Her fingers were stinging.

Jack Speerman looked as if he wanted to hit her again, and not in the hand this time.

"So you know Mary's alive," he said softly, "and you probably know by now that I was with her when you called. And if you know that . . ." Jack paused and shook his head. In a voice heavy with sadness he continued, "What have you done, Anna?" He glanced past her at Woody, who was standing now, the picnic forgotten. "What in God's name are you two doing here anyway, snooping around?"

"You invited me," Woody said, sounding hurt. "You said to stop by sometime and take pictures—"

"A year ago. Things have changed since then." Jack's gaze moved to the gray rooftop beyond the trees and then back again, and Anna saw the heartache in his eyes. "What are the odds?" he murmured. "Couldn't you have left well enough alone?"

Woody, Anna could tell, was beginning to understand. He had backed up several paces, his eyes narrowed and alert. He looked at the house too, then at the well behind him, and at the wheelbarrow tracks between the two. Putting it all together. Last of all, he turned again to stare at the pain and guilt on his old friend's face.

Except for the regular screech and creak of the windmill, the scene had gone dead silent. Anna could feel her heart thundering in her chest.

"It's you," Woody said, with something like awe in his voice. "You're the Night Stalker. He looked like someone impersonating a policeman because he *was* a policeman."

Jack ran a beefy hand over his face. He had perspired all the way through his uniform shirt. "No," he replied miserably. "It wasn't me."

"It was *me*," a voice said, from off to the side. All three swiveled to look.

Standing there on the rutted path to the house was a carbon copy of Jack Speerman. The eyes, mouth, even the build was the same. The only differences were hair color and height: this brother was darker, and shorter. That, and the fact that there was something odd in his eyes.

And a gun in his hand.

"Stuart?" Woody said.

"Hello, Woody. Lotta water under the bridge." Stuart Speerman turned to Anna, his face grave. "I don't believe we've met."

"But I know who you are," Anna said. She felt strange, and disconnected. It was as if she were watching all this from someplace else. At this point she was beyond surprise.

At last everything made sense. The violent, unbalanced brother, living here with Jack, staying out of sight except for an occasional drive down the road behind the house to intersect with Highway 25 and the unsuspecting motorists traveling there. The perfect hideout, for both himself and the bodies of his victims. The perfect opportunity to strike and take cover and strike again.

"Why?" Anna managed to ask.

Stuart's face grew even more solemn. "Voices," he said. "They told me to do it. I had no choice."

She shook her head. "Three innocent people. You're insane."

He shrugged as if that might indeed be a possibility.

Anna turned to Jack. "And you helped him."

"I protected him. There's a difference."

"Was it your car that stopped those women?"

"No," Stuart said. "But it was his light bar. It fits pretty well on the top of his other car. The one the voices told me to drive." He grinned then, and for a moment Anna could clearly see the gleam of madness in his eyes. "It's amazing—nobody worries if there's no uniform, or markings on the car. That flashing light's all it takes. Besides, I work at night."

"Worked," Jack corrected. "You promised me it was over." He turned to Anna and Woody and said wearily, "It's over now."

"Well, it will be." Stuart's smile was back again. "After we do a little cleanup."

Woody was staring at his old friend. "How could you do it, Jack? I mean, you're a *peace officer*."

The muscles in Jack's face seemed to slacken. "He's my brother." As if that explained everything.

"So you're going to shoot us both? Is that it?"

"*He* won't," Stuart said. "Somebody from the gas station might hear it." Slowly, casually, he took a noise suppressor from his pocket and screwed it onto the end of his pistol. "Besides, there's no real need for that. That well's ninety feet deep." Stuart grinned again. "Minus maybe ten feet of dirt and bodies. Still a long way to the bottom."

"Wait a minute," Anna blurted. "You're forgetting about our other friend. Mary. I told her what I suspected—she'll call the police. The *real* police, I mean." Even in her terror she gave Jack a withering glare. "And she knows where we are."

Jack shook his head. "No, she doesn't. I never mentioned your location when I spoke to you on the phone, and I heard most of what you said to her just now. All she knows is what I told her—you and Woody had car trouble somewhere." Jack still had a haunted, sorrowful look, but there was no fear of discovery there. He was in control, and he knew it.

But Anna and Woody were about to die, and Anna knew it.

As if to confirm this, Stuart raised the silenced automatic and pointed it at Woody. "Gentlemen first," he said.

And Anna did the only thing she could think of to do. Moments earlier she had unbuttoned the cuff of her left sleeve so the collapsed steel bar resting against her forearm could be easily removed. Now she snatched it out with her right hand, flicked it to its full length even as she spun around, and hit Jack Speerman with it, square in his left temple. As he went down, she turned again and threw the heavy bar as hard as she could, end over end, at Stuart.

"Run, Woody!" she shouted. "RUN!"

But Woody didn't run. He didn't run and he didn't attack. He didn't do anything but stand there, frozen and wide-eyed. Stuart Speerman, who had frantically ducked the bar Anna had thrown at him, stood straight up again, aimed the pistol, and shot Woody once in the chest.

Anna screamed, a primitive, blood-chilling scream that made Stuart turn and point his gun at her this time. The problem was, this target wasn't stationary. Anna was sprinting toward him, face contorted and teeth bared in fear and rage, and in his surprise both his shots missed her. She crashed into him at full speed, biting and clawing, and both of them fell to the ground. But as short as Stuart Speerman was, he was not weak. He pulled his right arm free and clubbed her viciously in the forehead with the heavy automatic, and then hit her once more, on the left side of the head. Anna rolled off him and onto her stomach two feet from Woody's sprawled body and four feet from the edge of the well. She was still conscious but was so stunned her world was spinning and full of stars. She tried to move but found she couldn't.

At the edge of her fading eyesight she saw Stuart's shoes take a step toward her, heard him say, "Good try." And knew, although she couldn't see his hands, that his gun was now aimed at her.

In those final seconds, a dozen thoughts ricocheted through her brain. Memories, loves, thrills, regrets. One was the realization that she should've gone for Jack's gun after hitting him, should've tried to grab it off the ground or out of its holster or wherever it was, and shot Stuart with it. But she suspected that wouldn't have worked either. The only difference was, she'd have died already, and twenty feet farther west.

It was all over now anyway.

Just as she was wondering whether to close her eyes or leave them open, another pair of shoes, these black and gleaming, stepped into her field of vision. She heard a grunt of great effort, and saw Stuart's brown loafers rise an inch or two off the ground. With a huge push she managed to force herself onto her side so she could see, and when she looked up she saw Jack Speerman, bright blood oozing from his ear and nose, lifting and squeezing his brother from behind. Stuart's arms were pinned to his sides, his gun useless. Grunting, the two men struggled there for several long seconds.

Then something happened that Anna would never forget. Jack looked down at her, looked down past his shorter brother's shoulder, and Anna saw a strange peace deep in those eyes. A moment later, Jack moved slowly past her, still holding Stuart in a bear hug, and stepped into the well.

Neither of the brothers screamed, or said a word. They just vanished into the pit. After what seemed an extremely long time, she heard a muffled thud as they hit bottom.

She turned her head to look at Woody, lying beside her in a

spreading pool of crimson, and thought, *Help him. I have to help him.* But she couldn't. She couldn't even help herself. A moment later her eyes clouded, the incredible pain in her head washed over her—

"—and she passed out."

Little Charlie was still asleep in his car seat, but Deborah sat and stared at her mother with eyes as big as quarters.

"You passed out?" she said. "What about Woody?"

"She—I—didn't know, for a long time. I woke up two days later, in a bed at Baptist Hospital in Jackson. I barely pulled through, they said. Woody was in a room down the hall. It took five months for him to heal, but the bullet had missed his heart, and he made it. Both of us made it, physically speaking. But . . ."

"You didn't stay together."

"No." Anna McDowell looked at her daughter, then back at the road ahead. "Thinking back on it now, I realize that I could never in a thousand years have suspected your father of having done what I—incorrectly—suspected that Woody Prestridge had done. If you truly know and love someone, those doubts just wouldn't be there, no matter what. I think Woody and I were never able to get past that."

"And then you met Daddy."

Anna nodded. "Six months later. We got married right away, and a year after that, a precious little girl named Deborah came along."

The girl thought about all that for several minutes. "I still don't understand. Who rescued you? Did someone hear you scream?"

"No. No one from the station, or the nearby area, heard or saw anything at all. We survived only because of a quirk of fate. The phone Jack Speerman slapped out of my hand stayed on, and the connection stayed open. Mary didn't hear everything, but she heard enough. She called 911 and the cops and ambulances were there within fifteen minutes. Mary saved our lives."

"A lady you'd just met earlier that day."

"Yep. An angel, according to your dad."

"But—like Speerman said—how did she know exactly where you were?"

Anna grinned. "The windmill. That rusty old windmill, squawking away in the background. She heard it through the phone."

Deborah was frowning again. "But to have heard the windmill noise earlier—to know where it was—Mary must've been in the woods after all."

"She was. Just like the cashier at the station said. She told me later that she'd crossed the street and the field all the way to the woods after coming out of the restroom—but then turned around and went right back to talk to the folks who wound up letting her ride with them. Woody never saw her until she called out to him a few minutes later."

"So you were wrong. He wasn't lying."

"I was wrong about a lot of things," Anna said. "Turned out Woody's odd behavior *was* because of his new position. He later transferred from sales to desk work." She took in a long breath and blew it out. "Nobody was lying that day except Jack, and nobody had killed anyone except Stuart."

"But Jack was guilty too, right?"

"Yes, he was. And he knew it."

Deborah blinked twice, her eyes still wide. "Whoa." She looked a little overwhelmed. "Has Daddy ever heard this story?"

"Oh yes."

"What about Aunt Penny?"

Anna smiled again. "There's something you probably don't

know about Penny. She used to be a nun. Or at least she trained for it. Then she changed careers and moved to Tennessee."

Deborah gaped at her mother. "What?! You said you were telling me the truth!"

"I was."

"But you said your friend that day . . . you said she was named Mary Patrick."

"That was the name the church gave her—they do that. Her real name was Penny McDowell."

Deborah turned and stayed silent for several moments, watching the countryside glide past the windows. "So Aunt Penny didn't just save your life; she wound up introducing you to her brother."

"And by doing so, made sure she would have a niece and nephew to come visit her once a year."

Deborah giggled. It was a good sound, Anna thought, after what they'd been talking about for the past hour.

She thought about what Officer Keller had told her, after the incident with the would-be carjacker this morning. Was it true? Had what happened to her that day long ago really made her tough?

Maybe it had. But right now she didn't want to be tough. She wanted to be a regular mother, the kind her kids could love and trust and play with before the world around them tried to make *them* tough. That would come soon enough.

"Mom?" Deborah said.

"What, honey?"

"The story you told me. Do you think about it much?"

Anna waited a long time before answering. Because the truth wasn't the answer she wanted to give, or the one Deborah wanted to hear. Of course Anna thought about it, those things that had happened there in the piney woods beside the highway.

She would always think about it. Sometimes, late at night, she could even hear the windmill again, the sound of those ancient, rusted blades turning around and around and around. But maybe now, now that the story had been told, she would think about it less. Who knew?

"Yes," she said. "Sometimes I do."

Deborah nodded, as if to acknowledge that the truth was always the best approach, honestly the best policy. They exchanged a knowing smile, Anna popped open another Coke, and little Charlie woke up in the backseat and rubbed both eyes with his chubby fists. Outside, State Highway 25 became 82 and then 45 and then pointed them north toward Tupelo and Corinth, straight as an arrow. Just south of the Tennessee line the sun broke through the clouds, waving them on.

It was a good day for traveling.

ANGLERS OF THE KEEP

BY ROBERT BUSBY

Olive Branch

Hunched over my ex-father-in-law's front yard, molding a layer of pine straw around the purple lilac hedges and crawl-space grates wrapped around Lafayette's sprawl of a brick one-story rancher, I heard the tires of Erin's rental car massaging the gravel drive leading up to the carport. Erin had found a new breath of life after our divorce, quit her job as first-grade teacher at Bodock Elementary to pursue her PhD in American folklore at Oklahoma State University. Except for the semester she took off after Betty, her mom, was murdered a year and a half earlier, she'd been in Stillwater for four years of the five we'd been divorced. I was between gigs. Holding out for a management position, as they say.

Erin eased the car to a stop just short of the carport even though her father's El Camino had not been parked there when I pulled in this morning. I'd assumed Lafayette was at the Feed Mill on Main Street, slugging coffee and shooting the shit with the other old-timers. Lafayette's lungs were bad sick, figured he'd want to get in all the breakfasts he could. But it wasn't like him not to welcome Erin home. The car door slammed. I stabbed the shears through the pallet of pine straw into the red clay underneath, made my way around the house along the stone path embroidered with monkey grass I'd planted for Lafayette last spring.

"Thought you might be over here," she said.

She pushed herself off the hood of the blue Saturn. She wore a black wool turtleneck and when she uncrossed her arms her tits became ambitious. Her teeth gripped a peppermint candy. I folded my work gloves into the back pocket of my jeans and gave her a hug.

"I just came from the hospital," she said. "Dad shot himself last night."

"He all right?"

"He was cleaning that damn .22 revolver of his," she said. "He forgot to unload it first. I flew in as soon as I got the call from the hospital." She removed her plaid-lined parka from the car hood. "The bullet only got his ear."

"Shit," I said. "Should've called."

She tumbled the set of keys around her finger. "Wasn't so bad he couldn't drive himself to the hospital. They're keeping him there another night. I came by to get him a change of clothes."

Erin invited me inside. A short, lopsided pyramid of empty beer cans squatted next to the garbage bin. Towers of newspapers and dirty plates had been erected on the dining room table when the kitchen sink had refused further occupancy. Erin reheated the leftover coffee in the carafe on the burner while we rinsed the dishes in the sink and sorted them into the dishwasher. Erin had always been attractively one diet away from what might be considered thick or hungry, filled out her jeans as if she'd been dipped up to her waist in a vat of liquid denim and left to air dry. Considering she'd flown into Memphis the night before and had immediately driven two hours south to the North Mississippi Medical Center in Gum Pond, twenty-five miles east of Bodock, and slept all night in a hospital room because her father had grazed a bullet off his head, she looked pretty damn good.

The first thread of steam rose from the coffee. Erin poured two cups and leaned against the counter. She grimaced at the stale, scorched Folgers. Said she needed a favor.

I smirked. "You wanna get remarried? Want me to be Lafayette's emergency contact?"

Erin fingered some coffee off the edge of her lips and said, "Found Lafayette a donor."

The night Betty was shot, Lafayette had ambled into their house after work to find a pair of men jacked up on methamphetamine holding her at gunpoint in their living room while robbing the place. Lafayette startled the man training the .357 on Betty into pulling the trigger. The other one, a black guy, managed to make the back door, but the ol' boy who put a bullet into Betty's sternum tripped and fell. Lafayette had just enough time to retrieve the revolver and put a round through the back of the man's skull as he scrambled away. Lafayette chased the other meth head down two backyards over, lodged a bullet in his spine while he climbed over a limestone retaining wall I'd installed for Gray Sherman, the neighborhood queer, the summer before. The man fell unarmed and off Lafayette's property. Before the trial was over, the black one died in ICU at the hospital, which elevated the case from attempted murder or manslaughter, to committed. Lafayette probably would've won against either charge given the circumstantial grounds of his case and his standing in the community. He stunned everyone when he insisted on a plea bargain, took two years for involuntary manslaughter. The best most of us could figure was Lafayette just wanted to move past the ordeal.

Erin and I were already three years into our divorce when Lafayette was admitted to the minimum-security wing at Parchman. A little over six months into his two-year sentence he nearly keeled over during a physical. His blackout led to a biopsy and the diagnosis that sarcoidosis had completely scarred his upper respiratory system. Lafayette's sentence was commuted to probation by Governor Fordice, courtesy of the urging of Judge Polk, who'd played football with Lafayette at Ole Miss. The convenience mattered little: as a seventy-year-old felon still technically serving out a manslaughter sentence, Lafayette had a lung allocation score—determined by a number of variables set forth by the United Network for Organ Sharing—that was too low for any viable shot of finding a donor in the seven months the doctors gave him to live.

Erin sipped her coffee and explained how she had discovered this loophole called the Good Samaritan clause, which allowed a donor to bypass any UNOS regulations and choose whatever nonfamily recipient he or she wanted at her own discretion. In Lafayette's case, that donor was a Pentecostal preacher dying of liver disease. The preacher's church had burned down last year. Erin had set all this up over the phone from Stillwater. Said the man was crazy, obsessed with all the old martyrs or something, had agreed to donate his lung to Lafayette on the grounds he turn over the deed to his house to the First Pentecostal Church of Bodock so that the ministry could continue in his absence.

"Huh." I nodded at the rest of the house. "So this place is going to be filled with snake-handlers this time next year?"

"They're not those kind of Pentecostals."

"So you want Lafayette to trade his house for a lung," I said, "and you explained all this to Lafayette over the phone yesterday morning, after which he shot himself in the head?"

"It was his ear." Erin considered the window above the sink, the white oak limb framed there like a pillar of cigar ash. "What am I supposed to do, sit on my fat ass and do nothing? He's all I've got."

Our marriage had not so much dissolved as imploded after a streak of impulsivity landed me between the thighs of a stripper named Sugartits one night a month shy of our five-year anniversary. We'd married young, while she was still studying elementary education at Ole Miss, a compromise I wasn't aware of until she enrolled at OSU. I was still building pinewood couch frames then at National Furniture out on Highway 54. We weren't living hand-to-mouth, but I'd lost out on a supervisor promotion one Friday afternoon to a man I still regard to this day as a fundamental douche bag. Because I was young and dumb-ass enough back then to think Lafayette was the barometer by which Erin measured me, I said hell with it and drove a few counties over to DeWerks La'Rey—spelled backward: Yer Al Skrewed—and spent a good chunk of my paycheck crafting a dollar-bill hula skirt out of Sugartits's thong. Got drunk and self-deprecated enough for it to seem perfectly justified to hand over what was left of my paycheck if Sugartits would just accompany me to a nearby motel.

Erin explained her favor. There was no guarantee she would be granted enough of a heads-up to fly back in time. I assured her I'd see that Lafayette made it to the transplant center two hours north of here.

Sometime later we ended up on the kitchen floor, our clothes on to protect against the cold brown linoleum. It wasn't the first time since the divorce: every couple of months or so when she came back home we'd get together to fulfill the more carnal of marital conditions that somehow manage to slip through the cracks of a divorce.

"Have you thought about starting a landscaping business?" she asked. "You've done a hell of a job on my father's yard. Seriously."

I told her I hadn't.

Erin stayed at Lafayette's through the weekend to get everything squared away with the preacher, make sure things with Lafayette were settled down. Monday morning she headed back to Stillwater to teach her evening composition class. The class canceled on account of some arctic front from Canada pairing up with a wet weather system before sweeping through and shutting down the whole state of Oklahoma, delaying all incoming and outgoing flights. The storm then wound its way southeastward, gathering strength the entire time.

The preacher went into a coma Wednesday evening about the time the storm reached Mississippi and dumped six inches of ice and knocked power out across the Mid-South. Hospitals would retain electricity but the Pentecostal preacher had a living will instructing not to put him on life support. The preacher lasted thirty-six hours before he suffocated early Friday morning. The Memphis International Airport was closed when the lung was harvested a little after eight a.m.

When I wheeled into Lafayette's yard Friday morning his lung was hurling through the air in a helicopter a few thousand feet above us. Lafayette was standing on his roof in a pair of Clorox-stained boxers, a loosely knotted noose around his neck, the end of the rope tied to a branch of the sweet gum stretching its bare, knotty limbs out over the front of the house. His wrists were cuffed behind his back. Gumballs from the tree overcrowded the gutters and piled up the slanted roof, accumulated around his bare feet. The tree had largely survived the storm but the branch he'd tied the rope to had sustained substantial damage. Probably Lafayette would take the branch with him to the ground and fracture a hip instead of stopping midair and snapping his neck in that pivotal moment when the rope and gravity became acquainted. *Well goddamn*, I thought. Lafayette's efforts to mount the roof had pulled loose the stitches in his ear; skinny swirls of blood colored the white bandage like a peppermint. I stepped out of the truck and asked him what the shit it was he thought he was doing.

"Had been contemplating killing myself," he said.

"Yeah, I gathered that much. You forget about us fishing?"

"Nah," he said. His breath pulsed like a chimney pipe in the chilly morning air. This was the dead of February, when fish hunkered down at lake bottoms, barely moving in their dormancy. But Erin had insisted on the fishing euphemism, something about perceived reality and helping her father to feel as comfortable as possible about not riding with her to his transplant surgery. Last night, I went over to check on Lafayette after the hospital pager Erin had given me alerted us that the next page would mean the lung had been harvested. Instead of sticking around after a supper of hot dogs roasted on clothes hangers over the gas heater in his living room, I headed home to bed. Did not give thought to leaving the old man unsupervised and fending for himself in a powerless house, only the specter of his murdered wife for company.

"Nah, guess not," Lafayette said again. "Suppose we can go *fishing* now."

Lafayette's operation was scheduled for noon. He was due in Olive Branch at 11:15 to get prepped for surgery: blood tests conducted to determine the type and strength of anesthesia, a tissue test to make sure his body wouldn't reject the lung. It was 8:45 now. I'd filled the gas tank that morning on a generator-run pump at a buddy's farm, which left Lafayette and me plenty of time to make the hour-and-a-half haul up US 78 to the transplant clinic just outside Memphis. I called up to Lafayette to get a move on then. He stepped forward and twirled his fingers to remind me of the predicament he'd gotten himself into. "Be right up," I said.

I retrieved the ladder lying out in the front yard and propped it against the house. When I reached Lafayette he had his head down. The plow lines of his gray comb-over revealed freckled sections of scalp. Erin could write a thesis on the number of tales her father contributed to the community mythos, like when he very nearly pummeled the testicles of an unfortunate rival while in a dog pile on the thirty-yard line during the county football jamboree. Rode through pharmacy school at Ole Miss on an athletic scholarship, played for the legendary Johnny Vaught. Returned to our good town after graduation to open Bodock's second drugstore. That was all before I was born, thirty years ago about. But Lafayette wasn't indomitable. The inflammatory lung disease and his wife's murder and six months in a low-security prison wing had left him a pathetic reflection of the man he used to be.

When I removed the noose from his neck and asked what pocket the handcuffs key was in, it was hard not to show my frustration when he raised his head and said, "The yard, somewhere."

"You not think to tell me that before I got up here?"

"Shit, Topher. This ain't exactly one of my best days."

The key had landed on some plastic sheeting I'd covered the hedges with when news of the possible storm first reached Bodock. After I got him off the roof, I brushed the asphalt grit from my hands on the legs of my jeans and looked at him bent over in the lawn. The scar on his calf from when he last went hunting and his bare feet positioned on the spiny gumballs. Chest heaving whatever was left of his lungs.

When he was finished coughing, I said, "You ready to go?"

Lafayette Cummings, standing straight as he could in the front yard, wiped a spot of blood from the corner of his mouth on his boxers and said, "Been waiting on you."

While Lafayette was in the house getting dressed, I waited out in the truck, honked the horn once, rested my arm on the Igloo cooler I had forgotten to unload.

It wasn't quite nine o'clock, but I appreciated the obvious

sense of urgency lent to the task of escorting a transplant patient. I honked again.

Gave it exactly two minutes. Then honked a third time.

Lafayette appeared on the front porch then. He wore a denim jacket over an Old Milwaukee T-shirt tucked into his beltless jeans and a pair of sunglasses draped around his neck by a red Croakie. Boat shoes on his feet. I retired the cooler to the backseat. In one hand Lafayette had a Shakespeare rod and reel he set in the truck bed. In his other hand was a half-case of Old Milwaukee which, when he tucked the box between his feet on the floorboard, I saw held only four bottles.

"Lafayette." I nodded my head as I turned over the ignition.

He inspected the cab as I backed downhill out the long drive. Just the walk from the house had spent him. What the hell sort of adrenaline had to have pumped through his old arteries this morning, allowing him to climb up on his roof without keeling over?

"Notice you ain't brought any fishing gear with you," he said. "Don't you think it would've helped the illusion some if you'd at least put a fishing pole in the back there? A tackle box at least?"

I forced a laugh. "I think you got the imagination for it, Lafayette."

"Shit. You got the cooler though, I see. I guess that could work. Coolers're essential for a day on the lake."

At the end of his street I threw the truck in park. "You want, I can go back and get my damn fishing gear, Lafayette."

"Nah," he said and winked. "I'm just yanking that rod and reel you did bring with you."

I shifted back to drive. "You was easier to get along with on the roof."

I made a left out of the neighborhood and then hung a right, which put us northbound on Highway 54. Lafayette cracked

open a beer, the bottle sneezed. He cleared the neck and said,
"Want one?"

"They ain't going to use anesthesia on you if you're drunk."

He bent down and handed me a beer. "So help me drink 'em
then."

I imagined the shit storm of arriving in Olive Branch only
to have Lafayette denied for surgery because I didn't deny him a
preop beer, a mock-fishing-trip beer. Figured I should be less worried with whatever condition he arrived in so long as I got him
to the surgery. Besides, there were all the stories of Lafayette's
drinking exploits before a pregnant Betty ultimatumed him into
sobering up. Hauling ass down back roads with a fifth of Evan
Williams between his legs, the green cap discarded out the window miles behind him as a sort of insurance the bottle would
be emptied in that single sitting. Usually it was. That kind of
tolerance doesn't desert a man. Further, he only had four beers
on him—two if we split them—which I reckoned would leave
plenty of time in the next couple of hours or so for him to piss it
all out before surgery.

I nursed the Old Milwaukee and we rode up Highway 54 in
silence except for the news station out of Memphis and something between a wheeze and a growl from Lafayette's chest.
According to the news lady's voice, power had been restored
in Nashville and parts of Memphis that morning, and some of
the larger towns in north Mississippi: Corinth, Gum Pond, Oxford. We hit the US 78 on-ramp in New Albany at 9:15, which
would take us north all the way to Olive Branch. Out on the
four-lane we saw not one wooded acre that had been spared.
Many hardwoods—oaks and hickories, some of the older, more
resilient gums—were still standing, but even their spread had
diminished some. The bright wood of their exposed flesh marked
their shed poundage, a pallet of broken trunks and branches car-

rying for miles across the roll of ridges. Besides the occasional eighteen-wheeler, there wasn't much traffic. Cleanup crews were set up every ten miles or so, removing branches or the occasional utility pole that had fallen onto the highway.

"Be better if we could keep them beers cold," Lafayette said at some point, and nodded toward the backseat. "There ice in that cooler?"

I told him no.

"Too bad we couldn't transport the lung ourselves. Would've appreciated seeing what a Pentecostal lung looks like."

"Perhaps they'll let you look at it just before surgery."

Lafayette gulped the last of his first beer as we passed a group of orange vests catapulting branches into a dump truck. Then northbound US 78 relaxed back into two lanes and Lafayette rolled down his window and sailed the empty beer bottle at the Myrtle corporate limit sign. The bottle missed high, swallowed up by the kudzu spilling from the tree line, where some of the more flexible pines made top-heavy by the ice collected in their branches were bowed over toward the highway like the Pentecostals who'd soon be congregating in Lafayette's living room. He took a handkerchief from his back pocket and coughed violently into it, wiped his mouth, and folded the handkerchief back behind his wallet.

"Be too drugged up then to remember."

The .357 that drilled Betty's chest belonged to Lafayette. He wore the piece everywhere as if it were a nickel-plated watch: Sitting in the concrete stands during high school football games, depositing his pharmacy's weekly cash flow at the Peoples Bank. Fighting off sleep in the back pew at Bodock Baptist where Betty dragged him. He even pulled the hand cannon on a customer once for being generally disruptive because the man didn't want to wait five minutes over the estimated hour for his prescription to be filled on account he was a distant cousin of Mayor Duff's.

But Lafayette would leave the gun at the house that morning, probably for the first time in years. That evening two unarmed men, high on crank and thinking the house vacant, would break in. A kitchen light sparking to life, perhaps, Betty's voice addressing whom she assumed was Lafayette home from work. And instead of abandoning their mission, one of the men would see an opportunity in Lafayette's pistol on the side table next to the recliner.

It was nearing ten o'clock when we passed Hickory Flat, about halfway to Olive Branch.

"How bad did that hurt?" I asked, pointing at his bandage in the side mirror.

"Ashamed to admit I cried some," Lafayette said. "Was a lot like getting your ear flicked in cold weather, except instead of thumping you with their finger, someone shot you. Still hurts like hell. I ain't never fallen asleep with my head in a fire ant bed before, but I'd venture a guess that the two was comparable."

"You mean to do it?"

"Why the shit would I mean to shoot myself in the ear?"

"Meant why'd you have a loaded revolver pointed at your head in the first place?"

Lafayette reached down to get his second beer, popped the cap, and offered it to me. I declined. He shrugged and hooked his fingers on the oh-shit handle above him. "Don't get me wrong," he said. "I'd do anything for Erin. She's my daughter. If she'd requested back then to fillet your pecker with a rusty boning knife or to simply shoot you in the face, I'd've obliged her. No questions asked. No offense." He pulled on the bottle. "So if she wants me to get my sternum cracked open or my side split like the underbelly of a bream or however the hell them doctors plan on fitting that crazy Pentecostal son of a bitch's lung inside me just so all his hair-legged-and-armpitted, ankle-length-denim-skirt-wearing female disciples can speak in tongues like retards, so be it. But it's not what I want for myself, and I ain't about to feign enthusiasm for it."

"So how was jumping off your roof this morning with a noose around your neck doing what's best for Erin?" I asked.

"Ain't what I said."

"Huh?"

"Ain't said I'd do what's best for Erin. Said I'd do what she wanted." Lafayette stared out the window and took two quick pulls on his beer. Said, "I admit I wasn't in the most logical of frames of mind this morning." He held his bottle up to me. "Stayed up last night drinking the other eight of these."

"Shit," I said.

"What? Power was off. Didn't have *Sanford and Son* reruns to distract me, I guess. Guess at some point I thought it was a good idea. Thought better of it once I got up there on the roof."

"You would've taken that branch down with you anyway," I said. "I suppose it's good you ain't gotten any better at committing suicide."

"Keeps me entertained at least," he said.

"How long was you up there this morning?"

"Couple hours. Maybe four. It hit me what extent of a bad idea it was soon as I tossed that key out in the yard."

I felt pretty shitty for pressing the issue and waited for Lafayette to say something else, but he seemed done with that talk. My beer had gone lukewarm. I finished it and held it between my legs and waited until we'd passed another cleanup crew before rolling down the window. For all the debris we'd passed, it seemed the crews' efforts at present were futile and they'd caught on to that fact as well. The crews this far north simply removed the fallen timber from the highway into brush piles ten or so feet high instead of fighting to stack each piece in a dump truck. The rush of air through the window was a welcome relief to the silence that'd swelled the cab.

It was twenty minutes after ten when we passed the Holly Springs exit. Thirty, thirty-five minutes from the transplant center. I asked Lafayette to hand me the last beer.

"What?" he said.

I pointed down at the box.

"Roll that window up," he said. I obliged. He popped the cap and handed the beer to me. On the radio, reports on the storm's aftermath continued. Some of the more rural areas of the state would be without power for upward of a month. Lafayette turned the volume down.

"Tired of hearing about that damn storm."

"All right," I said. Beads of sweat big as ball bearings had formed on his brow. "You all right?"

He fiddled with the heater some, trying to turn it down. I intervened.

"That better?" I asked. "You want, I can roll the window back down."

Lafayette said, "I ever tell you the story about the time I lost that old bird dog of mine?"

He had on several occasions. About how he and his black lab, J.R., were headed in from the field when a pack of feral pit bulls intercepted them, appearing from the tree line like gray ghosts. How Lafayette couldn't have taken them all on at the same time by himself, how the lab's efforts distracted the other bulls long enough for Lafayette to defend himself, first with the over-under, then with the .357 which was easier to load, more efficient. He had to put the lab down right there in the hay patch, not fifty yards from the safety his truck offered. Would end the story each time by showing where a large chunk of his calf was missing from where one of the pits stayed latched onto him even after he mowed the top of its head off point-blank with the over-under.

"I'm a little blurry on the particulars, tell you the truth, Lafayette."

"Was going to make you listen anyway," he said. He hung his arm on the oh-shit handle above him and commenced his detailed account. "Not thirty yards from us I remember J.R. and see him fighting the good fight but just getting tore at by about half the pack. Four of 'em had abandoned the crowd around J.R. and was headed my way. I popped off one of them with the over-under and abandoned it for the .357 because the over-under's too slow, too bulky. Get three of the cocksuckers before the other one runs off. Then I hobble toward J.R. but only make it a few yards because of the pit that's jaws're still attached on my leg like some badass tick. I shoot the two pits around J.R. but can barely see him for the pit on top of him. Looks like it's already dug into J.R.'s throat, only a matter of time. So I put a bead on the pit.

"But let's just say," Lafayette went on, tapping his middle finger on the dash twice for dramatic effect, "let's just imagine for a moment it only looked like that pit got ahold of J.R.'s throat, and just as I feel the trigger in the bend of my finger, that J.R., in some impressive maneuver and demonstration of resiliency, somehow manages his mouth around that pit's fat face and the pit rolls over to break free and it's my round that goes right into J.R. So that it's me who kills my dog out of no necessity whatsoever." He paused and looked for me to answer.

I said, "It'd change the whole dynamic of the story, I guess, Lafayette."

"About would, yes," Lafayette said.

Out of the corner of my eye I saw him drape back his denim jacket to make for the handkerchief again. Then I directed my attention back to the road. When my eyes drifted toward Lafayette again, I saw a black semiautomatic pistol resting on his leg. Had never known Lafayette to own the pistol—just the revolver and shotguns, hunting rifles. Knew he couldn't've bought the pistol anywhere legally.

"Why the hell did you bring a gun with you, Lafayette?"

Before he could answer, he suffered another violent coughing episode, this time before he could reach the handkerchief. Traces of blood and phlegm sprayed on the glove compartment. Lafayette's beer tipped over onto the floorboard. In his fit I grabbed the gun away from him. He didn't fight me for it. He took out his handkerchief and wiped the dash.

"Shit. Sorry about that," he said.

I felt the heft of the gun in my hand. "Why the hell did you bring a gun with you this morning?" I asked again.

When he was finished smearing his muck off the dash, he dropped the handkerchief into the empty beer carton, deposited the bottle he'd knocked onto the floorboard in the carton as well.

"Don't know anymore," Lafayette said and moved the carton to the backseat. He closed his eyes and leaned into the headrest. "Don't know. Had my .357 on me as always, Topher." He pointed at the gun in my left hand. I could tell he was fighting back tears his chest was trying to convulse out of him. "So that white-trash piece of shit was holding that gun on her instead. Didn't know there was another man in the house, so when his Negro buddy saw me, sumbitch registered his friend's surprise, moved just as I pulled the trigger."

Ahead of us an exit sign bounced like a green buoy in the waves of cool air thawing off the highway. I took the exit, turned right on Hacks Cross Road. Power still hadn't been restored. Truck stops sat squat and dead and empty. The only life, some smoke pillaring from the side of one of the stores. I pulled around. It was 10:45 and we were only ten minutes away from the transplant center. Olive Branch was the next exit down 78. But the beer in my empty stomach reminded me how I hadn't eaten anything yet that morning. I felt claustrophobic.

A red horse-trailer was parked back behind the truck stop. A gas generator growled power into the trailer, *MALONE'S CAT-FISH AND OTHER FINGER LICKIN GOOD STUFF* painted on the side of the truck. Only a few customers were standing in line. I pulled back around the building and parked in a space facing the large panes of glass at the front of the store. The tires nudged the curb. A pay phone stood just beyond the truck grill.

"Shouldn't've told you that," Lafayette said, then opened his eyes. "Don't tell Erin."

"Of course."

"We there?"

"Sit tight," I said. "Got to get some food in me. You want something?"

"Probably shouldn't eat before surgery."

"But you can drink beer?"

"Just a little something to snack on then. A biscuit, pack of Nabs. Whatever they got."

Two ladies were working the truck. The black one manned the register and the other one, a Mexican, held a pair of tongs over matching beige Crock-Pots. Both women were wearing hairnets. Not so much the smell of frying catfish wafted from the truck as chorizo and what I recognized as tamales. The first man in line paid and carried away a Styrofoam box. Two customers remained in front of me. The next customer ordered. The Mexican lady with the tongs waited for her coworker to indicate which Crock-Pot. The black lady pointed with three fingers at the one on the right. Aluminum foil draped from the Crock-Pot. The Mexican lifted the lid and produced as many tamales.

Perhaps the pay phone actually worked, fed from lines below the ground, immune to the storm. What would I tell Erin then? That the best possible result today would be the operation going just about textbook and Lafayette living out the five years his new lung might afford him at a retirement home, all while the guilt over having shot Betty continuing to consume him much less quietly than the sarcoidosis had or ever would. Blame laid as much with me for how far this had gone. I ignored what Erin could not see with Lafayette's first suicide attempt because I still and always would love her enough to harbor some hope of a past revisited despite what all another man, who had not just broken his wife's heart but had gored it with a bullet, would be wrung through.

My reflection caught in the rear glass window of the quick stop. I needed some time I didn't have to figure this out. I focused past my reflection and examined the inside of the vacant store. All the usual suspects of quick-stop merchandise were present: junk food and beer, videocassettes and country music and gospel and gospel-country music cassette tapes and CDs. CB radios and wiring, exaggerated antennas and bracket mountings. Several cheap brands of fishing poles hung on the wall.

To hell with the phone. Better I didn't find out if it worked.

Back behind the wheel I told Lafayette we had some time to kill, that the black lady at the food truck said the store owner's catfish pond was nearby, a place we could cast a few quick lines in while we ate the tamales. They were selling hot dogs from the other Crock-Pot and I'd bought an opened pack of raw ones to hook on our cheap lines from the quick stop. A couple of miles down the frontage street I made a left onto a narrower gravel road, maneuvered the truck like the lady said her old man some-times did around the padlocked gate that did not stretch across the entire width of the path, wasn't met on either side by fencing. Branches slapped and scratched the side panels of the truck.

The path yawned into a cove and a man-made lake of about fifteen square acres sprawled out before us. At the far end two tractors held between them a seine which would drag the length of the lake during harvest. A wire-netted hopper waited at the other end of the lake to lift from the water the catfish caught between the seine and the bank. I parked. Tall pines untouched by the storm darted from the ground around the rectangular perimeter of the lake like the makeshift walls of a medieval keep. There was some cloud cover and from the truck the water looked murky. Lafayette tried opening the door of the truck while balancing the hot dogs on top of the box of tamales in his lap.

"Don't worry about all of that," I said, reaching for the food. "I can get it."

"I ain't completely helpless yet." He swung open the door and stepped down and the opened pack of hot dogs slipped off the Styrofoam and landed in the grass. Two of the hot dogs rolled from the plastic. Bits of dirt clung to them. "You can get them," he said.

We walked to the far end of the floating pier that would retract onto the bank during harvest. Lafayette's breathing was labored and he set the tamales and his pole on the dock, propped himself up on his knees, and wheezed. When he could manage his respiration he sat down on the pier. I handed him my pocket-knife. He cut up one of the hot dogs against the pier and baited his hook. Cast out into the lake. His arm jerked the rod in his hand, the other reeled the slack out of the line. I offered him another tamale.

"Can't say I've had any of these before," he said.

I told him the first time I'd ever tried them was when Manny, a coworker when I was a produce clerk at the Jitney Jungle, offered me one from his lunch box left over from dinner the evening before.

"They ain't bad." Lafayette licked tomatillo salsa from his fingers. "You know? A little different but taste good. You still got that Ruger on you?"

I slipped the gun out of my pants, wanted to tell him I didn't feel comfortable with him having a loaded gun, but he'd been through enough. "Long as you ain't fixing to shoot me or you with it."

He cast the line again. "Would you believe they broke in with only one bullet in that gun?" He swiped a finger across the bandage on his ear. "Used it to pull this here van Gogh what's-his-face."

I broke the breech of the gun, ejected the clip. The chamber and clip were empty so I handed the gun to him. He looked at the unloaded Ruger and tossed it off into the water. Then my father-in-law cast once again, the line clicking as it unreeled and stretched fifteen, twenty feet from us. "Way the wind's moving this water, kind of looks like we've launched out from land," he said. "Always appreciated that particular illusion."

I said I had as well and bit into another tamale. I was killing time, was aware of as much, waiting there for Lafayette to give the word to head out or, if he never did, for some explanation why to arrive at me.

Sometime later, most of the hot dogs gone and nothing to show for them, I joked that it was too bad we didn't have the organ with us. That if we planned to stick around out here, we could've changed our strategy some. Maybe have given his lung a go.

JERRY LEWIS

BY JACK PENDARVIS

Yoknapatawpha County

An open box of doughnuts on the coffee table. Little bullets lined up in a pretty little row. The girl working on the chamber of a revolver with a little tool like a Q-tip expressly designed for the purpose. Her yellow hair hanging in her eyes.

Girl with a half-fastened holster, like a male gangster in a movie.

Girl in a sleeveless corrugated T, low-scooped neck, like a male gangster in a movie.

Girl in striped boxers, like a male gangster in a movie.

She looked up.

Humphries jerked back his head, away from the dirty window into which he had accidentally peeped.

What was he supposed to do now? Something?

She opened the door.

"Hi," said Humphries. "I'm looking for a cat." His eyes went to the empty holster. "Are you a policeman?" he blurted.

"What gave me away, the doughnuts?"

"What doughnuts?"

She laughed like a sexy crow. The way she talked was also like a sexy crow, one of those crows that can talk. But sexy. Her teeth were so white they were almost blue. They looked like happy ghosts. She said, "Have you ever seen the movie *Hardly Working*?"

"I don't think so. What's it about?"

"Jerry Lewis is on a job interview at the post office. He's really hungry. He hasn't eaten for days. So while the guy's trying to interview him, all he can see is this box of doughnuts on the desk. He's not listening at all. The guy finally asks him, *Do you want a doughnut?* And Jerry goes, *Where ARE DEY?* Just like that. *Where ARE DEY?*" She laughed some more.

Humphries made himself laugh. He was nervous because where was the gun? In the dewy small of her back, tucked in the waistband of her boxers? He had seen something like that in a movie.

"I'm not a cop," said the woman.

"My wife's cat is missing," said Humphries. "He's orange? Sometimes I see a black cat on this porch, sitting on this thing." He pointed to the rusted glider, its filthy vinyl cushions illustrated—defiled—with big blotchy flowers. "I don't know, I felt my wife's cat might have sought out the company of another cat? He's not used to being outside and she's very worried, understandably. We recently moved here to Mississippi from Vermont, which is generally considered a more civilized state, no offense, and my wife is understandably concerned that there might be some barefoot children who have reverted to some kind of savagery and walk around trying to shoot little cats with a bow and arrow."

"I'm from Chicago, dude. I don't give a shit. Want to know what I would have told you if you hadn't seen the gun? My cover story is that I'm looking for a place to live out in the sticks because I want to have a baby. I'm thirty-nine. If I wait any longer, there's some danger involved for the baby. I mean, there's a pretty good chance of something going wrong chromosomally, am I right? Where am I going to bring up the baby I want to have? Chicago? All the neighborhoods are getting too expensive, even the bad neighborhoods. There was a torso on a mattress. Where we lived. In the alley below our apartment. They found a headless torso on a mattress. And the place was still too expensive for us. Is that where I'm going to raise a kid? Like, *Look out the window, there's a torso on a mattress.* Like, *Mommy, what's a torso?* And we can't even afford *that.* Like, *Sorry, lady, the torso on the mattress is extra.* Jocko had some prospects down here—my cover-story husband who doesn't actually exist, that's Jocko—so here we are, anyway. He wants to do voice-overs. He wants to be a voice-over guy, my made-up husband does. He can do that from anywhere. He just needs a good microphone and a special phone line."

Humphries couldn't believe she was thirty-nine. She looked like a girl, like a college kid or something. Like an inspirational young teacher fresh from the academy with a lot of exciting notions about how to change the world. She had a gun.

"Come on in," she said.

"I really need to keep looking."

"Could be I have some information about your cat. Sorry. Your *wife's* cat." She said it like she didn't believe he had a wife.

"Really?"

She shrugged.

Humphries was scared but titillated. He followed her inside.

The place was dank. It smelled the way other people's places always do: like the long-unwashed pillowcase of a much-sought-after courtesan—sour milk and violets.

"What'll it be?"

"Ovaltine?" said Humphries.

She turned from him without humor and headed for the kitchen, scratching her ass in an elegant way.

Humphries sat on the couch where he had seen her sitting. The bullets and pistol were magically gone. The doughnuts remained. There were two flies walking on the doughnuts. He thought the seat cushion felt warm from her, or maybe everything was warm.

Who was she? Why did she need a cover story? Obviously she knew nothing about Mr. Mugglewump. Chicago was where hit men came from. Something awful was going to happen and Humphries would never be seen again. Part of him thought that would be okay.

She came back with a couple of Rolling Rocks and handed one to Humphries. It was fairly warm, like everything else.

She sat catty-corner to Humphries, on an armchair that looked to be upholstered in some sort of immensely uncomfortable material, like tweed. It would make little red marks on the backs of her bare legs, he thought. Fascinating crosshatched patterns.

"This place is a hole," she said, then twisted the switch on a shabby lamp. It seemed to have a brown bulb. At least it leaked a brownish light that made things darker.

"Please, officer, I'll tell you whatever you want to know," joked Humphries. He shielded his eyes as if from the bare bulb of a searing interrogation.

She didn't get it.

When Humphries and his wife were trying to find a place, they had attended an open house for which the realtor had decorated the gates with brown balloons in welcome. Brown balloons! It was an odd choice. It was odd that expensive factory machinery would be put into place to manufacture brown balloons.

"Stay right there," she said. "If you ever want to see Fluffy again, ha ha." She got up and went back to the kitchen. For cigarettes, Humphries assumed somehow. His hands were sweating.

There were sexual feelings mingled with terror. He got up and ran out the door, knocking over a small table, clattering.

He ran down the street. He hadn't run anywhere since boyhood.

Thank goodness Mr. Mugglewump came home that night.

"Where have you *been?*" Humphries cooed over him, as did his wife, Mrs. Josie Humphries.

The cat couldn't tell where he had been. Neither could Humphries.

Now I have a terrible secret, he thought.

He lay in bed next to Josie and had private visions of torment.

It was a small neighborhood. He would run into the mysterious siren. Maybe Josie, who loved a pleasant stroll, would be on his arm when the confrontation occurred! All scenarios were distasteful.

He couldn't sleep.

Humphries read the *New York Times* on the Internet every day like a big shot. He disdained the local rag. It was a way to get back at his wife, who had moved to this Podunk burg for a job. Humphries was a landscape painter, so he could live anywhere. That's what Josie said. But what was he supposed to paint around here? A ditch? He stood on the back porch every day and painted pictures of turds for spite. Josie said they were good.

She was all right.

She noticed that Humphries had started walking down to the drugstore in the morning and picking up the local paper. She made knowing faces at him. Now that Mr. Mugglewump had survived on the streets, Mississippi was looking okay to her. Humphries cringed and shuddered at her implicit optimism and got back to the paper. He was looking for a story about some local jerk getting assassinated.

On the third day he almost gave up because he didn't want to give his wife the satisfaction. But he rose in the first smeary light, while Josie was still asleep, and walked to the drugstore. He didn't have to bring the paper home. Without that clue, Josie wouldn't be able to guess he was happy. Because he was happy. He was happy being miserable. He was happy that living in Mississippi would give him a great excuse to be a failure.

There were some old codgers spitting in a cup for some reason. Humphries stood on the corner reading about Buddy Wilson, who had owned a struggling poster shop. He was a large, fat man who had been found at the county dump, his head nearly severed from his body. Police suspected garroting by banjo string because there was a banjo lying nearby with a missing string.

It was cool out. Humphries's palms were sweating. He threw the paper in a trash can and wiped the slippery newsprint on his pants. For the first time, he went back to the house where he had spotted the girl with the gun.

The window glowed. He could see everything from the street. It was like a different place, draped in fabrics, oranges and pinks, full of light and life. There was a homey smell of bacon in the air.

A young couple—nothing like the yellow-haired girl with the gun—pulled a twee red sweater over their little white dog. They had a string of white Christmas lights blinking along the mantle, though Christmas was miles and miles away.

The dirty old glider was still on the porch. It was the only thing to convince Humphries he wasn't crazy.

He had a bad day and couldn't get any turds painted.

That evening, just before the sun went down, he went back to the odd little duplex. The young couple had put up curtains. The black cat, a fixture of the neighborhood, was back in its place on the soiled glider. The white dog in the red sweater stood smugly on its hind legs between the curtain and the window with its white forepaws on the window ledge, safely behind the glass, staring at the cat with sick superiority.

CHEAP SUITCASE
AND A NEW TOWN

BY CHRIS OFFUTT

Lucedale

Betsy had been raised to hold grudges forever, but long ago realized it required more effort than she cared to exert. She remembered the very moment when she'd understood that forgiveness had nothing to do with an adversary, but would benefit solely herself. Her entire worldview had shifted, like discovering her house contained a new room full of light, a chamber she wanted to occupy forever.

Ten months before, Betsy had moved to Lucedale and found work in a breakfast café, becoming the very person she detested most—a woman in a shapeless uniform serving eggs to workingmen, the oldest waitress in the place, alone and not wanting to be, living in a dump and drinking herself to sleep. She was not yet forty. She thought she should know better and felt worse for it.

An eighteen-year-old girl named Thadine joined the breakfast crew. Betsy envied her youth and vitality, the cheery optimism, her slim hips twitching among the tables. Betsy had been the same as Thadine twenty years earlier in another town and had progressed nowhere. Worse, Thadine actively sought Betsy's attention, craving approval, trailing behind her like a pup who'd been kicked but never with severity.

During the midmorning lull before lunch, their side work included refilling salt and pepper shakers, marrying half-empty ketchup bottles, and topping off the sugar containers. Thadine chattered about inconsequential subjects, a running narrative of what lay immediately before her, a commentary on the obvious. Occasionally she tested safe opinions. She laughed readily. The boss liked her and the cooks strove to conceal her errors. In another context, Betsy might have found her adorable—slight and needy in old loafers—but Betsy was reminded of all that she herself had lost: everyone she'd ever loved, a familiar landscape, the security of deep belonging, but most of all the naïveté of seeing life as fraught with promise.

For two weeks the girl had gotten on Betsy's nerves. Fed up, her voice hard, Betsy finally said, "Get away from me. I'm your coworker, not your friend."

Thadine's face turned red as if she'd been slapped. Her eyes, formerly as brimful of hope as an egg is of yolk, filled with tears. She hurried to the kitchen and Betsy ignored her during the rest of the shift, grateful for the efficiency of working alone. She counted her tips at the Formica breakfast bar, cashed her change into folding money, and left.

The incessant heat pressed against Betsy as if she'd stepped into the sea. Though mid-September, there was little autumn to behold. In the parking lot Thadine was leaning against Betsy's car, her face downcast.

"Why do you hate me?" Thadine said. "I only want to be like you."

Betsy's knees seemed to give, as if the struts that held her upright had become elastic. Her polyester uniform clung to her skin, smelling of bacon, stained along the perimeter of her apron. She was tired. Perspiration sheened her face. This was the girl's hometown. She no doubt wanted out, same as Betsy had wanted out of her own. It never occurred to Betsy that seeing her young self in Thadine was a two-way enterprise. Thadine's life must feel drastic for Betsy's to appear worthy of emulation.

The unforeseen arrival of forgiveness relieved Betsy of a burden she didn't know she carried, an invisible shawl of stone. She'd felt the burn of betrayal many times—lied to, taken advantage of, abandoned—left alone with the numb opacity of loss. But she had done her share of hurting people too. It all worked out in the end. The balance of life was achieved by weighted extremes. She had no appetite for moderation, no patience for people who did.

With the stunning clarity of sunup after a fierce storm, Betsy realized that her life wasn't a case of failing to learn from her mistakes, but one of repeating the same patterns again and again. Waitress shoes, a narrow bed, a damaged man. A cheap suitcase and a new town. She wanted to warn the girl, to give her advice Betsy had never received: *Don't let them hit you, don't drink on an empty stomach, don't cry alone.* But Betsy knew it wouldn't have done her younger self any good to hear it, no more than it would for Thadine.

Only two things ever helped in life—love and money. Any love Betsy could muster was reserved for the next reckless man, not this waif weeping in the harsh light. She offered the day's tips.

"You're wrong," Betsy said. "I don't hate you."

Thadine started to speak, then didn't. She took the cash.

"You hate this town," Betsy said. "Get out before you hate yourself."

She got in her car and drove past a fancy house with a large expanse of grass, automatically watered at night. The grass didn't actually grow, but had been unfurled from trucks and pressed into place. Few people trod upon the slim shards of yard.

A mile farther she entered her own neighborhood of cement and asphalt, a used-car lot and front yards of weed and dirt. Betsy parked and climbed an exterior staircase composed of premade concrete to her one-room apartment. She removed her greasy waitress smock and cursed herself for the day's work with nothing to show. What kind of life was she leading? What kind of name was Thadine?

The last time she lived in a house had been in Alabama. She'd gotten mixed up with a man who'd spent three years hand-building a stone enclosure of water for koi fish. He was proud of his project, which Betsy considered a lot of work simply to maintain overgrown carp. In the afternoons they drank beside the pool. He liked to talk and she didn't like to be alone. He fired a BB pistol at neighborhood cats that skulked about, attempting to prey on his fish. Betsy asked him to stop and he set wire traps instead. One trap caught a gopher, which drew a coyote that ate all his precious koi. He blamed Betsy. She left him and quit living in houses, returning to single rooms.

In her apartment, she poured vodka and drank it, facing a fan in her underwear. The AC was a window unit that didn't actually cool the air, just barely cut the heat and blew dust that made her sneeze. After two drinks she laughed at herself—she'd gone from saving cats in Alabama to giving her money away in Mississippi. She closed her eyes. Awhile later she awoke disoriented from a dream she'd had consistently since childhood—lost in a vast house, wandering long halls, opening doors and encountering people she'd met in different places. They were quite friendly with each other, but ignored her as if she was a ghost. She ran down a long hall, trying to ward away the awareness that something serious was amiss.

Betsy sat in the chair, blinking herself fully awake until the imagery faded. Each time she had the dream, the house was bigger, as if her continued existence furthered its renovation. After a shower she ate leftover food from the refrigerator. She packed her clothes, loaded the car, and left for New Orleans.

Each time she began a new life she momentarily wished she had a pistol, a small one. She didn't know why. She supposed it was about confidence and fear. If she'd bought one, she'd have pawned it by now. Someone else would own it, and no telling what they'd do with it, who they'd shoot, maybe Thadine. Betsy hoped the girl would get out before someone did. It could happen easily. Anything could.

ABOUT THE CONTRIBUTORS

MEGAN ABBOTT is the Edgar Award–winning author of seven novels, including *Dare Me*, *The End of Everything*, and *The Fever*, winner of the ITW and Strand Critics Award for best novel and chosen one of the best books of 2014 by Amazon, NPR, the *Boston Globe*, and the *Los Angeles Times*. Her stories have also appeared in *Queens Noir*, *Phoenix Noir*, *Wall Street Noir*, and *Detroit Noir*. Her latest novel is *You Will Know Me*. Abbott served as a John Grisham Writer in Residence at the University of Mississippi in 2013–14.

Drew Reilly

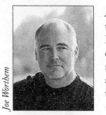

ACE ATKINS is the *New York Times* best-selling author of nineteen novels, including *The Redeemers* and *Robert B. Parker's Kickback*. He has been nominated for every major prize in crime fiction, including the Edgar Award three times, twice for novels about former U.S. Army ranger Quinn Colson. A former newspaper reporter and SEC football player, Atkins also writes essays and investigative pieces for several national magazines including *Outside* and *Garden & Gun*. He lives in Oxford, Mississippi, with his family.

Joe Worthem

WILLIAM BOYLE is the author of the novel *Gravesend* and the story collection *Death Don't Have No Mercy*. He is from Brooklyn, New York, and currently lives in Oxford, Mississippi.

Katie Farrell Boyle

ROBERT BUSBY was born and raised in north Mississippi. He has worked as a band saw operator, a produce clerk, a bookseller, a driving school instructor, and a satellite television technician. His stories have appeared in *Arkansas Review*, *Cold Mountain Review*, *PANK*, *Real South*, and *Surreal South '11*. Currently he lives, writes, teaches, and eats much barbecue in Memphis, Tennessee, with his wife and their two sons.

Jorden Cunningham

JIMMY CAJOLEAS grew up in Jackson, Mississippi. He earned his MFA from the University of Mississippi, and now lives in Brooklyn, New York.

Mary Marge Locker

DOMINIQUA DICKEY, a former stage manager, paralegal, and deputy court clerk, was born in Chicago, raised in Grenada, Mississippi, and became an adult in Los Angeles. Her Southern upbringing and West Coast affinity are reflected in her work, as well as her love of history and its effect on common folk. She is pursuing a MFA at the University of Mississippi while applying the finishing touches to a short story collection and mystery novel.

LEE DURKEE drives a cab in Oxford, Mississippi. He is the author of the novel *Rides of the Midway* (WW Norton), and has published short stories in such places as *Harper's Magazine, Tin House, Zoetrope: All-Story*, and the *New England Review*.

JOHN M. FLOYD's work has appeared in more than two hundred different publications, including the *Strand Magazine, Alfred Hitchcock's Mystery Magazine, Ellery Queen's Mystery Magazine*, the *Saturday Evening Post*, and the *Best American Mystery Stories 2015*. A former air force captain and IBM systems engineer, he won a Derringer Award in 2007 and was nominated for an Edgar Award in 2015. Floyd is the author of five books: *Rainbow's End, Midnight, Clockwork, Deception*, and *Fifty Mysteries*.

TOM FRANKLIN is the author of *Poachers: Stories* and three novels, *Hell at the Breech, Smonk*, and *Crooked Letter, Crooked Letter*, which won the *Los Angeles Times* Book Prize for mystery/thriller, the Willie Morris Prize in Southern Fiction, and the UK's Gold Dagger Award for Best Novel. His latest novel, *The Tilted World*, was cowritten with his wife, Beth Ann Fennelly. They live in Oxford, where they teach in the University of Mississippi's MFA program.

MICHAEL KARDOS is the Pushcart Prize–winning author of the novels *Before He Finds Her* and *The Three-Day Affair*, an *Esquire* best book of the year, as well as the story collection *One Last Good Time*, which won the Mississippi Institute of Arts and Letters Award for fiction. He grew up on the Jersey Shore and currently lives in Starkville, Mississippi, where he codirects the creative writing program at Mississippi State University.

Nick Ulmer

MARY MILLER is the author of two books, *Big World*, a short story collection, and *The Last Days of California*, a novel. Her second story collection, *Always Happy Hour*, is forthcoming from Liveright/Norton. A former James A. Michener Fellow in fiction at the University of Texas, she most recently served as the John and Renée Grisham Writer-in-Residence at Ole Miss.

Melissa Ginsburg

CHRIS OFFUTT grew up in Haldeman, Kentucky, a former mining town of two hundred people in the Appalachian foothills. He is the author of two memoirs, *The Same River Twice* and *No Heroes*; two collections of short stories, *Kentucky Straight* and *Out of the Woods*; and one novel, *The Good Brother*. His latest book is *My Father, The Pornographer*. He lives on fourteen acres in Lafayette County, Mississippi.

Jamie Paige

JAMIE PAIGE was born in Meridian, Mississippi. He is a graduate of the MFA program at the University of Mississippi and currently studies at the Center for Writers at the University of Southern Mississippi.

Phil McCausland

ANDREW PAUL grew up outside Jackson, Mississippi. Some of his more recent work is featured or forthcoming with *Virginia Quarterly Review*, *Oxford American*, *VICE*, *Tablet*, and *The Bitter Southerner*. He currently lives in New Orleans.

Neko Case

JACK PENDARVIS is the author of five books. He is currently a writer for the Peabody Award–winning television show *Adventure Time*.

MICHAEL FARRIS SMITH is the author of *Rivers*, *The Hands of Strangers*, and *Desperation Road*. *Rivers* was named to "best of the year" lists by *Book Riot*, *Esquire*, Hudson Booksellers, and numerous other regional and national outlets. He is the recipient of the Mississippi Author Award for fiction, the *Transatlantic Review* Award for fiction, and the Brick Streets Press Short Story Award. He lives in Columbus, Mississippi, with his wife and daughters.

RASHELL R. SMITH-SPEARS grew up in Memphis, Tennessee. She is an associate professor of English at Jackson State University in Jackson, Mississippi. Smith-Spears earned a BA in English from Spelman College and an MFA from the University of Memphis. She has published creative works in *Short Story*, *Black Magnolias*, and *A Lime Jewel*. She recently completed her first novel.

Also available from the Akashic Noir Series

BROOKLYN NOIR
edited by Tim McLoughlin
320 pages, trade paperback original, $15.95

THE INAUGURAL TITLE in the Akashic Noir Series, *Brooklyn Noir* features Edgar Award finalist "The Book Signing" by Pete Hamill, MWA Robert L. Fish Memorial Award winner "Can't Catch Me" by Thomas Morrissey, and Shamus Award winner "Hasidic Noir" by Pearl Abraham.

BRAND-NEW STORIES BY: Pete Hamill, Nelson George, Sidney Offit, Arthur Nersesian, Pearl Abraham, Neal Pollack, Ken Bruen, Ellen Miller, Maggie Estep, Kenji Jasper, Adam Mansbach, Nicole Blackman, C.J. Sullivan, Chris Niles, Norman Kelley, Tim McLoughlin, Thomas Morrissey, Lou Manfredo, Luciano Guerriero, and Robert Knightly.

MEMPHIS NOIR
edited by Laureen P. Cantwell & Leonard Gill
288 pages, trade paperback original, $15.95

BRAND-NEW STORIES BY: Richard J. Alley, David Wesley Williams, Dwight Fryer, Jamey Hatley, Adam Shaw & Penny Register-Shaw, Kaye George, Arthur Flowers, Suzanne Berube Rorhus, Ehi Ike, Lee Martin, Stephen Clements, Cary Holladay, John Bensko, Sheree Renée Thomas, and Troy L. Wiggins.

"[A] collection of stories celebrating the underbelly of the city, its ghosts, and the characters that give Memphis its rich patina of blues." —*Memphis Flyer*

DALLAS NOIR
edited by David Hale Smith
288 pages, trade paperback original, $15.95

BRAND-NEW STORIES BY: Kathleen Kent, Ben Fountain, James Hime, Harry Hunsicker, Matt Bondurant, Merritt Tierce, Daniel J. Hale, Emma Rathbone, Jonathan Woods, Oscar C. Peña, Clay Reynolds, Lauren Davis, Fran Hillyer, Catherine Cuellar, David Haynes, and J. Suzanne Frank.

"All in all, the stories in *Dallas Noir* have an unsettling, slightly creepy presence that is not just appropriate but completely necessary for a collection of noir fiction. If you think Dallas is boring or white-bread—well, perhaps you haven't gotten out much and seen the dark edges of Big D for yourself." —*Dallas Morning News*

NEW ORLEANS NOIR
edited by Julie Smith
288 pages, trade paperback original, $15.95

BRAND-NEW STORIES BY: Ace Atkins, Laura Lippman, Patty Friedmann, Barbara Hambly, Tim McLoughlin, Olympia Vernon, David Fulmer, Jervey Tervalon, James Nolan, Kalamu ya Salaam, Maureen Tan, Thomas Adcock, Jeri Cain Rossi, Christine Wiltz, Greg Herren, Julie Smith, Eric Overmyer, and Ted O'Brien.

"*New Orleans Noir* explores the dark corners of our city in eighteen stories, set both pre- and post-Katrina . . . In Julie Smith, Temple found a perfect editor for the New Orleans volume, for she is one who knows and loves the city and its writers and knows how to bring out the best in both . . . It's harrowing reading, to be sure, but it's pure page-turning pleasure, too." —*Times-Picayune*

NEW ORLEANS NOIR: THE CLASSICS
edited by Julie Smith
320 pages, trade paperback, $15.95

CLASSIC REPRINTS FROM: James Lee Burke, Armand Lanusse, Grace King, Kate Chopin, O. Henry, Eudora Welty, Tennessee Williams, Shirley Ann Grau, John William Corrington, Tom Dent, Ellen Gilchrist, Valerie Martin, O'Neil De Noux, John Biguenet, Poppy Z. Brite, Nevada Barr, Ace Atkins, and Maurice Carlos Ruffin.

"[An] irresistible sequel to Smith's *New Orleans Noir* . . . Anyone who knows New Orleans even slightly will relish revisiting the city in story after story. For anyone who has never been to New Orleans, this is a great introduction to its neighborhoods and history." —*Publishers Weekly*, starred review

ST. LOUIS NOIR
edited by Scott Phillips
272 pages, trade paperback original, $15.95

BRAND-NEW STORIES BY: Calvin Wilson, LaVelle Wilkins-Chinn, John Lutz, Paul D. Marks, Colleen J. McElroy, Jason Makansi, S.L. Coney, Michael Castro, Laura Benedict, Jedidiah Ayres, Umar Lee, Chris Barsanti, Scott Phillips, and L.J. Smith.

"Featuring a baker's dozen of original stories, plus one 'poetic interlude,' this new entry in Akashic's globetrotting anthology series explores the 'collision of high and low' that makes St. Louis so interesting to crime writers." —*Booklist*